I0693122

THE ENFORCER AND HIS HEART

THE KINCAID PACK BOOK FIVE

KIKI CLARK

Copyright © 2022 by Kiki Clark

Cover Designer: Natasha Snow Designs
www.natashasnowdesigns.com

Editor: Sandra Dee, One Love Editing

All rights reserved. No part of this book may be reproduced in any form or by any electronic or mechanical means, including information storage and retrieval systems, without written permission from the author, except for the use of brief quotations in a book review.

This book is a work of fiction. Names, characters, places, and incidents are products of the writer's imagination or have been used fictitiously and are not meant to be construed as real. Any resemblance to actual events, locales, persons, or organizations is entirely coincidental.

This book contains sexually explicit content which is only suitable for mature readers.

❀ Created with Vellum

THE ENFORCER AND HIS HEART
THE KINCAID PACK BOOK 5

With Keegan's safety on the line, there is nothing Nico won't do to protect him.

The mysterious Keegan has been haunting Nico's dreams.

Ever since the night he stormed through the pack's protections like they were nothing, Nico hasn't been able to forget the powerful young witch. Not his scarred face, his loyalty, or his fierce but sad eyes.

Nico just wished he'd caught Keegan's scent. He ached to know if his fated mate is a witch stuck on the other side of the country.

No one will stop him from finding out.

The Kincaid Pack is trouble.

Everyone knew that, and Keegan's coven forbid contact with them.

But Keegan broke the rules, and now he can't stop dreaming about a shifter he barely caught a glimpse of the night he'd helped the pack. The teasing smile he sees every time he shuts his eyes is becoming a near obsession.

One he isn't sure he wants to stop.

The Enforcer and His Heart is the fifth book in the bestselling Kincaid Pack series, best read in order. This installment features a pack Enforcer who's the epitome of sunshine, a grumpy witch who never planned on being a single parent but would do anything for his child, a three-year-old who thinks wolf snuggles are the best thing ever, inept and allergy-inducing wooing, and a dangerous cross-country trip guaranteed to end in a happily ever after.

🐾

This one is for you.

THE KINCAID PACK SERIES

Free Prequel: A New Pack for New Year
(Victor & Cole)

The Alpha and His King
(Rick & Kai)

The Second and His Bonded
(Bennett & Kieran)

The Deputy and His Enforcer
(Marcus & Robson)

The Hunter and His Mates
(Drake & Jamie & Gabriel)

The Enforcer and His Heart
(Nico & Keegan)

The Witch and His Doctor
(Doc & Damien)

CHAPTER ONE

"You shouldn't be here."

Nico pushed to his feet, eyes locked on the young man across the room from him. A room filled with greenery and bright blossoms all around them. He had to imagine that the scent would have been overwhelming, though it was beautiful.

But not as beautiful as *him*.

"You're acting like I have any control over being here."

Keegan's lips twisted, his face turning away. Where he stood, most of him was shrouded in shadows from what looked like some sort of fruit tree, but Nico didn't need to see him clearly to know exactly what he looked like. Keegan haunted his every waking moment as well as his dreams.

He wasn't quite as tall as Nico or as broad, but he wasn't small by any means, his body a well-honed weapon that showed in the firm lines of his muscles. His dark brown skin came from his African American mother and Haitian father, and his dark brown eyes tended to be serious. When he was annoyed, they'd turn downright breathtaking. His black curls were always a little wild-looking, and Nico yearned to touch them.

There was a thin scar on the left side of his face that went down to his jaw. Nico hadn't learned where it came from, but he hoped whoever had given it to him was still alive so he could have the honor of killing them.

Not that he'd told that to Keegan. He had a feeling his strong, independent witch wouldn't appreciate Nico's need to protect him.

"If you didn't want to be, you wouldn't," Keegan argued.

Nico shrugged, grinning. Keegan's surliness couldn't fool him. "Maybe, maybe not. Of the two of us though, I'm not the one with magic."

Slowly, he stepped forward, being careful not to move too fast. He'd made that mistake in the past. If he approached with any sort of speed—or even too much eagerness—Keegan would flee. It had been... too long since he'd seen him, and he refused to have it be over so quickly. He'd take every stolen moment he could get and hold them to his heart like the greedy fool he was.

"What is this place?" he asked, reaching out to run a finger over a large orange blossom but not actually feeling it.

"Alpha Davis's solarium. I used to visit it quite often when I was in his territory."

"You're not there anymore?" Nico knew he wasn't. Keegan was very careful not to share where he was during their nighttime meetings, which was probably smart. Because if these conversations were *real*, impending threat or not, he wouldn't be able to stop himself from going to find him.

And he wasn't sure what he'd do once he had Keegan in front of him again.

And *that* was why he hadn't asked the pack's coven to find him.

When he got within a few feet of where Keegan was half-hidden, he paused, frowning at the way Keegan's body tensed, and knew he'd reached the limit of how close he could get.

But goddess, he wished there was no limit. He wished their time together was real and he could touch the man. Hold him in his arms. Scent him.

"Are you safe?"

He always asked. Even when he told himself over and over not to pry or pressure Keegan, he couldn't help but ask that. He wouldn't be able to live with himself or go about his day once he woke if he didn't.

And like always, Keegan answered, "I am."

But Nico knew that it was a lie sometimes. He didn't need to hear Keegan's heart or catch his scent to know it. Not when he could see for himself the edges of bruises and scrapes. The occasional limp. Whatever work Keegan did for his coven—he would never really tell Nico that either—it was dangerous, of that he was sure.

They stood in silence for a few moments, but Nico didn't really mind. Just being in Keegan's presence, even if he wasn't *really* with him, was enough to soothe his wolf and ease a little of the ache in his soul. Their moments together were all he'd had for months, and as long as he reminded himself frequently that it wouldn't be like this forever, it was enough to get through each increasingly long day.

Except when he couldn't stop the voice in his head from whispering that all of these dream meetings were just that: dreams. Figments of his imagination and nothing more.

Those ended up being days where he holed up in his office in town and avoided everyone until he could get his game face back on.

When Keegan scraped his teeth over his bottom lip, his eyes darting away like they did when he was getting ready to leave, Nico took a step back, giving him just a bit more space and turning to one of the exotic plants next to him.

"This place is really nice," he offered, smiling at the prickly plant. Beautiful and unapproachable—just like someone else he knew. "I can see why you enjoyed visiting. I have no idea what most of these plants are, but they're nice to look at."

"That is a castor bean plant. Its seeds contain ricin—it's one of the most deadly toxins known to man."

Nico snorted at his dry tone, eyeing the spiky red flowers and purplish-brown leaves. He cast a look around the rest of the greenhouse, wondering what other poisonous plants were hiding in plain sight. He wasn't sure if he should be more worried about why a pack had such a dangerous plant or why Keegan had enjoyed visiting the murder flowers.

He watched Keegan out of the corner of his eye, unable to completely look away. All he ever wanted to do was look at Keegan. Talk to him. Just be in his presence.

Goddess, he prayed he wasn't just dreaming up all of their interactions. He wasn't sure what he'd do if all the little bits and pieces of information he'd gleaned over the months turned out to be nothing more than things his brain had invented.

Because he liked this Keegan. A lot. He liked that he was serious and brilliant and gorgeous. And he knew that if their dream dates were real, that meant Keegan couldn't stay away from him either, and that... that made every day they spent apart worth it.

Well, almost.

When he spotted Keegan fidgeting with his clothes, he felt a bolt of panic, casting about for something to say to keep Keegan from leaving. "So you spent a lot of time here? When you were in the Davis Pack's territory?"

Sighing, Keegan shoved his hands in his pockets, eyes

downcast. Like every other night, he was wearing some variation of what he'd had on the night they'd met. Tonight, he had on khaki cargo pants instead of jeans, but the baggy hoodie was a staple.

Nico wondered if it was part of the illusion, his brain filling in what he'd seen Keegan wearing before rather than showing him the reality of his witch's day-to-day. He didn't really understand how the spell or whatever worked. He just said a prayer every night before he went to sleep that he would dream of Keegan, the witch who'd enchanted him without so much as a word.

The night Keegan had broken through the protective warding around the Kincaid Pack lands, they'd locked eyes for a second. The span of two heartbeats. It had been so brief, it shouldn't have mattered. And yet…

Months later, he could still clearly remember the way it had felt like he'd been kicked in the gut by a horse. When Keegan had turned away to leave, Nico had stepped forward, his instincts clear on the fact that he needed to get closer to the mysterious man, and Nico wasn't one to ever ignore his instincts. He was closer to his animal side than most, having grown up in a pack that revered that connection.

And if Colt hadn't grabbed his arm, Nico would have chased after him. As soon as their gazes had connected, he'd known the truth. Even after all the time that had passed, he still felt it, deep down in his soul where his wolf prowled, angry that they hadn't chased after him.

Keegan was his mate.

He also knew their love would not come easy. He was sure of that. It was a damn good thing he was a patient man.

"I did," Keegan finally said, and Nico could have crowed in triumph. Some nights, no matter what he did or said, Keegan would barely speak and then disappear abruptly. Those nights were almost worse than the ones where they didn't see each other at all. "My assignment there was... complex and required I stay for nearly two months. The pack itself was quite busy with a lot of pups running around. So there was always chaos and noise."

"And you liked to get away from all of that," Nico finished for him.

Keegan nodded, his chin tipping up just enough that his intense eyes caught Nico's and held for a few seconds, heating the blood in his veins and stirring his wolf.

It made sense that Keegan would like the quiet isolation of the solarium. He'd discovered that while Keegan was young and powerful, he was also smart and had little patience for people he felt were foolish. He also seemed to be very careful about what he said, at least to Nico, weighing each of his words.

Sometimes, it drove Nico crazy. He wanted his mate to be able to speak freely, to say whatever he wanted without having to worry. But he knew that would take time. A lot more time than they'd had with their stolen moments in their dreams.

Or none of what they'd experienced together was real and his brain just loved to torture him.

Nico cleared his throat, trying to dislodge the painful lump that had popped up. "I get that. Sometimes the manor is so loud nowadays I can barely hear myself think."

Head cocking to one side, Keegan studied him. "You like it though."

It wasn't a question, and Nico couldn't help but be elated that Keegan was getting to know him too. He chuckled and ran a hand through his hair. "I do, most of the time. Playing with the pups is an acceptable excuse not to get work done as far as I'm concerned."

Something painful flashed across Keegan's face, and Nico

took a step toward him without thinking, a low growl building in his chest.

"What's wrong?"

Keegan shook his head harshly, curls tumbling around at the movement. "Nothing. It's... It's nothing."

Nico had to look away from him and take a few steps back to quiet his agitated wolf. He looked around the solarium, noting all the dark corners inside the glass walls. It was pitch-black outside, a large array of stars shining above them with just a sliver of a moon.

It occurred to him with a jolt of jealousy he couldn't control that the greenhouse, with all its hidden corners and mass amounts of foliage, would be the perfect place to meet a secret lover.

The fact that he never knew where they were when he opened his eyes had been the one aspect of the dreams that had made him hold out hope that they were real. That Keegan was choosing places he'd visited in the past rather than Nico's brain making up something random.

But if Keegan was choosing places that reminded him of men or women he'd fucked or cared for in the past...

A snarl ripped from his throat, and he coughed to try and cover it, rubbing at his eyes to hide their telltale glow and accidentally pricking himself with a claw. Shit. He was losing control in a damn *dream*. "Did you use to bring anyone else here?" he asked, working hard to keep his voice level and dreading the answer.

When only silence met his question, a sourness grew in his mouth, and he wondered why he could taste that but not smell the flowers or hear Keegan's heartbeat. There an odd pressure on his arm that startled him. He looked down and stilled when he realized that long fingers were gripping his forearm.

Black, intricate tattoos trailed around each finger. Nico followed the line of his arm up to his shoulder. Then to his throat. His stubbly jaw and lush mouth. When he landed on Keegan's dark brown eyes, he couldn't help but lick his parched lips, dying for a taste. His wolf wasn't used to being denied.

Nico's gaze dropped back down to Keegan's bobbing Adam's apple, the nervous tell more than he usually got and somehow stirring his wolf even more.

There was no stopping the glow of his eyes as he met Keegan's once more, dying to ask if all of this was real. If *any* of it was. At the sight of his wolf peeking out, Keegan sucked in a breath, and Nico wondered if he had his answer or just the one his brain wanted so desperately.

"You silly wolf," Keegan whispered, trailing his fingers up Nico's arm to his shoulder. He still couldn't really feel it, just that strange pressure, but it was more than he'd ever experienced in one of the dreams. What that meant, he wasn't sure.

Keegan gave his head a shake just as his fingertips hit the side of Nico's neck and causing him to shudder. It wasn't real, but it was something.

He had to believe this was really Keegan, that his mate was using magic to bring them together because he couldn't stand not being able to see Nico either.

He had to believe it.

It was all that was keeping him sane.

Nico held his breath as Keegan leaned closer, their bodies a bare inch apart. His hair fell over his forehead as he lowered his head just a little. Keegan was staring at his mouth, Nico's heart about to beat out of his chest...

But then Nico felt *the tug*. The one he always dreaded and always came far too fast.

Deep in the pit of his stomach, like a hook snagged in his intestines, it pulled him backward without actually moving his body. He felt the loss of Keegan's touch like a punch to the face as everything around him began to fade.

"No!" he snarled, fighting like he hadn't since that first time before he'd learned there was no stopping the tug. "Not yet!"

But, of course, it didn't stop. The last thing he saw before everything went black was Keegan's face and his sad eyes.

"Nico, man, are you okay?"

Waking with a jolt that shot him halfway out of bed, Nico panted and stared at his closed door, breathing in José's familiar scent and letting it ground him in reality.

The reality of Keegan not being there. Of maybe never being there.

And Nico having to continue to pretend he was fine.

"Yeah," he finally said, but he had to clear the sticky emotions out of his throat before he could continue. "Just a dream."

It was always just a dream.

José hesitated, like he was going to ask if he could come in or if Nico wanted to talk about whatever had caused him to wake up screaming—again—but he just sighed and walked away. Nico waited until he heard him start down the stairs, then let himself flop back on his bed, his sheets twisted around him like he'd been thrashing.

Which he was sure he had been.

He stared at the ceiling of his sage-green bedroom for a minute, trying to recall every moment of the dream. The words Keegan said and the ones he hadn't.

But *only* a minute.

It was all he ever allowed himself when he woke from the dreams or whatever he was having with Keegan. Or about

Keegan. Whichever it was, whether real or not, he couldn't let himself have more than the few brief moments when he first woke up, or he knew he'd obsess all day, trying to find an answer... or try and find Keegan.

It had been more than half a year since they'd locked eyes for that split second, and Nico's wolf had nearly burst out of his chest. He'd never experienced anything like it. A bone-deep certainty that the defiant witch standing toe-to-toe with his alpha was the most important person he'd ever met.

Then their gazes had broken, and the feeling in his chest had subsided. Within a few moments, the blazing intensity had disappeared—along with Keegan. He'd shaken off the feeling, telling himself he'd imagined it, thanks to all the magic in the air that night.

And he'd almost convinced himself.

Until the dreams started.

The first one happened about a month after Keegan had stormed into the pack's territory and through their coven's warding like they were made of caution tape. It had been fuzzy though, nothing like they were now. The only thing he'd seen had been Keegan, the edges of his form blurry like an out-of-focus picture.

His mouth had been moving, but Nico hadn't been able to hear him. When he'd woken up, he'd told himself that it had just been a weird dream and nothing more.

But then he'd had another one, and then another. Gradually, they started to become clearer, more defined. Three months after their eyes connected that night in the woods, Keegan finally spoke to him for the first time: "Hi, Nico."

After that, Nico had craved their nighttime conversations, even if Keegan didn't share a lot with him. Just being near his mate eased the strain his wolf felt during the day, knowing he was so far away and maybe in danger.

Over the months, the settings of the dreams changed

often, but it was always just him and Keegan, which made Nico think they really were real. But he hadn't told anyone about them because... well, if they were real, he wasn't ready for anyone to know that he had some sort of magical connection to a witch that wasn't part of their coven. Was, in fact, part of a coven who hated parahumans by all accounts.

But the other reason, the bigger one that had kept him from even telling his best friend, Marcus, was that he was *terrified* they weren't real. That it was all in his head. That it was his brain's way of making him feel better over the fact that he hadn't seen or spoken to Keegan since the night they'd locked eyes. Hadn't even gotten a chance to speak to him that night either.

But the dreams were becoming more frequent and more intense. He'd never felt anything before, and he'd tried touching things often—even Keegan once or twice while he wasn't looking. He'd run a finger over the back of his hand or shoulder, but it hadn't registered, and Keegan had never reacted.

So he wasn't sure what it meant that he had felt some sort of sensation when Keegan had grabbed his arm. Maybe it was because Keegan was the one who wielded the magic and had been the one to do the touching, or maybe it was nothing more than his brain filling in because he wanted it so badly.

Either way, his minute to mourn the loss of the connection was over. He sat up and took a deep breath, tucking away his feelings.

By the time he was downstairs in the kitchen pouring himself a cup of coffee, he had his regular smile fully in place, flashing it at José as he came into the kitchen. The beta gave him a once-over, then shrugged and went over to the fridge to grab the orange juice.

Nico used to live alone—all of the Enforcers did. Most of the betas had also had a place, or at least an apartment, to

11

themselves. But with the influx of people into the area—between the former McAllister members who'd chosen to stay on and the Keshena Pack temporarily seeking refuge after being attacked last fall—housing was in short supply. Those who were able and willing were doubling and tripling up; even some mated pairs had taken in roommates until the pack was able to get more housing built. One of Nico's many headaches.

Fiona and Colt had offered to let him move in with them, but he'd been sort of attached to his house and decided he'd rather open it up to somebody else to join him than share space with the BFFs. He would have always been the odd man out if he'd moved in with them. Fi may have been ace, but Colt was one hundred percent her person. And Colt was a gentle giant, the slow-to-anger type, except if somebody threatened those he considered his. Fi had moved in with him years ago after Colt's brother had died, and they'd been inseparable ever since.

Nico had honestly lucked out when it came to a roommate, he figured. José was young, but he was smart and capable. He was also a great beta and had taken on more responsibilities lately, partially because he never saw a job as beneath him. Rick and the Enforcers valued that desire to serve the pack in whatever capacity was necessary. Nico had no doubt he'd make an excellent Enforcer one day as well.

They'd had another beta living with them for a while, but she'd found her mate the month before when one of the new hunters had arrived. That had been... complicated. Despite the fact that a pack Enforcer and Rick's personal assistant were both mated to the hunter Gabriel, it had still caused quite the stir. Though part of that had been because the new hunter hadn't even made it through the full screening process yet.

Another of Nico's headaches.

Somehow, Gabriel had convinced Rick that the pack needed hunters to help protect them from any upcoming conflicts with the Council. It was right after they'd found out the Keshena Pack, along with a handful of other allies, had been targeted and threatened for offering to stand with the Kincaid Pack. Despite being a large and prosperous pack, they didn't have a ton of fighters to protect the civilians and humans if they were attacked.

But bringing in retired hunters or those who wanted to leave their clans and pledge allegiance to Rick had caused some to question his leadership—a few going so far as to leave the pack.

"Are you ready?" he asked, shaking off his heavy thoughts and draining the last of his coffee. He'd stop at the café on Main Street on his way through town and grab the biggest cup they had. He felt like he hadn't slept much last night, but that was common after one of Keegan's visits.

He and José were hitting up a few places before heading to the manor, including the housing development site and the training facility Gabriel had also talked Rick into. It was attached to the bunker where most of the hunters were staying but open to the whole pack, and Nico had to admit the place was sweet. He loved sneaking in a training session with one of the experienced hunters whenever he could— they kept him on his toes in a way the other Enforcers couldn't anymore, since they were all so used to each other's fighting styles.

José looked up from his phone and shook his head. "Actually, no. I'm going to have to go straight to the manor."

"You're bailing on me? How rude."

José chuckled as he chugged the rest of his juice and tucked his phone away. "Hardly. I just got a text that I got tapped to be Kai's shadow today."

Nico nodded. "I suppose protecting the alpha-mate is a *little* bit more important than running errands with me."

"Maybe a little," Jose said, already heading for the door. "Ericka is picking me up in a minute. Let me know how the meeting with the city planner goes. Hopefully he finally signs off on the last of the permits."

"Hopefully." Rick had assured him that the mayor had leaned hard on the man to get him to finally approve the development plans so they could finally break ground. Everything else was ready to go. "Good luck with Kai."

José wrinkled his nose as he pulled on his shoes. "Thanks. He's gotten better about the protection detail."

Getting Kai to accept protection had been a weeklong fight that Nico had made sure to avoid as much as possible. Rick had been adamant though. Outside the manor, his family could be too easily targeted even with all the pack members and magical protection around the territory.

Nico and the other Enforcers had agreed but were all too busy to take on the duty. Gabriel had offered to set up a schedule for the hunters to cover Kai and his siblings, but Rick had nixed that immediately. He wanted shifters with all their enhanced abilities to be the ones protecting them. Using the betas stretched them thin, but Rick had finally approved a new batch to help fill out the ranks.

Sighing, Nico stared into his empty coffee mug, wondering if anyone would notice if he just... took the day off. Maybe stayed home and took a nap. Almost as soon as the thought crossed his mind, his cell phone started to ring.

Glancing at the screen, he set his mug in the sink and answered, "This is Nico."

"Hey, man, can you help me out with something?"

Forcing a smile, Nico headed for the door. "Of course. What do you need?"

CHAPTER TWO

K eegan was playing with fire.
       An irresistible and beautiful, but ultimately doomed, fire. But he couldn't stop himself. Even as he tried to go about his day, he kept thinking about the night before and the look on Nico's face when he'd asked if Keegan had ever brought anyone else into the solarium.

Why did the idea that his wolf was jealous heat his blood and quicken his breath?

It shouldn't matter. Nothing about Nico would ever truly be his business. Nico would never be his to care for and protect—or be cared for and protected by. No matter what *fate* had decided, he knew it could never come to pass. And he also knew that it was only making things worse for Nico, their midnight dream walks. That the more time he and his wolf spent time together, the harder it would be for him to let Keegan go.

And Keegan wasn't fucking fooling himself. Nico would have to let him go.

Despite what he'd felt that night when he'd busted through the warding around the Kincaid Pack land and his eyes had met Nico's for that split second. He knew it was a fraction of what Nico must have felt, but his magic had been so thick in his veins, ready to defend himself at a moment's notice, that it had reached out for Nico, yearning for a taste. He'd barely been able to hold it back from latching onto the wolf.

He was pretty sure the leader of the Kincaid Pack's coven, Tashmica Torres, had felt it when his magic had surged inside him, about to break free. The look she'd given him right as he was leaving had been knowing... and also pitying. He was sure that she'd heard stories about his coven and knew without him having to say anything that any feelings he had or could have for Nico were destined to come to nothing.

It didn't matter if they were mates—fated or not. His coven—fuck, his *mother* would never allow such a union. In her eyes, mating a shifter was no better than mating with a common dog. They were beasts not to be trusted, unable to control themselves. Most of the elders in the La Fleur Coven believed the same.

Of course, it had been decades since any of them had even left New Orleans except to meet with like-minded allies. He and the others who were sent out to investigate and punish parahumans who posed a threat to humans were the only ones who ever encountered shifters. And he had learned the truth long ago. That despite what his coven had taught him his entire life, just as there were good and bad witches, there were good and bad shifters.

And he knew, in his heart of hearts, Nico was *good.*

He could see it in his sweet, unassuming smile and hear it in his easy laughter and the way he talked about Rick's pups. And the quiet yearning he had for a family of his own one day. Every time they met at night, Keegan barely allowed himself to speak, too afraid of what would come out of his mouth. But Nico… He would talk and talk, filling the space with stories and laughter, slowly coaxing Keegan closer and closer. Winning his heart even though it was not his to give. Not anymore.

It hadn't been for years.

He needed to let Nico go. He told himself every night, and sometimes he resisted. Sometimes, he wouldn't take the herbs and whisper the spell right before he went to sleep that would allow him to dream walk and bring Nico to him.

But more and more often, he couldn't fucking help himself. It was an itch beneath his skin that no matter how often he scratched could never be satisfied until they were truly together. Their midnight meetings were only making it worse because that could never happen.

To make matters worse, his friend Gabriel kept pestering him about translating some journal for the Kincaid Pack. When Gabe had first asked if he'd be willing to translate something for him that was in Haitian Creole, Keegan had agreed without thinking much of it. But then Gabriel had explained that it was a whole journal that couldn't be mailed to him, and it was actually for the pack his friend had joined. The same pack where Nico was an Enforcer.

Bad idea.

Because he knew the pack "representative" Gabriel wanted him to meet with at some remote cabin in West Virginia would be Nico. He wasn't sure if Nico had told anybody about them or their dream walks, but if he knew his wolf, there was no way he'd let anyone else bring the journal to him, considering he'd been hinting at them meeting for months.

But if they were alone together, holed up in some out-of-the-way place, how long would it be before they gave in? Before Keegan had to have a taste?

What would it do to Nico when Keegan inevitably had to leave him behind?

So he'd been putting Gabriel off, trying to come up with a way of getting out of doing it, but he had a feeling his old friend was starting to figure out he was dodging him. He'd been using his coven as a convenient excuse because he really did need to be careful about when and where he could meet someone. While he was technically allowed to come and go as he pleased, he risked a harsh rebuke if he wasn't available when needed by the elders—or worse, if they found out who he was meeting with.

If anyone other than Gabriel had asked him for a favor like that, he would have said no immediately, and he would have to be more careful in the future about favors he did for the hunter now that he was a member of the Kincaid Pack. His coven *didn't* work for a pack or with them. Period.

To do so, he risked expulsion from his coven. Or worse.

If they decided he was deliberately aiding an enemy of the coven, he could face a whole hell of a lot worse. He'd heard stories of witches having their magic bound against their will, of others who were tortured and had their magic ripped from their bodies, and still others who disappeared and never came back. It was all whispers, of course, and it was rare for anyone in the coven to speak openly in front of him anymore.

Either way, he didn't kid himself into thinking that being the heir of the leader of the La Fleur Coven would mean fuck-all if someone found out he was helping the Kincaid Pack. In fact, there were a number of witches who would joyfully report him to his mother or the elders just to watch him get taken down a few pegs.

The work he did for the coven... he tended not to make a ton of friends.

Well, the work he did and his inability to put up with dumbasses.

Still, even before the recent falling out with the Council and whatever the hell had gone down with Jericho McAllister, the Kincaid Pack was considered bad news even by other covens. Not because of anything terrible they'd done, at least not as far as Keegan was concerned. It was more of the way Rick Kincaid took in strays and runaways without a second thought, giving shelter to those other packs that would have preferred to stay out in the cold or to have never left their family to begin with.

He wasn't an expert in pack politics, that was for sure, but even he'd heard rumblings because it wasn't just shifters that Kincaid took in. And when a coven expelled you, they expected you to stay distressed and unmoored, weakened by a lack of connection to others.

If anyone was even worse at making friends than him, it was Rick Kincaid.

"Keegan, are you ready?"

He sighed and closed the book he hadn't been reading, looking up at his mother. She was tall and slender and beautiful. Dark skin always flawless, hair and makeup perfect. And powerful beyond measure. She could proudly trace her family line back over five hundred years to a famously influential and powerful coven from an area of Africa now known as Ghana.

Whereas his dad's mom had been the first in her family with any true abilities, and she and his grandfather had left Haiti to join the La Fleur Coven, long before it had become the most dominant coven in the entire Southern half of the United States.

When he didn't respond to her question, she raised her impeccably sculpted brows at him, so he slowly rose to his feet. She rolled her eyes at his obvious reluctance, checking her lipstick in a small mirror from her purse. "Jasmine is from a good family and a strong coven. She would make a lovely match. I expect you to be on your best behavior."

Keegan had to stop himself from rolling his own eyes. His mother would *not* appreciate that. The last thing he wanted was to piss her off so early in the evening, but goddess, he was tired of these dinners. For the last year, she'd been setting them up and forcing him to attend.

She—and his father, though he seemed almost as reluctant a participant as Keegan—would pick out a prospective wife, contact her parents, and then set up a dinner for all six of them. They'd meet at a carefully selected restaurant, make polite conversation, and all act like it wasn't weird as hell that his parents were trying to set him up with an arranged marriage.

He did his best to play along. Truly, he did. He had to if he didn't want her digging into why he was so reluctant. It was becoming fucking tedious though.

If he didn't though, if she found out his plans or discovered his secrets, she'd make him pay.

Him and his daughter.

It wasn't that he had thought his mother was trying to find him a love match. But more and more, he was beginning to think his mother didn't actually care if he was even *happy*. That's the only explanation he could come up with for why each prospective bride he was set up with was worse than the last. More dull and self-centered, and he'd be surprised if—despite their excellent lineages—a single one had any sort of active power.

Worst of all, they were the complete opposite of his Nico.

All night, he bit his tongue and refrained from any caustic remarks.

And it was damn hard.

He thought about telling her that he was already taken. He thought about rolling his eyes when she started another story about something she'd bought earlier that day. He even refrained from telling her how she should lead with her parents' money and influence in the future because her personality was shit.

When they all stood from the table to leave, Keegan pasted on a smile, shook her hand, told her it was a pleasure to meet her, and walked away without a backward glance, getting no small amount of joy out of her outraged gasp.

His mother wasn't happy though. When she and his father slipped into the back of the car, she asked Willie to close the partition, the old driver doing it without hesitation. Even with it closed, she didn't say anything the entire way back, and Keegan knew it wasn't because she was aware that Willie could still hear everything. He'd been with their family for over a decade—he'd seen and heard worse than her scolding him for being rude to some twit.

No, Willie wasn't the one she wouldn't lash out at him in front of it. It was his father.

As much as she ruled the La Fleur Coven, she still seemed to love and respect his father, and he wouldn't abide by her harsh words for Keegan.

But he also didn't speak the whole way home either. As much as their marriage had started based on love and affection, the more powerful his mother had grown, the quieter his father had become. These days, he rarely left his greenhouse, toiling over his plants and herbs like they mattered more than the state of his family.

Keegan would sometimes think about how differently their family had been when he and his sister, Jocelyn, were kids. His mother had always been strict, but she'd indulge his father, letting him take him and Jocelyn out to explore the city and swamps. They'd visit his father's parents in their little house out in the bayou, spending all day with his grann and papa cooking griyo and plantains. Grann made sure he and Jocelyn knew Creole, not wanting them to forget their Haitian roots.

After they passed, Keegan's father grew quieter, more isolated and eager to follow his wife's lead. Even when it meant ostracizing their coven from others in the region and Jocelyn from their family.

When they reached the house, his father shot him an apologetic smile and then... disappeared. Keegan knew without having to ask that he would head right upstairs to change before going out to his precious garden.

Sighing, Keegan tried to follow, wanting nothing more than to lock himself in his bedroom and meet Nico in his dreams and just forget everything his mother was trying to do to him. But her clipped "Wait" froze him at the bottom of the steps.

She didn't say anything else, simply turning and stalking toward her study. He knew better than to ignore her. Silently, he followed, closing the door behind him and leaning against it. He watched as she stepped behind her enormous desk, deceptively delicate hands landing on the back of her executive chair, and raised her pointed chin just enough to look down her nose at him.

He'd spent many hours in her study getting looked at like that. Half disappointment and half annoyance. Like he was a fucking pet that shit on the rug—you couldn't *really* get mad at them; they didn't know better.

The room was full of research and reference books, as well as at least a dozen grimoires, and the scent of incense was heavy in the air. In front of the large picture window, there was a small table with a worn cloth bag and some candles. He knew that inside the bag was his mother's most cherished possession: her tarot deck.

She'd been gifted many other decks over the years, but when she really had questions to ask, she used that one and always kept it close at hand. Her father had given it to her when she was a child, she'd told him once when he was young and not such a failure in her eyes. Back then, she'd shared things with him, including that the deck had never steered her wrong. She'd said that thanks to it, their family would become powerful and wealthy beyond measure. That other covens would fear them, and parahumans would tremble at their feet.

As a child, that had sounded terrifying. Why would he want that when he could just have his family happy and in their small house where he and his sister caught crawfish and swam and learned to harness their magic?

But like always, his mother had been right.

When he visited other covens on official business or went to investigate unruly packs, he was watched with trepidation and distrust. Sometimes, downright fear.

"I didn't appreciate your attitude at dinner tonight," she finally said, nails digging into the leather back of her chair.

He held her gaze, but his insides trembled. "I didn't say a single improper or rude thing to that incredibly dull woman."

"No, but you were thinking plenty of them."

The bottom of his stomach fell out, but he firmed his jaw. "My thoughts are my business, Mother, and I would thank you to stay out of them."

That was the truly scary side of her.

For as well as she could read her tarot cards, she could read others even better. It was a rare ability and one that was revered by other witches. The elders had been so impressed,

23

they'd made her the leader of the coven at thirty-five, ousting the previous leader without hesitation when his mother helped negotiate a truce with a neighboring coven they'd been feuding with for years with one conversation.

Of course, since then, she'd orchestrated a toppling of that coven and triumphantly added their territory to the La Fleurs', not even bothering to hide the fact that the leaders of the other coven had "disappeared" and the rest of the members had fled in terror.

One of a million reasons he'd kept his daughter hidden from her since her birth.

He had learned when he was a teenager how to pack away certain thoughts, but he couldn't completely block her out. He doubted he'd ever be strong enough to do that. And even if he could, it would only raise her suspicions. He'd witnessed firsthand what she did to those she suspected of lying or betraying her.

So he let her hear the mundane things, the everyday thoughts and complaints and musings, and kept his secrets locked away where not even she could reach them.

"As my heir," she began, "it is your duty to me, to this family, and to this coven to marry and have children with an appropriate match."

Keegan's hands clenched at his sides, the reminder a familiar one. He wasn't the oldest, but Jocelyn was gone, happily married to a witch from an *inappropriate* coven.

He swallowed, trying to force down his anger. "I'm only twenty-four; I have time. Why are you pushing this suddenly?"

He had a feeling he knew, but he wondered if she'd admit to it.

She flicked her fingers in annoyance, a tiny spark lighting up at the ends and making him flinch against his will. "Your father and I were married at twenty-two, and I was pregnant

24

within the year. You are plenty old enough, *and it is your duty.*"

There was such finality to her words, like it was just a done deal that he'd fucking do as he was told and produce another generation of powerful witches to lead the La Fleur Coven for her. But it wasn't a duty he wanted, one he refused to live up to, in fact. He didn't voice the words, keeping them locked away behind his wall, but he knew that she knew. She wasn't stupid. Goddess, no. She was brilliant. She could anticipate others' moves like a seasoned general or brilliant chess player.

There was no way she *didn't* know it wasn't what he wanted.

And she had to know that he had a plan to get out of it.

He just prayed she never learned the true driving force behind his need to escape her, and her plans for him sat in his sister's house on the West Coast, already showing signs of her magic even at three. His sweet Rosie had been his reason for living and not giving in to his mother's demands since he'd first looked into her squishy, red face.

She was also the reason he could never have Nico, not if he wanted them all to escape his mother's wrath. He could only see one way out, a plan he'd been putting off executing, knowing it would devastate his wolf and wanting every last moment he could have with him.

But after years of sneaking away to visit Rosie and Jocelyn as often as he could, he knew he couldn't continue to risk everything for a few more dream walks with Nico.

He needed to stop, to give him up and let him move on and forget about Keegan. The terrifying light in his mother's eyes was proof enough he couldn't put off leaving any longer.

He'd bet every dollar he had tucked away that his mother was pushing the parade of dates on him because she thought if she could lock him down in a marriage to an appropriate witch from an appropriate coven, she could keep him under her thumb until she'd molded him into the next La Fleur Coven leader.

He just prayed he'd manage to get away before she found out the truth.

CHAPTER THREE

As Nico trailed through the woods behind Gabriel, he thought about trying to ask him again about Keegan. The couple of times he'd tried to bring him up, Gabriel had just given him his smart-ass smile and told him to mind his business, but Nico had never tried to talk to Gabriel about Keegan as anything other than a pack Enforcer.

Maybe that was where he'd gone wrong.

He carefully stepped over a downed log, senses all on high alert as the two of them moved nearly silently through the night. Only another shifter would hear the soft footfalls they couldn't completely erase, but another shifter wasn't who they were expecting to come across. He watched Gabriel's big form and thought about approaching him another way.

Gabriel and Keegan had the kind of bond most pack-mates strived for. They protected each other, fought for each other, lied for each other. Maybe Nico needed to be honest about why he was trying to ask instead of letting Gabriel assume that Nico was speaking in an official capacity, trying to hurry things along. Anxious for Keegan to get going on the work for the pack.

It was no secret that Rick wanted the journal Gabriel and his mates had found in Massachusetts translated and was growing impatient for it to get done. Unfortunately, the only person they knew and sort of trusted who could do it couldn't just waltz into the Kincaid Pack territory. And, according to Gabriel, was being vague about when they would be able to meet at a neutral location.

Rick wasn't waiting. Plans were moving forward without the journal and whatever knowledge was in it, but nobody really liked it. There were too many unanswered questions. The fact that a councilman had died trying to get it to Rick had to mean there were answers in it about *how* the Council was destined to be defeated. The seer who the journal belonged to, Angeline Pierre-Louis, had lived a hundred years ago and been renowned for her abilities. She'd also been famously half-witch, half-seer, and had predicted her own reincarnation.

Unfortunately, they were pretty sure a young witch in their coven, Jessica Macey, was Angeline's reborn spirit. How that played into what would happen, no one really knew, but Jess hadn't exactly taken it well, blaming herself for everything bad that had happened in the last year.

Whether the journal got translated or not though, war was coming. They all knew that. It was why he and Gabriel were traipsing through the woods—again—in the middle of the night.

When he cleared his throat, Gabriel chuckled, pausing to look back at him. The moon barely penetrated the thick, late-spring foliage, but Nico's eyes were strong enough to clearly see the former hunter just fine. And behind his thick blond beard, Nico was pretty damn sure he was smirking.

"Finally get the nerve to ask me whatever it is you've been stewing about?"

Nico cocked his head. "How did you know I've been stewing?"

That just made Gabriel laugh a little more. Once Nico was next to him, they continued on their way, shoulders brushing. "Because we've done this... what? Almost ten times now?"

Nico shrugged and nodded. "Almost."

"This is the only time you haven't talked my ear off."

That was probably true, and Nico couldn't help but smile at the big hunter's words.

A lot of the Enforcers—and betas—weren't big fans of Gabriel still, despite one of his mates being an Enforcer or that he'd finally revealed his scent in a bid to get Rick to trust him. And they weren't the only ones. There were a lot of people in the pack who still avoided Gabe because of who he used to be and how he used to make a living. Hunters killed parahumans, and some in the pack couldn't get past that.

Since meeting Gabriel and getting to know him and about his world, they'd learned that wasn't all they did anymore though. Gabriel had revealed to him and the others that many hunters, himself included, were hired for jobs by the Council.

A fact which other packs had found infuriating when Nico had started spreading the information around, contacting people he had met over the years during his travels and letting them know what was actually happening. How apparently for years, the Council had used hunters to take out shifters and other parahumans they deemed *prob-lematic*. He also told them about the Keshena Pack getting attacked and having to flee to Michigan, as well as the truth about what had actually happened with Alpha McAllister.

Many of his contacts were shocked, having heard very

different versions of events or not heard anything at all. Through these backdoor conversations, Nico had been able to secure quiet pledges of support from other packs that hopefully wouldn't put them in the crosshairs of the Council. Considering none of them had been attacked like the Keshenas or the few others who'd openly supported them, he was feeling a little more optimistic.

As far as Nico was concerned, a lot of what he and the other Enforcers had been able to accomplish in the last few months was a direct result of the information Gabriel had provided.

In fact, Nico had always kind of liked the guy. He and Robson Medina were both humans mated to powerful shifters and yet managed to go toe-to-toe with anyone who threatened their mates. Plus, they had wicked senses of humor, which Nico appreciated. He'd always been the kind of person to appreciate a good laugh, not taking himself or others too seriously. Even after joining the Kincaid Pack after years of traveling and never putting down roots, he'd done his best to stay upbeat and positive in spite of more and more responsibilities landing on his shoulders.

So he'd had no problem chatting with Gabriel during their trips into the woods, but it was getting harder and harder for him to pretend like everything was fine. Day in and day out, he was finding it difficult to be his normal self.

He knew he was getting slower to smile, and he was quieter, always caught up in his head and thinking about Keegan. He also knew the others had to have noticed, but they hadn't said anything, probably attributing it to the stress they were all under. It was almost funny to him that Gabriel of all people was the first to say something to him about it, even in such an offhanded way.

Of course, it didn't help that his best friend had been isolating himself for months, all tied up in knots over whatever was written in a mysterious note from the same councilman who'd made sure the pack had gotten the original Council charter and the seer's journal of prophesies. Whatever Marcus had learned, it was personal, and that was all he'd shared, even with Nico.

"You caught me," Nico said, giving Gabriel a half-hearted smile. "There's something I've been meaning to ask you."

"Alright."

Words wouldn't come. He was as sure as he could be that Gabriel wouldn't give him a hard time or blow him off. But for some reason, it felt almost like a betrayal to talk to someone else about his feelings for Keegan before he actually got to talk *to Keegan* about them, but it had been a week since their last shared dream. Something was starting to feel... off.

There was an itch under his skin that wouldn't go away. No matter how often he shifted and ran for hours, his wolf sensed something. Something Nico couldn't quite see yet.

"Kind of making me start to worry," Gabriel said with a chuckle when the silence stretched out to a full minute.

"Sorry, it's just—" He froze, tilting his head back and inhaling. At first, he just smelled the forest and Gabriel, the occasional critter... But then he caught it again. The scent of someone he didn't know floating in the air. He pushed his worries and their conversation into the back of his mind and focused, pointing in the direction the scent was coming. "He's there. A hundred yards or so."

Gabriel nodded, and they changed course in unison, closing the distance between them and their visitor.

As they drew closer, the tenser Gabriel became. Nothing about him visibly changed, the subtle shift in his scent the only indication something was different about him. It was like a switch had been flipped, putting him into the hunting mode he'd tried so hard to forget.

Colder, deadlier. An unapologetic killer.

31

Nico put a hand on Gabriel's arm when they were about ten yards away. They stopped, Nico calling out, "You've entered Kincaid Pack territory. Show yourself and present your invitation."

There was a pause and a tiny rustle, and then a tall, lean man with dark hair and a short beard stepped between two trees just ahead of them, his arms out to the sides and empty of any weapons.

"I don't have an invitation," he said, speaking clearly and slowly. His eyes bounced between Nico and Gabriel, like he didn't want to take his attention off either one for too long.

He felt Gabriel's arm move next to him, reaching for one of his many weapons. "That's not Trevor."

"You're trespassing." Nico watched the man carefully, sifting through his scent to try and get a better read on him and why he was there. To know the exact spot where Nico and Gabriel met the defecting hunters, the man had to know Trevor or one of the others Gabriel had reached out to. There was no blood or anger in the air—just a spike in his adrenaline and heart rate, along with a healthy dose of trepidation.

"I was told this was the place to come to if I wanted out of the life." The man shifted on his feet, taking a deep breath and adding, "If I wanted peace."

"Who told you that?" Gabriel barked, all of the friendliness from his voice completely stripped away. "How did you know where to come?"

There was a trip in the man's heart just before he said, "There's whispers. About finding a place among a pack. A strong one. One not afraid to stand up against witches or hunters or even the Council."

Nico tapped Gabe's arm once with his fingers, their signal that he'd detected a deception. The man might have been telling the truth about there being rumors, but it wasn't the whole truth. He was hiding something.

"Who told you to come here?" Gabriel said, pulling one of his knives free. The sound was soft, but the quiet of the woods meant it carried. When Nico saw the hunter's muscles in his shoulders and arms tighten, he knew he'd heard the weapon leaving its sheath. "Don't make me ask again."

"Trevor. Trevor told me."

Two taps. *Truth.*

"Where is he?" Nico asked

The guy lifted his chin, face hardening as his hands fisted at his sides. The anger souring his scent put Nico on edge, and he tensed as well, preparing in case the man did something insanely stupid like attack them. Gabriel's scent and heart rate stayed steady as hell, but he moved his arm forward, reacting to either Nico or the stranger's aggressive stance.

Sucking in a deep breath, Nico narrowed his eyes. If he hadn't been one of the best trackers in the pack, he probably would have missed the scent lurking beneath the man's anger. He was trying to look fierce and pissed off. But it wasn't the whole truth.

The guy was terrified.

"Trevor's dead."

"What were you going to say before?"

Nico turned his head toward Gabriel without actually taking his eyes off the hunter ten feet from them. He was sitting on the ground in the exact same spot he'd been standing, hands tied behind his back. He hadn't resisted or argued about waiting despite the chill clinging to the nights that spring, simply nodding and falling silent as Nico called Rick and let him know about the situation. Rick had told them to hold tight and that he'd be there with Tashmica, the head of their pack's coven, as quickly as possible.

"What was I going to say when?" he asked and then realized what Gabriel was talking about. "Oh, that." He ran his fingers through his hair and scratched at his scalp. "I was just..."

He hesitated. The hunter was doing a good job of pretending like he couldn't hear them, but Nico was pretty sure he could. Human senses weren't *that* weak, and he wasn't comfortable sharing his concerns in front of some stranger.

"We can talk about it later."

Gabriel eyed the bound man, then jerked his head in the opposite direction, stepping away a little farther. Nico followed but never let the hunter out of his sight. "Alright, we're out of earshot. What's going on?"

"It's Keegan," he finally admitted, grateful for the darkness and Gabriel's human eyes that hid his warm face.

Gabriel sighed. "Listen, I'll tell you what I told Rick three days ago—something's definitely up with him."

That was news to Nico. Rick hadn't shared with the Enforcers about that conversation. "What do you mean?"

Gabriel scratched at his beard and shook his head. "I knew it would be hard for him to get away from his coven without them finding out what he was up to, but it's been more than six months of excuses. I know he's gone out on missions for the coven, so it's not like he's on lockdown in New Orleans after helping me get Wendy here."

Heart squeezing, Nico tried to ask as casually as he could, "What kind of missions does he go on?"

"Depends on the situation," Gabriel said, shrugging. "Mostly he gets sent places where the La Fleurs suspect humans are being harmed by parahumans. If he finds enough evidence, he... punishes the guilty party. Or calls for more help if he needs it—but he prefers to work alone."

Alone. That wasn't a concept Nico could fathom. Even during his nomad days, he traveled from pack to pack because the drive to be around others was strong in shifters, especially wolves. They were social creatures and depended on their bonds with their packmates to keep them happy and healthy.

That Keegan preferred to go off into dangerous situations by himself was concerning to Nico. It made him question for the first time whether he could ever truly make Keegan happy. Was that why he was hesitating to meet? Because he wanted to put off telling Nico they weren't a good match?

The last dream they'd shared though, the way he'd grabbed Nico and called him a silly wolf, had seemed... different. Intimate in a way that was hard to explain.

Gabriel continued, having not noticed how much Nico was freaking out. "Regardless, there's no reason why he couldn't have met up with you someplace to start translating the journal. Even if it took a few trips to get it done, I don't know why he's putting it off. He just keeps making excuses."

It felt like a fist was squeezing Nico's heart. "Like he just doesn't want to do it? Or..."

Gabriel shook his head, long hair catching in the moonlight. It was too dark even for Nico's eyes to see the small braid with purple beads that he still wore. Every hunter wore their clan's color in some form, and even though Gabriel had left his clan and retired from hunting, he'd told Nico once that he kept the beads because they were a reminder of his past. That he didn't want to forget. He just wanted to move on. "I'm not sure. He could have just said no, but he's being cagey as fuck instead. He has to have at least guessed at how important this is."

Nico raised his eyebrows. "How much have you shared with him?"

His beard twitched. "Probably more than I should have, definitely more than Rick told me to, but not everything."

Nico rolled his eyes. "You know I'm an Enforcer, right? You can't just say shit like that to me."

"Please." Gabriel scoffed, crossing his arms over his chest, knife still in one of his hands. "Rick was being an unreasonable hard-ass about it. I trust Keegan with my life."

He paused, looking at Nico steadfastly until he nodded in understanding.

"I don't know what's up, but for him to be dodging me like this has me more than a little worried."

Nico watched the hunter sitting quietly between two tree trunks across the way. "Could you find out the next place he's going to be sent so I could meet him there?"

"I suppose we could try. He doesn't usually tell me until after he's finished with the job, but sometimes I can guess where he's going to be sent. There's something brewing in South Carolina. I wouldn't be surprised if his coven sends him there."

"What do you mean something's brewing?"

Gabriel didn't get a chance to answer. The sound of crashing and a feminine voice muttering about the inconvenience of being woken up in the middle of the night grew in his ears, and he held up a hand. Gabriel raised a brow as he lowered his arms and glanced around them.

"They're here."

Gabriel nodded, correctly guessing Nico would want to keep their conversation secret, and stepped back over to the hunter. The man looked up at Gabriel, but when nothing else happened, he dropped his gaze back to the ground in front of him.

Before Nico saw them, he caught their scents—annoyed but also a little worried.

It only took a few minutes for the figures to appear, Rick's sun-kissed white skin and gray T-shirt like a giant beacon next to Tashmica's dark skin and clothes. Even still, Nico would hear her coming a mile away. He grinned as he heard her curse and then thank Rick, guessing she'd tripped and nearly fallen.

Rick moved through the forest silently despite his large size. The alpha was one of the tallest and biggest men Nico had ever met, and he radiated power like no one Nico had ever seen, thanks to the strong bonds of his pack. Packs drew strength from their alphas, but it worked the other way too— the bigger the pack, the more power an alpha had access to. But if the alpha didn't have the strength to hold his pack together, it could wither and die around them.

They'd seen it happen. The former McAllister Pack hadn't had a pup born in years—a direct result of weak pack bonds. If it went on too long, pack members would start to struggle to shift until they eventually lost the ability altogether. In most cases, members left long before then, or another more powerful, shifter took control of the pack and became the new alpha.

Tiny next to Rick—and still making a hell of a racket— was Tashmica Torres. She'd taken over leading their coven about a year ago, but even before then, she'd been the one he and others trusted and called on for help. As they drew closer, he noticed her curls were covered with a black silk hair bonnet, and she had a royal purple robe tied over what looked like pajamas.

For some reason, he found it utterly charming and grinned as she looked up at him in aggravation, stalking past him to the bound hunter. He'd seen her in action in the middle of the night before, but usually she looked completely put together rather than like she'd just rolled out from between her sheets.

"Sorry to drag you out of bed," Gabriel drawled.

Tashmica huffed as she stepped closer to him, crossing her arms under her breasts. "Why don't I believe you?"

"You could have gotten dressed," Nico offered, trying not to smile when she whirled on him with narrowed eyes. "We would have waited."

She straightened her shoulders and raised her chin. "Why bother? I plan to wrap this up in five minutes and then get back in my bed for the rest of the night."

"Rick got dressed," Gabriel said, nodding at him where he stood staring at the hunter.

Tashmica rolled her eyes.

"I sleep naked," Rick said, stepping closer to the stranger and crouching down in front of him. He didn't say anything for a long moment, just studying him with a hard look. "What's your name?"

"Aiden," he said, watching Rick warily.

"Well, Aiden, you want to tell me why I shouldn't just kill you now for interrupting my beauty sleep?"

Gabriel snorted a laugh, and Nico had to press his lips together to stop himself from chuckling too.

"I heard you were looking for fighters," Aiden said, holding Rick's gaze.

Nico had to give him credit—not a lot of people outside the pack could do that. It was instinctual, even for humans not aware of parahumans, to recognize Rick's authority and dominance by averting their gaze. The primal part of their brains recognized him as the apex predator and uncon-sciously submitted rather than risk challenging him. He'd seen visiting alphas struggle to hold the man's gaze.

"Why would Trevor tell you that?" Gabriel asked, stepping closer, all traces of humor gone. "I knew Trevor; I trusted him. I don't know you."

For a minute, the guy didn't say anything or look away from Rick. Finally, he sighed, so softly Gabriel and Tashmica probably hadn't heard it. They definitely would have missed how he swallowed before saying, "Trevor was going to bring me with him. We were... together."

A new scent filled the air, burning Nico's nose. *Sorrow.*

Rick stood, rocking back on his heels, hands on his hips. "You loved him?"

Aiden's jaw clenched. "I did."

"Who killed him?"

"I thought it was our clan because they'd found out we were planning on leaving, but..." He shook his head, dropping his eyes back to the ground. "I snuck into where they were keeping him until his parents could get there. I wanted to... say goodbye."

When Aiden tipped his head back up, Nico wasn't surprised to see his eyes were glassy with unshed tears or the pain creasing his face. There was no deception left in him, every word true and heartbreaking. His grief wrapped around Nico like an oppressive cloud, and he had to work harder than normal to keep it from affecting him.

"What'd you find?" Nico asked, voice low.

"He was... shredded. I've seen hunters mauled by shifters before, and this wasn't that." He swallowed again, running his tongue over his lips. "Something literally tore him apart. I... couldn't even recognize him anymore."

"I'm so sorry," Tashmica whispered, tears shining on her dark cheeks.

Nico knew the others had to be thinking the same thing he was, that whatever had attacked Trevor had to be the same kind of beast that had been sent after Gabriel and his mates. And Wendy, the woman Keegan had rescued and brought to them at Gabriel's behest.

Nico chanced a glance at Gabe, and his face was hard, jaw set, no doubt remembering the attack on him and his mates. Sidling closer, he surreptitiously gripped Gabriel's shoulder, offering silent comfort and reminding him that he wasn't alone anymore.

They'd hunt down whoever was behind the beasts— behind everything—as a pack and make them pay.

"All I could think about was how the clan elders had said a shifter had killed him," Aiden was saying, sounding incredulous. "I stared at his mutilated fucking body and realized they must have known what had really done that to him. They had to. There was no way an experienced hunter could mistake that for a shifter attack."

Rick grunted in agreement, rubbing at the stubble on his chin.

"And if they were hiding it, that meant they were responsible for his death." Aiden's voice and face hardened, his sorrow lessening and turning to pure, white-hot anger.

"Why'd you come here?" Rick asked evenly, watching the man closely.

Fierce, dark green eyes met Rick's. "I'll help you with your Council business or whatever, but then I want you to help me."

"To get justice for Trevor?" Nico asked, though he was pretty sure that wasn't what Aiden was getting at.

"No. To help me fucking kill them. All of them. I want to burn my clan to the ground."

CHAPTER FOUR

"Daddy, do you see?"

Keegan smiled and nodded, even though he couldn't actually see what his daughter was holding. She was standing so close to the spelled mirror at his sister's house that all he could see was half of her chubby, happy face. That was all that mattered to him though.

He wished more than anything he could be with her every single day and hoped he would be able to make that happen very soon. He'd reached out to a witch he knew who was already a member of the Council's coven and was just waiting to hear back. The idea that very soon he wouldn't be stuck under his mother's thumb filled him with cautious relief, but he also mourned for his sweet wolf. He'd kept his promise to himself, resisting every night for a week to keep from dream walking with Nico.

But, goddess, the *guilt*.

He wrestled with one last trip into Nico's dreams, to try and explain why they couldn't meet like that anymore and that they'd never see each other in real life unless it was Council business, but each night, he chickened out. He knew

Nico could never understand why he was making the choice of applying to join the Council's coven, and even if Keegan explained about his daughter and his mother's terrifying power, his wolf would fight the decision. Maybe even come to New Orleans to try and help. And probably get himself killed in the process.

No fucking thank you.

Keegan didn't know the full extent of what was happening between the Council and the Kincaid Pack, but Nico had shared enough—as had Gabriel—for him to understand that Nico wouldn't just not understand, but he'd see Keegan's decision as a betrayal.

And he was too cowardly to see the look on Nico's face when he found out what Keegan was doing.

His nephew, who was a couple of years older than his Rosie, came careening into the room, laughing. Their dog was on his heels, woofing in excitement. He chased Rosie right out of the room, her bright giggles at once a balm and a stab to his heart.

His sister called after them to settle down and that it was almost bedtime, but he wasn't sure they'd heard with how loud they were being. He wished he was there more than anything.

"Those two," Jocelyn said with a sigh, and even though she looked tired, he knew that she was happy. Her hair was wrapped in a flowery turban, and she didn't have a speck of makeup on—and he was pretty sure there was a food stain on her shirt—like she hadn't had a second of peace or a moment to herself all day, but her smile was always wide when she looked at her husband or kids. "When do you think you'll get out to see her? It's been three weeks."

He sighed and rubbed his face. He was sitting cross-legged on some poor schmuck's crypt, inside a mausoleum so filled with cobwebs and crumbling stones there was no way anyone but him ever visited. It was isolated, on a piece of property not owned by the coven, and long forgotten.

The perfect place for him to contact his sister every day or two to check on Rosie and talk to her. They spoke on the phone too, sending coded texts as well, but the enchanted pair of mirrors they were currently using was the most secure way to talk. They regularly respelled them to make sure no one had tampered with them. He also kept a duffel bag of clothes and another of books and grimoires he'd collected since he'd started traveling for the coven. Since he didn't trust his mother not to go through his things if the whim struck her, he hadn't kept anything he really valued there in years. And the clothes were his insurance in case he needed to bolt.

He prayed that wasn't the case, but he believed in being prepared.

"I'm not sure, Jos." He ran his thumb down the scar on his face absently. "Beatrice has me meeting with all these different witches and going on these weird family dates. Without a job to cover my absence, she'll get too suspicious, and the last thing we want is her digging into me and my secrets."

Jocelyn didn't comment on him calling their mother by her first name, too used to it by that point. As far as he was concerned, she'd lost the right to be their *mom* a long time ago. Her face wrinkled in disgust though. "Family dates? That sounds... really disturbing."

"Trust me, they're even weirder than you'd expect. All of these women are..." He hesitated, not sure how to describe them. "Their families are powerful, without question, and so are their covens, but I'd be surprised if a single one of them could scry worth a damn. None of them have any real magic, that's for sure."

"Why would she think they're *appropriate*, then?" The

scorn she put in that single word was impressive. Their mother had been awful to Jocelyn when she'd fallen in love with her husband, Zeke. He was a witch and from a respectable coven, if not a particularly powerful one, but he didn't have any active powers, and their mother had been horrified when she'd found out. Even gone so far as to try and end the relationship. "She's all about more power."

He shrugged, running a finger through the pattern he'd created in the dust on the crypt ages ago. "I'd ask her, but it's not like she'd actually tell me."

"Still, after the fuss she made about Zeke's magic?"

"My best guess is that she's decided solidifying an alliance to another powerful coven is more important to her overall plans than gaining more magic." He rolled his eyes at her. "It's not like we don't have that coming out of our ears."

She snorted a laugh. "I suppose that's true. There was that one time—"

"I was eight." He groaned.

She kept talking like he hadn't said anything. "You made that boy who kept teasing me shoot rainbows out of his ears. He cried every time he saw me after that."

"And he and his friends never bothered you again."

"That's true," she said, smile softening. "My hero."

He grunted. "Hardly. But I fucking hate bullies."

"I know," she murmured, and he knew she was thinking about how the biggest bully in their lives had ended up being their own mother.

"Anyway," he said, clearing his throat. "I'm hoping I can get away in the next week or so. There's been rumblings about a pack in South Carolina."

"That's in the opposite direction, dear brother."

"Never stopped me before." He waved a hand. For three years, he'd been forced to see his daughter in secret every few weeks, whenever he could sneak away or had a job that got him out of New Orleans. If he hadn't had his sister to lean on when Rosie was born, he wasn't sure what he would have done.

But there had been no way he was going to let his mother raise another generation, not after everything she had said and done to him and Jocelyn. And that's what she would have done—taken Rosie from him, claiming he was too young to be a parent, and brought her up as her own.

Being away from Rosie was like living with his heart outside his chest, but he'd sacrifice anything to keep her safe and make sure she never went through the pain and fear he had growing up with his mother.

But he couldn't do it much longer. He was missing so much of her life, so many milestones, and it killed him each and every time Jocelyn told him another story. Or when she told him about Rosie's bad days when she was inconsolable and asking for him, her voice hushed because she was holding a sleeping Rosie, who'd cry every time Jocelyn tried to put her down.

He had a feeling those bad days were made worse because of her magic starting to come in. He and Jocelyn had both been young too, and it could be scary. Not having control of something so powerful that reacted to big emotions.

He just wished he could be there to hold her when she needed soothing.

When she was born, he hadn't really had a plan other than to keep her away from his mother and figure out a way to get himself out of the La Fleur Coven. Of course, that ended up being easier said than done. The one time he'd brought up the topic of leaving the coven with his mother, thinking maybe if he just told her that he didn't want the life she'd laid out for him, she'd respect that. Maybe even want him to be happy.

Looking back, the idea that she'd want what was best for him was laughable.

The explosive rage she'd flown into was how he'd gotten the scar on his face, and he'd decided subterfuge was the only way out. She'd been very clear that there was no *other life* option for him like there had been for Jocelyn. He might not have been the firstborn, but he was more powerful, and it was his one and only job to take over the coven one day and produce his own heirs. In her mind, they would become a dynasty. A legacy she had built from the ground up.

She would not let him go.

He couldn't help but think about a certain wolf in Michigan, probably wondering when Keegan would slip into his dreams again and getting frustrated that he kept putting off translating some journal. He forced himself to shake off the thoughts though. Nico and his pack might be powerful, but they'd be no match for the La Fleurs when his mother came for him.

And she would.

The strict but kind mother from his earliest memories had been completely obliterated by the woman who only ever sought more power. He wasn't sure when exactly she'd stopped caring about him and his sister as anything other than pawns to be used to get what she wanted, but at some point, something inside her had broken. Or maybe been corrupted.

Either way, his only chance to get away and not have his mother or the coven hunting him down and dragging him back—or worse—was to join another coven. But not just any other one. It had to be one more powerful or held in the highest of esteem by the coven elders. If they gave their approval, there wouldn't be much his mother could do.

It was just bad luck that the only option he could come up with—after researching and visiting packs and covens for years, some of which were led by witches or alphas even worse than his mother—was the fucking coven attached to the shifter Council. Their job was to protect the Council and enforce shifter law when necessary, but they were also highly respected even by covens like his own who stayed out of shifter business.

His mother wouldn't be able to put up a fight without raising the elders' suspicions because it would be considered a great honor to have a member of the La Fleurs on the Council's coven. She'd have to bite her tongue and pretend to be happy for him.

But he needed to score an invitation first. That was where his friend was hopefully going to come in handy. She couldn't bring him into the fold herself, but if he could get in front of the leaders of the coven, he knew he could impress them with his magic and knowledge and score a position.

Keeping everything from his mother before things were a done deal would be the tricky part though.

Jocelyn yawned, holding the back of her wrist to her mouth to cover it. His eyes caught on the tattooed sigil on the palm of her hand that perfectly matched the ones on his own, as well as everyone else in their coven. The mark was used to amplify and target their magic. He'd added more spelled tattoos to his hands over the years, but every witch of age in the La Fleur Coven had the palm sigils. "Alright, so you're going to come here after you take care of whatever's happening in South Carolina?"

He nodded. "Fingers crossed, I'll have to make a pit stop in Montana on my way through or before coming back home."

The Council was located in an isolated area of Montana, warded up the ass and surrounded by nothing but magic and wildlife. Living there would be a huge change from what he was used to in New Orleans, but it would be worth it.

It had to be.

She tipped her head back and stared at the ceiling of her home office. "Kee."

"Don't," he said, knowing if he didn't stop her before she got going, he'd be subjected to a twenty-minute lecture about how he was *throwing away his life*. "It's the only way to guarantee mine and Rosie's safety."

"No, it isn't," she said, voice breaking with her exasperation. "Just leave. You can come here; you can join this coven. She can't actually stop you."

He shook his head before she even finished. "She would come after me, Jos."

"I know she's powerful, but it's not like she would take on an entire coven just to get you back."

He probably should have shared more of the horror stories he'd collected of their out-of-control mother since she'd left, but he never wanted her to feel guilty for leaving him behind, not even for a second. Hell, he'd never even told Jocelyn the real story of his scar. She knew how demanding and controlling their mother could be when they were kids, but she had no idea the violent outbursts she'd become prone to having anytime she was challenged or felt like she'd been insulted.

And anything could become a slight if she was looking for a fight.

He'd had her lash out with her magic, striking him or choking off his air, for looking at her "the wrong way."

"You don't know that" was all he said. "The way she talks about my duty to her and our family... She would see it as a personal betrayal, Jos."

"What do you think she'd do? Drag you back kicking and screaming?" She snorted at the idea.

He looked away, staring at a crumbling cherub on a built-in shelf just inside the door of the mausoleum. "Maybe," he whispered. But what he really wanted to say was "No, Jocelyn, I think she'd kill me."

Jocelyn spent a while longer trying to convince him that he was wrong, but he knew the truth. She hadn't been there the last few years, watching as their mother became harder, more power hungry, more violent. He'd seen her discipline other coven members for the tiniest of transgressions as well, not just him, and leaving wouldn't be tiny by any means.

It would be the biggest offense he could commit in her eyes.

He let Jocelyn think he would wait to reach out to his Council coven friend so they could try and come up with another plan when he got there. Even if he could tell his friend to wait, he wouldn't, and it was too dangerous to reach out to her again anyway.

As he stepped into his parents' quiet and dark house, the hour later than he'd realized, he admitted to himself the true devastation of his plan had nothing to do with betraying his mother or the coven he had grown up in and helped him nurture and grow his magic and skills.

No, the part that twisted up his insides and brought tears to his eyes when he thought about it too hard was the loss of Nico. He'd held back from dream walking with him for a week, and it felt like he could barely catch his breath. But it wasn't fair to his wolf to keep holding on.

He needed to let him go.

As soon as Nico found out he joined the Council's coven, Keegan suspected he would never forgive him or want to speak to him again anyway. That he'd feel he could no longer trust Keegan. Gabriel had shared some hints of what was happening between the Kincaid Pack and the Council, and

Keegan had made some quiet inquiries of his own, but in the end, it didn't matter. It couldn't. It was the best option for him and his daughter, so he needed to sever his connection with Nico now.

He just prayed to the goddess that Nico would understand one day. Maybe even find another mate and be happy.

The thought of Nico with someone else hurt, more than it should have considering they'd never truly met or come close to bonding, but he steeled his spine as he walked up the stairs. It had to be done.

Maybe if he told himself that enough, he'd start to accept it

If it was just him, if it was just his life in the balance, he would have run already. He would have run to his sister, or to Nico, or to another continent. He would have used the skills he'd trained and worked hard for his whole life to hide for as long as he could.

He would have been his own person, lived his own life, the consequences be damned.

But it wasn't just him.

Keeping Rosie's birth a secret had been the most difficult thing he'd ever done. He'd been a twenty-year-old kid who'd gotten drunk with his best friend, Rose Ellen, had sloppy, less than satisfying sex they'd both laughed off the next day, and then a couple of months later, she'd come to him in tears, terrified of what her parents would say if they found out. Or even worse, what the coven and elders would think. Her parents were high-ranking members and had an ambitious future planned for her, and she was so scared she'd lose everything she'd worked hard for.

They'd both been so young and nowhere near ready to be parents, so deciding to head to a clinic to terminate the pregnancy had seemed like the obvious choice. He'd held her hand as she'd made the appointment and promised to go with her, but a few days before they were supposed to go, she told him about a dream she'd had that had felt more real than any dream she'd ever had before. Rose Ellen said she'd never had premonitions before, but that was what it felt like.

She said she'd seen Keegan walking toward a little girl, her curly hair in messy pigtails and wearing a bright yellow dress with a purple stain on it, as she was pushed on a swing. She was calling for Keegan and laughing, and as soon as he was close enough, she let herself sail right off the seat of the swing and into Keegan's waiting arms.

She told him he'd looked happier than she'd ever seen him.

And then she'd asked him, point-blank, if he wanted to be a dad. She'd said, "I don't want to be a mom right now, maybe not ever, but I can't shake that dream or the look on your face. If you want this baby, I'll do this for you. You're my best friend, and I love you."

The idea, once he actually let himself think about it, had been terrifying. But also thrilling. He'd almost said no. He came from a fucked-up family and wouldn't know the first thing about being a good dad, and there was no way he'd want any child of his raised in the La Fleur Coven.

But he couldn't quit thinking about her dream either. He'd lain awake for days imagining what the purple stain could be, wondering who was pushing her, trying to figure out if he could actually say yes...

In the end, even though it would be hard, even though it would be complicated as hell, he knew it would also be worth it.

He'd told her yes. He absolutely wanted to be a dad.

So, they'd hidden her growing belly as long as they could, and he'd made a plan to bring the baby to Jocelyn in Oregon after she was born until he could figure out how to get away from his mother. The last few months of her pregnancy, she'd had to spend with her cousin a few hours north of New Orleans. Rose Ellen's parents had thought she was just spending time with her cousin and learning under the small coven there for a little while and never seemed to be the wiser even after she returned home.

For Keegan, it had been the first big test he'd had for his ability to truly hide something from his mother. Something way more important than what he'd gotten up to during his spring break senior year with the Gallagher twins. He'd spent as much time away from her and the house as he could, but there had still been a few times where he'd had to implement his wall in his mind, focusing on making it as strong as he possibly could.

Of course, Rose Ellen had gone into labor while he was stuck in Alberta, dealing with a witch who'd been cursing the locals to die nasty and unnatural deaths. Not something he could exactly leave without putting innocents in danger and drawing major suspicion from the coven and his mother.

Jocelyn had been trying to find someone to watch her kids so she could fly out, her husband out of town as well, but not having success. Rose Ellen's cousin had been calling him every fifteen minutes, pissed as hell he wasn't there and wanting to know what to do since she didn't have anything at her place for a newborn, and Rose Ellen, after a hard labor, was in no condition to take care of the baby.

Freaking the fuck out, he'd called the one person he thought he could depend on to keep his baby safe and pay for his silence.

Gabriel had, thank the goddess, been between hunting jobs and able to get there in three hours somehow. Untraceable vehicle loaded up with supplies and with a promise to call Keegan every hour on the hour, he'd set off with little Rosyln Esther Toussaint, named for his sister, her mama, and Keegan's grann.

As soon as Gabriel had arrived in Oregon safely, Keegan had finally taken a breath, beyond grateful when the hunter had agreed to stay until he could get there too. And he'd also refused payment, asking Keegan for a special kind of spell instead in exchange. One that made his scent undetectable by shifters.

He'd gladly done it.

Holding his sweet Rosie in his arms for the first time, he'd looked into her face and known he would do anything to keep her safe and give her the best life he possibly could. That he'd sacrifice anything.

He hadn't known at the time that would include his sweet wolf.

If it hadn't been for that moment when he'd met Nico's eyes across that clearing and felt the earth move beneath his feet, he would have reached out to his friend on the Council's coven as soon as he'd come up with the idea. He'd been selfish, pretending he needed more time to get his plan in place, but he just hadn't been able to stop visiting Nico, knowing not even he was cruel enough to keep dream walking with him after he'd betrayed him.

As much as he missed his baby girl, he couldn't actually regret the time he'd spent with Nico. Maybe that made him a terrible person—definitely made him a terrible father—but for once, he'd taken something for himself.

He'd known the dreams he shared with Nico would be the only time they would get together and that they'd have to get him through the rest of his life, so he'd taken every moment he could, soaking up the sight of him and listening to him laugh and talk.

The injustice of knowing he had a true mate out there, someone who was the perfect match for him, and not being able to be with him had to be the most tragic thing to ever happen to him.

But severing the connection had to be done. For both their sakes.

It wasn't the only tie he needed to cut though.

Pulling out his phone, he found his text thread with Gabriel and read the last few his friend had sent, asking for updates and if Keegan was okay. Heart in his throat, he typed out a message and hit Send before he could stop himself.

Keegan: *I'm sorry. You'll have to find someone else to help you with the journal. Thank you for... everything. Please don't look for me. Goodbye, Gabe.*

Not letting himself stop to reconsider, he blocked Gabriel's number and then deleted it from his contacts. He'd have to dump his phone when he left anyway, but that would buy him a little time, hopefully.

He rubbed his stinging eyes as he reached the end of the hallway and opened the door to his bedroom. Before he turned on the light, he knew she was there. Nothing good could come of her waiting for him in the darkness, so he braced himself.

He used his magic to flick on a lamp, and his mother's hard, cold gaze met his as she lifted a hand. He swallowed, scrambling to lock down his thoughts and not show any reaction to the fact she'd somehow found the small velvet bag containing the herbs he used when he cast the spell to visit Nico.

They were the only incriminating thing he kept in his room because he had to use them right before going to sleep. But they'd been hidden in a spelled book that he'd hollowed out and should have only been able to be opened by him.

"Keegan," she said lowly, "who have you been dream walking with?"

Oh fuck.

CHAPTER FIVE

Nico loved running as his wolf.

His best friend, Marcus, resisted it as much as he could, trusting the man part of him more than the beast. And while Nico understood why he was like that and the trauma he'd gone through growing up in the pack that he had, it was still such a foreign concept to him.

He felt sorry for his friend, though he never told him that. He felt bad for anyone who couldn't understand the pure, unadulterated joy of embracing the most primitive parts of themselves and letting them run free. When he was his wolf, the voice that was always rattling off the list of things he needed to attend to became silent, all his worries drifting away.

His wolf didn't worry about the future or regret the past. He just… was.

The pack Nico had grown up in had been more on the hedonistic side than conservative, like Marcus's. They hadn't gone so far as to ban human inventions and luxuries like some fundamentalist packs did, but there had also never been any shame in following their animal instincts or embracing that part of themselves.

He was taught to listen to what his wolf needed and trust in him.

It wasn't until he left his family's pack when he was eighteen and started traveling as a nomad that he discovered some of the things they did were... different than how other packs interacted. His first lunar celebration he attended after leaving, he'd waited hours for the real celebration to begin, for the joining of mates around the campfire, but it never happened.

The more he traveled and learned, the more he realized how fortunate he had been.

He couldn't imagine growing up any other way. And even though he wasn't close with his family, he respected their traditions and valued the lessons they had taught him. Thanks to them, he'd always hoped that when he found his mate—whether by choice or by fate—he would be able to embrace some of the customs he'd left behind.

As he raced through the trees toward the manor, the air thick with flowers and tree pollen and mating animals, he couldn't help but imagine what it would be like to chase Keegan through the woods, stalking him and claiming him out in the open.

Warning away anyone who'd dare to covet what was his.

Would Keegan let him do that? A lot of other shifters weren't as interested in public matings as Nico was—would a witch who didn't even grow up around a pack even understand the animalistic drive to rut and knot his mate in the open air, staking his claim for all to see?

It seemed like too much to hope for, especially considering Keegan's resistance to meeting in person. After his conversation with Gabriel, Nico couldn't help but worry, especially since he still hadn't seen Keegan in his dreams.

They were nearing two weeks since the last time, and it was making Nico's wolf edgy as hell, the need to track him down and make sure he was okay driving him to distraction as the days went on.

Was Keegan pulling away, or was he hurt?

The not knowing was killing him.

He had a finance council meeting in less than an hour, but he hadn't been able to focus and had decided to go for a run. His skin felt too tight, and his stomach churned with worry constantly—his instincts screaming at him that something was wrong, that Keegan wasn't just busy.

He had no evidence to back up the feeling, but he had learned long ago to trust his instincts. It was one of the first lessons his parents ever taught him: to trust himself and his wolf. And both sides of him *knew* something was wrong. He just wasn't sure what to do about it.

Or if he had the right to go digging into Keegan's life.

In all their dreams together, they'd never once talked about being mates or what that meant for them. Nico hadn't wanted to push, hoping Keegan would relax and open up to him if he gave him space.

He sighed, the top of the manor coming into view, and resigned himself to begging Gabriel for help. He had a suspicion he'd have to confess the full truth of his connection with Keegan, and the idea made him bare his teeth, his steps slowing. It wasn't that he didn't trust Gabriel or want anyone to know how he felt about Keegan. He just hated the fact that he was being forced to confess before he was ready and, worse yet, that he had to depend on someone else to take care of his mate. Even if it was just to get his phone number.

When he broke into the clearing behind the manor, he veered toward the play area, where Rick and Kai's kids and a few others were playing. Callie screamed in delight at the sight of him, jumping off her swing before she was as close to the ground as her brother probably would have liked, based on Kai's small gasp. She didn't even pause though, taking off toward him at a run.

Nico stopped near the sandbox, where little Henry was, and let Callie come to them as the small toddler pulled himself up and over to him, burying his sandy hands and face into Nico's fur without hesitation. Callie hit his other side a little harder than he would have liked, but he was no dainty wolf and absorbed the impact without disturbing Henry where he was rubbing his cheek against Nico. The instinctive scent marking from pups he cared about so much settled him somewhat, and he turned his head to nose at each of them in turn, leaving his own scent on them.

Callie chattered at him, sharing everything about her day so far and petting his neck and ears. Every once in a while, she'd take a second to press sweet baby kisses to his face, giggling furiously when he licked at her in retaliation.

Some of the other children made their way over to say hello, gently touching his sides or legs—one adventurous young man pulling his tail and getting a gentle nip in reprimand. None of them had quite the same exuberance as the King siblings, but Nico wasn't offended. Most of them were pups from the former McAllister Pack, they and their parents still forced to live in the manor as they waited for housing to become available.

It was good for them. Nico remembered spending time with shifted adults in his pack growing up, long before he could shift himself. It helped strengthen the bonds between the kids and the rest of the pack. A lot of the other Enforcers didn't seem to want to take the time to indulge in extra snuggle time with the pups, but Nico loved it.

It felt infinitely more important than any meeting, to encourage the connection between him and these tiny packmates.

Especially since the McAllister kids had been so scared when they'd arrived. It was easier for them to play with him in this form than to try and talk to him as a man. He was just nosing in behind a small girl's ear to give her a quick scenting when a door at the back of the manor burst open, smacking against the wall with a hard bang.

He turned toward the noise, instinctively placing himself between the pups and the possible threat. He relaxed immediately when he saw that it was Bennett Young, the pack's second-in-command. He glanced at his mate, Kieran, who was holding his niece up so she could reach the monkey bars, and his stern expression softened for a second.

"What's wrong?" Kieran called, scent spiking with anxiety. Ever since he'd helped take down his father, the alpha of the McAllister Pack, he'd taken all of his former packmates under his wing, helping them acclimate to life in the Kincaid Pack and becoming very protective of them.

Bennett shook his head, then turned to Nico. "Get in here. Something's happened."

Shifting immediately, he pressed his hand to each of the kids still crowded around his legs as he exchanged glances with Kieran and Kai, who both shrugged.

"Something must have just happened," Kai said, the alpha-mate's shoulders straightening as he came over to pull a clinging Callie off Nico's leg. "We've only been out here fifteen minutes or so, and everything was fine when I left Rick right before that."

Nico nodded, his wolf still on full alert and just beneath the surface. He hurried into the small room just off the kitchen, where he'd left his clothes, and pulled on his jeans and T-shirt. Running a quick hand through his hair, he bent and tied his shoes as fast as he could.

It was midafternoon, so the kitchen was in full swing, preparing for dinner, but he didn't bother pausing to see if

Beth knew what had happened. The housekeeper was usually pretty up to speed with everything inside the manor, but with so many people in residence, she was busier than she ever had been.

He ran into Robson in the hallway outside the kitchen. His best friend's mate was a human—and a former deputy—who worked for the pack, stepping up their training and tactics. The sight of him looking and smelling as agitated as Nico felt didn't help calm him down.

"Do you know what's up?" he said before Nico could ask him the same question.

"No, Bennett said to get in here and then took off."

Robson pulled out his phone. "I got a 911 text from Marcus that said to meet him in the war room."

Nico's stomach dropped as they turned in unison toward the Great Hall, where they'd been meeting regularly since last fall to discuss different plans to handle the Council and whoever was the magical influence behind them. Since Rick had invited more than just his Enforcers and betas to the meetings, they'd needed the extra space.

There were raised voices that could be heard from behind the closed doors as they approached, and Nico's bad feeling from before grew worse. He tried to tell his wolf to stay calm, that they had no reason to believe any of this had to do with their mate.

He didn't really believe it.

As soon as he pulled open the door and stepped into the large room, he found Gabriel, and the hunter met his eyes, jaw firm. His scent was muted, like he was controlling himself so tightly it was affecting even that, but Nico's nose was sensitive enough that he still caught it.

Fear.

"What's going on?" Robson asked the room at large as he

made his way toward Marcus, where he was already sitting with Gabe's mates in the circle of chairs.

Gabriel hesitated, eyes still on Nico, and he realized that the hunter knew—or at least suspected—that his interest in Keegan went beyond what it should have been as a pack Enforcer. Clearing his throat, Gabriel turned to the group that had gathered so far and said, "My friend Keegan... he's in trouble."

Fuck. Sometimes Nico really hated being right.

"What do we know?" Rick asked as he burst into the Great Hall, a scowl on his face and Tashmica on his heels.

Gabriel turned toward him and began addressing their pissed-off alpha. "Not much. A few days ago, Keegan sent me a text stating he wouldn't be able to translate the journal after all."

"What? Why didn't you say anything?" Rick barked, stopping behind the chair he usually sat in but not making a move to actually sit.

"I should have," Gabriel said, lifting his chin. "I'm sorry. It just... It was a weird text."

"What do you mean?" Nico asked, taking a few more steps toward the circle. He hadn't even realized that he'd frozen just inside the room after meeting Gabe's eyes.

"It read like a goodbye. He thanked me and told me not to try and find him. Since then, my texts go unanswered, and my calls straight to voicemail."

Nico's wolf didn't like the sound of that, his claws itching to come out.

"What happened today?" Rick asked, crossing his arms. "Your message said Keegan was in danger."

"I have another contact in the La Fleur Coven," Gabriel said, taking a deep breath. "I reached out to her this morning to find out what was going on with Keegan, and she got back to me a little while ago. She said she and Keegan's sister haven't been able to get ahold of him in days—which is highly unusual—and she was worried for his safety. When she went to his house, no one could even tell her where he was."

Nico held his breath and watched Rick scowl at the floor and rub at the back of his neck. When he shook his head, Nico's stomach dropped before he even said, "I know he's your friend, but I can't risk starting a war with the La Fleur Coven. And that's what you're asking me to do, isn't it?"

"Rick," Gabriel said, voice scratchy, "I'm asking you to consider the fact that he risked his life to get us Wendy and the letter she carried. Plus, he's the only person we know who has a chance of translating the journal. Don't do this for me, do it for the pack."

Rick planted his hands on his hips, shaking his head again. "Fuck the journal. The Council is already making moves, attacking our allies. We need to come up with a plan of our own because we can't keep waiting for them to attack us head-on or for this journal to hopefully have answers." Sighing, Rick stepped forward, clasping a hand on Gabriel's shoulder. The hunter turned his face away, lips pressed tight together. "I'm sorry, but I can't risk losing any of my fighters on some sort of suicide mission. Especially when no one has officially asked us for help. We can't afford to make an enemy of someone so powerful."

Nico felt like his heart had dropped to his feet and been stomped on. A couple of people close to him were giving him weird looks, but he couldn't focus on anything other than to keep breathing and trying to come up with an argument to change Rick's mind.

When Gabriel didn't say anything, Rick turned away, gesturing at the rest of them. "Everyone, sit down. We need to have a fucking meeting and decide what we're doing."

Nico was frozen in place, staring at Gabriel. When the hunter met his eyes, he asked, "Is he still in New Orleans?"

He pretended like he didn't notice the way everyone stilled around him, the tension skyrocketing in the room. He didn't dare look at his alpha, knowing he wouldn't take Nico's question as anything other than straight-up insolence.

Gabriel licked his lips, then nodded. "As far as I know. I can try and get my contact on the phone and see what other information she might have. I think we could narrow down where he's being held—I've been there a few times, and Keegan pointed out some places that his mother kept off the radar of those outside her inner circle. My guess, we'll find him in one of them with her."

Nico swallowed, but before he could figure out what to say, Gabriel took another step toward him.

"*If* he's still alive, Nico. You need to prepare yourself."

He couldn't even let himself think of that, the words alone like an icicle to the stomach. He turned to Rick, who was watching him with narrowed eyes. "Alpha Kincaid—"

"What are you doing, Nico?"

"What I have to," he said, resisting the urge to bare his neck and apologize. "You would do the same if it was your mate."

No one in the room made a single sound, yet the silence was deafening. Every single heart began to race, breaths quickened, and the overpowering scent of shock, sorrow, and fear coalesced in the air around him.

"How long have you known?" Rick asked, his tone even.

Nico glanced away for a second, knowing Rick wasn't going to like his answer. "Since the night he was here with Wendy. My wolf recognized him."

"We are at war, Nico," Rick said carefully. "I need you."

"I know, sir, but I have to go. I understand if you don't want me to come back after defying a direct order though."

Marcus made a noise behind him, but Nico kept his focus on Rick. He was studying Nico, his face giving away nothing, his scent angry and... resigned?

"Tashmica," Rick said without looking at her, "what happens if Nico steals a La Fleur Coven member and brings him back here?"

Tashmica stepped forward, shooting Nico an apologetic grimace. "Most covens wouldn't dare to engage in a conflict with a pack and coven as powerful as ours, but the La Fleurs are different. They're powerful in and of themselves; their magical lineages go back generations." She hesitated and then added, "I think they would come for him, and I think they would fight to get him back."

"Even if he didn't want to go back?" Nico argued despite a part of him wondering if that would even be the case. Just because Keegan was in trouble, that didn't mean he'd want to move to Michigan and join their pack. To be Nico's mate in every sense of the word.

She nodded, her face sad. "Even then. Beatrice Toussaint, the leader of the coven, is Keegan's mother, and she would consider it a grave insult for us to get involved in what she would consider internal matters, and she is not known for her forgiveness. And from what I have learned from Gabriel and my own discreet inquiries, she wouldn't let go of her son without a fight. Keegan is extremely gifted and will be the next leader of their coven."

"Then we won't come back here," Nico said, his voice rising at the hopeless picture Tashmica painted. "We'll leave and go somewhere she can't find us."

"Nico," Tashmica said softly. "As powerful as Keegan is, there is nowhere you and he could go and nothing you could do to hide from his entire coven."

Nico shook his head. It didn't matter what she said. He couldn't do nothing. Simply standing there trying to have a rational conversation was driving his wolf mad. He needed to leave, to run and find Keegan, get him to safety and protect him. He needed to take care of him and claim him.

He needed the chance to love him.

To convince Keegan to love him back.

Gabriel cleared his throat. "Keegan won't be the next coven leader. He's been trying to leave for years and recently told me he had a plan to do it so his mother couldn't come after him."

A tiny flame of hope began to burn inside Nico. His mate wanted to leave. Had come up with a plan to get away from his coven. Nico would do anything in his power to help him.

"That doesn't change—" Rick started to say, then ground his teeth together when Gabriel interrupted him.

"The spell he created to hide my scent was payment." He glanced at Nico, and the flame of hope sputtered inside him at the look on his face. "He owed me because I… I helped sneak his newborn daughter out of Louisiana underneath his mother's nose. He's kept her hidden for three years with every intention of leaving. He would do anything to protect her. If he's in danger, I have to believe that his daughter is too."

Nico stared at Gabriel, shock reverberating through him as he shakily lowered himself into a chair. His mate had a child. Did that mean…

Did Keegan already have a mate?

Nico barely heard Rick through the buzzing in his ears when he sighed and ground out, "Fine. We'll help him, but we're going to be fucking smart about this. Someone get me some coffee and a computer. We need to find somebody that the La Fleurs either respect or fear to help us."

Did Keegan already have a mate?

CHAPTER SIX

"It's so peaceful here."

Keegan smiled and slowly peeled his eyes open. Turning his head to face his sister, he was filled with happiness at seeing her. He wasn't sure how long he'd been sitting on his grandmother's back porch, but it felt right that she was there with him. Everything felt... syrupy and smooth.

Like it was the perfect moment, and everything had slowed down so he'd be able to enjoy it.

It was warm and muggy, and insects were chirping noisily, but there was just enough of a breeze that it felt good to sit in the shade of the porch. He smiled easily. "When did you get here, Jos?"

She turned a familiar grin on him, just like the one she used to give him when they were kids, full of teeth and dimples, when she wanted to get into trouble. But her eyes... they were missing that mischievous glint.

As he focused on her harder, everything around him... flickered.

"What was that?" Why was she there? She wasn't supposed to be. She was supposed to be doing something else. Something important. He was almost sure of it, but his thoughts were jagged and out of order, and he couldn't remember what.

She laughed. "What are you talking about? I've been here the whole time. What have you been doing?"

The question seemed innocent enough, but for some reason, it stirred something in his gut. A warning telling him to be careful and to watch out. As quickly as it rose up, it was pushed back down by the feeling of comfort he'd always had at his grandparents'. His dad's parents had emigrated to Louisiana before his father was even born, leaving Haiti with the hope of building a better life for themselves and their kids.

Their house had always been Keegan's happy place. He and Jos would disappear there for huge chunks of time during summer break to get away from their mother's over-bearing pressure to constantly work and become better, stronger witches. Grann would always welcome them with a hug and cool drink before sending them out to play.

He hadn't been there in... a long time though. He was sure of it. But it felt so good to be back. Relaxing once more, he let his eyes fall shut once more.

"Keegan," Jos said, laughing again. "What are you doing?"

"Nothing. It's amazing."

"But there's so much to do," she insisted.

"Do?" he repeated, swatting at his arm where it burned a little suddenly. He didn't have anything to do, did he?

"Of course. That's why I'm here. You said you needed my help. Remember? It was something you couldn't tell Mom."

Something he couldn't tell their mother.

He forced his eyes open, his lids fluttering with effort. Some of the fuzziness along the edges of his vision cleared as he turned to focus on her. Something was wrong. "What are you talking about? What are we even doing here?"

He tried to sit up, but her firm hand landed on his shoulder, pushing him back into the deep recline of the Adirondack chair he was in.

"Focus, Keegan," she said. But there was something off about her voice. The inflection was just a little... too cheerful. "What was it you needed my help keeping from Mom? What is it you don't want her to know?"

Something was really wrong.

He looked around, trying to focus past the porch, but everything was a little blurry. When he tried to stand again, her grip on him fell away, and he darted toward the familiar screen door. He skidded to a halt once he got inside.

It was empty.

No furniture. No laughter. No people. No smells of his grann's cooking.

It was an echo.

"This isn't real," he said out loud, spinning around. He tilted backward, surprised to find Jocelyn right behind him. She was still smiling, but her face was... blank. "You're not really here, are you?"

"Don't be silly," she said. Her voice was still cheerful, but her face was unmoving, the mismatch disconcerting in the empty house. "You're the one who asked me to come here to help you with something. What was it? What did you need my help to keep from Mom? What are you hiding from her?"

Firming his jaw, he stepped into Jocelyn's face and said clearly, "This is bullshit. I know what you're doing. Get out of my fucking head."

He startled awake with a gasp, feeling light-headed and disoriented. He blinked at the harsh lights above him, his eyes watering. When he tried to sit up to try and figure out where he was, he realized he couldn't. His arms are outstretched on either side, and when he tugged on them, there was a metallic *clang* but little give.

Turning his head back and forth, he tried to see past the bright lights, his heart racing and breaths coming fast. He wasn't in an illusion anymore—he didn't think—but he was trapped and vulnerable in some unknown location.

It was dark beyond the lights, so he couldn't make out any details behind them. He wasn't sure if he was still in his parents' house or if he'd been taken somewhere else.

But he hated how fucking afraid he felt.

He searched his memory—his *real* memories—and the last thing he could recall was… talking to Jocelyn.

No, wait.

He closed his eyes and concentrated, his stomach dipping as he finally remembered finding his mother in his room, holding his herbs and asking him about his dream walking. He'd tried to deny it, to tell her that it was nothing, and she'd sighed like he was just so exhausting.

Before he'd known what was happening, someone had come up behind him, and… that was it. That was all he remembered. He wasn't even sure how long ago that was.

How long had she been trying to break into his mind?

Were Jocelyn and—

He stopped himself, not trusting his wall while he felt so… depleted.

He felt sore all over, and when he looked around again to try and gather as many details as he could, he realized there was an IV in his arm. He wasn't sure if it was just to keep him weak and compliant or if he'd been there so long, they'd worried about keeping him hydrated. He thought about calling for help, but he didn't think anyone around would actually answer.

He couldn't just lie there and do nothing though.

He took a few deep breaths and tried to center himself, searching within to find his magic. Usually, it came to him so easily, surging forward with eagerness and ready to spark out of his fingertips, but whatever herbs or drugs they'd given him was making his brain sluggish. He could barely focus.

Finally, he caught a wisp of his magic and tugged on it, gathering as much as he could into his chest. Taking a deep breath, he flung it out toward his hands, pushing his intention as hard as he could.

"Fuck!" he yelped at the painful zap he got from the manacles around his wrists. He bit his lip to try and muffle the sound.

He'd figured it wouldn't be that easy to get away, but fuck, that had hurt.

Footsteps approached, and he contemplated pretending to be asleep, but the click of the heels gave him a good idea who it was drawing near. He knew it wasn't worth trying to pretend with her.

He did his best to focus, and when she came forward past the lights, he met her angry eyes head-on. She looked as well put together as always, but he didn't even entertain the idea that that meant he'd only been there a short time. He was sure he could have been held for a month of her torture, and she'd still look like she was about to go out to a dinner party.

"I'll give you this," she said, sounding annoyed, and that gave him a perverse sense of satisfaction. "You're stronger than I anticipated. Why don't you do us both a favor and just come clean before I have to resort to ripping the secrets out of you."

They both knew that if she did that, there wouldn't be much of him left when she was done.

"Go to hell." Keegan had meant to say it aggressively, but his voice was raspy and his throat dry, so it came out as little more than a whisper. It still caused her eyes to narrow. He did his best to ignore the trepidation crawling over his skin.

"I don't know what game you're playing, but neither I nor

the elders take a betrayal to this coven lightly. Your only hope is to confess and beg for leniency. If you're lucky, we'll only bind your magic."

He shuddered and glanced away, the threat of what she'd do if he didn't tell her what she wanted to know hanging over him like a guillotine. "I've never betrayed my coven."

She shook her head. "If that were true, you wouldn't be dream walking with someone behind my back."

He couldn't help barking out a dry laugh. Licking his lips, he prepared to give her the fucking list of reasons why he kept secrets from her, but someone yelled something, and then he heard hurried footsteps.

"I told you not to come in here," she snapped without turning to look at whoever it was. The person had stopped just behind the lights, so Keegan couldn't make them out, but he recognized her voice when she spoke. She was a young witch in the coven and one of his mother's sycophants. She and the others followed Beatrice around like she was a goddess, hanging on her every word.

"I'm sorry," the girl said, sounding close to tears. "Councilwoman Voight is here and demanding to see you."

"We don't answer to the Council. Tell her she has no authority here and to leave."

Keegan raised his eyebrows at that. Unattached covens like theirs, ones that weren't part of a pack, liked to act like they were above shifter law and politics, but they both knew it wasn't true. The Council might have only been made up of former shifter alphas, but they were responsible for keeping *all* parahumans in check.

Something his mother clearly decided she'd ignore.

He could hear the trembling in the girl's voice when she said, "We tried, but it didn't work. She said... She said that all parahumans fell within the Council's authority, and that... that she wasn't leaving without your son."

"Uh-oh," Keegan singsonged, tilting his head back and staring up at the dark ceiling. Whatever they were pumping in his veins was making him dizzy and nauseous, but he'd be damned before he let her see it. "It seems like you have a choice to make, Mother dearest."

He imagined that he could hear her teeth grinding together.

"You can keep me here and continue to try and extract information from me—despite the fact that I've never been anything but a loyal and devoted member of the La Fleur Coven. Or... you can let me go with Councilwoman Voight and avoid an incident."

When only silence followed his taunting, he let his tired eyes fall closed. His mother liked to act like she was invincible, that their coven was. But there was a reason he'd chosen the Council's coven as the place to go when he left.

"Keep in mind, if you choose option one, you'll be pitting the coven against the Council. And while we've always prided ourselves on being independent, scoffing at the idea of building partnerships with others, they have a lot of packs and covens in their back pocket. They can call up any number of them to send here." He paused, his throat burning it was so dry. Coughing lightly, he said, "Are you willing to risk the annihilation of your precious La Fleurs on some herbs? Is risking being wrong worth losing everything?"

He smiled to himself when he heard her turn and stomp away, his dry lips cracking. A drop of blood ran down his chin as oblivion tugged at him. He fought it, wanting to stay awake and find out what was going to happen, but he was just too damn weak.

Within a few minutes, he faded into unconsciousness.

When he came to again, there was brightness again, but it wasn't the same harshness of the lights. No, it was... sunshine.

He slowly turned his throbbing head on the soft pillow it was resting on and found a window cracked open, sheer curtains fluttering at the soft breeze coming through. The room he was in was painted a pale blue and had a distinctive western style to it, all the way down to the border along the top of the walls featuring cowboy boots and horseshoes.

He was positive he'd remember if he'd ever been in the room before.

"Thank the goddess you're awake."

Keegan's breath caught in his chest at the achingly familiar voice. He almost didn't turn to check, certain his mind was playing tricks on him or that his mother was still trying to break him.

He squeezed his eyes shut and braced himself, then opened them again and tipped his head to the side. He pressed his lips together to hold back the broken sound trying to escape.

"Jocelyn," he whispered, "tell me this is real."

Her curly black hair was more disheveled than he could ever remember seeing it, and there were bags beneath her eyes. A brown coffee stain was on her pale pink shirt. He couldn't imagine why his mother would make him see his sister like this, and that gave him hope.

Even though hope was a terrible thing and would make him fall harder if it wasn't real.

"Oh, Keegan," she said, tears running down her face. She leaned over the bed and gently brushed his own unruly curls off his forehead. "You look like hell."

They both gave watery laughs at that, his turning into a cough. She scrambled to get a glass from off the table, holding the straw to his lips so he could take a few sips. Once he lost the feeling of sandpaper in his throat, he pulled back. "Pinch me."

"What?" She paused, the cup still a few inches from the tabletop, to stare at him.

"I need to know what's real. In that place…" He wasn't sure he could even describe it. The hell that she'd put him through, over and over again, trying to trick him into revealing his secrets. "It was always someplace peaceful or happy. There was never any pain. That's the only way I'll know for sure if this is real."

Sniffling, she swiped at her cheeks, then reached down and pinched his thigh through the covers. Hard.

"Ouch," he yelled, swatting at her hand. "That seemed unnecessarily painful."

She rolled her eyes at him and threw up her hands in exasperation.

But he was almost positive she was really there, that it was really over.

The longer he was awake, the more clearly he was able to think. He looked around the room again, but it was just the two of them.

"Is Rosie with you?" He needed to know she was safe, that his mother hadn't somehow gotten to her.

Jocelyn nodded. "Yeah, she's running around here some-where, making friends. I'll bring her by in a little bit."

As much as he wanted to hold her in his arms immedi-ately, he could already feel exhaustion pulling at him. He sagged back against his pillow, nodding. "Okay. Why am I so tired?"

Jocelyn's breath hitched in her throat as she leaned over to straighten his blankets. "You… need the rest. To recover. It's been three days since they got you away from her."

"Seriously?" He could barely even keep his eyes open. "How long was I… there?"

"About a week," she whispered, trailing the back of her fingers down his cheek. "The witches here say it could take some time for you to get back to your full strength. You need to take it easy for a while."

"Where's here?" he mumbled. "Are we in Oregon?"

He didn't think so. Nothing about the place seemed familiar, and he knew for sure he wasn't in her house.

"Kansas. About a half an hour from Topeka."

"What are we doing in Kansas?" He fought the drowsiness that was trying to pull him under.

"I'm not sure. He just told me to come here and to bring Rosie."

"He?" Keegan wasn't even sure he said the word out loud. "I thought… it was Voight…"

Jocelyn gently caressed his face again. "She got you away, but it was this other guy who orchestrated everything. Some friend of your friend Gabriel. He called me your wife though, so that was kind of weird."

Warmth filled Keegan's chest, and he couldn't help the tiny smile from pulling at his lips. He knew exactly who it had to have been. Then her words sank in, and he jerked, trying to fight the sleep pulling at him. *My wife?*

Jocelyn shushed him, soothing him with her soft touches, and he decided he could set his silly wolf straight once he got some more sleep. The thought of him, of finally getting to see him in person, sent a thrilling jolt of yearning through his whole body.

Nico had come for him, had rescued him and given him his family back. He wasn't sure how he would ever be able to repay him.

But he could think of a few ways to start.

CHAPTER SEVEN

"Honestly, dear," Councilwoman Voight said, taking a sip of her tea, "I'm just glad Beatrice didn't call my bluff."

"Me too," Nico said, trying not to imagine what would have happened if he'd had to go with his plan B to save Keegan, which had mostly just consisted of storming the warehouse where they were holding him and trying to take him by force.

Gabriel had looked at him like he was crazy when he'd confided in him his backup plan. It hadn't stopped Nico from flying to Louisiana and waiting just outside the city limits until Voight gave him the all clear after she was able to retrieve Keegan.

"I'm fairly certain if she hadn't been so weakened by her attempts to break into her son's mind, she would have been able to suss out my true intentions."

Nico grimaced. "At least it's over. I don't know how to repay you for your help."

She set her cup aside and waved a hand at him. She had to be at least seventy, but she still radiated power despite her small, wrinkled frame. "It's over for now, but I wouldn't count her and her coven out just yet. Especially if she finds out where he ends up."

She gave Nico a meaningful look, and he tried not to blush at the implication. He wasn't sure why it embarrassed him, but there was something about the older mountain lion's gentle demeanor that made him feel like he was talking to a maternal figure. Though not his own mother. She'd been brash and outspoken and raised him not to be ashamed of his wants and desires.

"I'm not sure where Keegan and his family will be headed after this," Nico said carefully after clearing his throat. "Once I hand over the journal, I'll be headed back home. Ericka will be staying, and she'll bring back the translation with her."

She frowned. "But I thought you and he…"

Nico knew exactly what she'd thought, but he forced himself to shrug like he wasn't bothered. "So did I. Until I found out about his wife and daughter."

When Gabriel had passed him the phone number, the name *Jocelyn* written above it, Nico had thought he would throw up. It had taken every ounce of strength he had to dial and wait while it rang, and he'd had to close his eyes and fight back his wolf when the soft, feminine voice had answered with an achingly familiar accent.

He hadn't told her who he was to Keegan, just that he and Gabriel were working on a plan to get Keegan away from his mother and that she should meet them in Kansas with… with Keegan's daughter. Gabriel had already texted her, letting her know she could trust him, and she'd agreed to come right away, no questions asked.

He was doing his best to avoid her and the small girl she'd been carrying since they'd arrived the day before, though he'd caught glimpses of them and been bombarded by their scents. It physically hurt him to see the family his mate had created without him, especially knowing that now that he'd helped Keegan escape from his coven, they could all be happy and together.

Without him.

Taking a sip of his own tea and trying not to grimace at the taste, he changed the subject. Rick had told him to get any information he could from the councilwoman while he had her away from prying eyes and ears, and it would help him to focus on that instead of the steady beat of Keegan's heart above them. "Have you or Garcia heard of any other packs being attacked?"

"No," she said right away. "I brought it up during the last Council session before the holidays last December, about how concerning I found these vicious and unprovoked attacks, and I haven't heard a single thing about any other threats or acts of violence." She sighed. "I doubt we spooked them that much, but whoever is helping Alistair and his puppets seems to be taking their time to make their next move. I've been quietly spreading word to other packs I trust, just in case though."

Nico hummed in agreement. That had been their conclusion as well. Rick was getting damn antsy waiting around for another attack. Their war council meetings had begun to take on a more offensive and aggressive tone, and a number of members—including Gabriel and Robson—were fully on board with taking the fight to the Council.

Nico wasn't quite sure that was the best move though. There were still plenty of packs out there unaware of the fucked-up things the Council had been a part of, and they would see an act of aggression by the Kincaid Pack as a declaration of war and would come to the Council's aid.

Tapping a finger on her knee, she said, "Have you had any luck capturing one of the beasts?"

"Not yet. Once the attacks stopped, the beasts disappeared too." Having seen the aftermath of one of the monstrosity's attacks, he wasn't eager to come face-to-face with one, personally. But Tashmica thought there was a chance she'd be able to unravel the magic that made them and figure out who was behind it. "Maybe there were only a few and they're all dead now."

She gave him an indulgent smile, and he couldn't help but huff a laugh as she said dryly, "I don't think we'll get that lucky."

No, probably not.

"Have you been able to find out anything about who might be pulling Kincaid's strings?" he asked, though his hopes weren't high.

She shook her head. "No, even during our breaks, he and a few others just stay in Montana. They don't seem to be consorting with any single pack or coven. Whoever's working with him is keeping their distance."

"I heard our sleeping beauty is awake." Liam Amato, the Silver Oak Pack's alpha, strode into the living room and offered a brisk smile. The distinctive claw marks peeking out above the neck of his shirt gave him a dangerous appearance, though they had faded to faint scars, but he'd been nothing but hospitable to their odd group.

Even still, Nico wasn't sure he liked the young, handsome alpha commenting on Keegan's looks. He bit back his wolf's instinctive growl for the sake of propriety and gratitude, considering the man had opened his territory and home to them knowing it could be dangerous.

Amato had just grinned, looking more like a pirate than a lion, and said that having the Kincaid Pack owe him a favor was worth the risk.

"Yes," Voight said, smiling warmly at Amato. "Jocelyn came down a little while ago and said he'd woken up about an hour ago, but he'd still seemed pretty weak and fallen back asleep quickly."

"Not surprising." The alpha crossed his arms over his chest and shook his head in disgust. "My witches said they'd never seen anyone in his condition before and that it would take a while for him to heal from the damage she did to him and his magic."

Voight tutted in disapproval, then turned to Nico. "Did you ever find out what caused her to suspect he had betrayed the coven? She must have been convinced of his guilt to have gone to such extremes."

Nico pressed his lips together, trying not to think about the torture Keegan had been put through. "No. Gabriel's contact hadn't known, and as far as we could tell, no one except her inner circle even knew what was going on. The rest seem to be in the dark about what she did to him."

"I can't even imagine doing that to your own kid," Amato said, a distant look in his eyes.

Neither could Nico. He couldn't imagine hurting anyone he loved like that. Someone he was supposed to protect. A part of him wondered what was broken inside Beatrice that she'd been driven to do something so horrible, but mostly, he was just glad that Keegan was away from her.

He was also grateful that despite everything else happening, the Kincaid Pack still had people they could rely on. He was about to thank both Voight and Amato again but hesitated when a beefy guy covered in tattoos appeared in the doorway, a couple of the black markings seeming to glow or pulse. Nico recognized him as one of Amato's Enforcers; he and a couple of others had been there when Voight had arrived with an unconscious Keegan.

"Alpha."

Amato nodded, and the guy disappeared. "You'll have to excuse me. I have a meeting. But please let me know if either of you or Keegan and his family need anything while you're here."

As soon as they assured him they would, he left, heading deeper into the strange house. The sitting room he and Voight had commandeered was right by the front door, and Nico hadn't been invited into any of the back rooms, where he suspected Amato met with his Enforcers and maybe had an office he worked out of.

Nico didn't take offense; Rick didn't like strangers in his personal space either.

"Seems like a nice young man," Voight said, still watching the empty doorway. "Unmated too, I believe."

Nico stared at her, not liking her implication. "He's definitely better than the old alpha. That guy was an asshole."

"I was surprised he was willing to allow us into his territory given the circumstances." She sent him a questioning look. "You did explain the risks to him, right?"

"Of course I did. He knew what he was getting into and decided it was worth it."

"I suppose having Garrick Kincaid indebted to you is quite the incentive. Still, people talk." She picked up her teacup once more. "A Kincaid Enforcer and a powerful La Fleur witch both just happen to be visiting the same small pack in Kansas? If word gets out…"

He grunted. "All the more reason for me to leave as soon as possible. Ericka will blend in much better."

The young beta was smart, strong, and trustworthy. Plus, she was a lioness and would fit in with Amato's pack of large cats. She was also more than capable of staying for as long as it took Keegan to translate the journal.

Nico would… Well, he'd head back home. Back to his life and his to-do lists. His paperwork and endless meetings.

His empty bed and quiet house.

Voight's face softened, and he realized he was spewing his

emotions all over the room. Clearing his throat, he said, "Thank you again for your help. It was invaluable."

"Of course. I'd like to think I've always been a friend to the Kincaid Pack, and I hope you feel the same." She paused, watching him closely, and he nodded. He understood what she wasn't saying—if the shit hit the fan, would they keep her from getting sprayed with it? As long as she continued to help them, Nico was sure Rick would do everything in his power to protect her and Garcia if it came to that. After taking another sip, she smiled and said, "By the way, have you met Alpha Amato's second yet?"

He'd been about to excuse himself, hands already planted on the arms of his chair, but he relaxed back into it at the way she asked him that. "The guy with the tattoos?"

"No." She leaned forward and said in a quiet voice, "The vampire."

Nico stared at her, positive he'd misheard. There hadn't been a vampire sighting in over a century, not since the hunter clans had banded together to find and kill them all, believing them to be too dangerous to be allowed to live. "Are you serious?"

She nodded eagerly, looking damn near giddy with excitement. "Yes. I met him the first night I was here. He was standing guard outside the house. We had a nice little chat."

He couldn't quit staring. "But... they're extinct!"

"Apparently, they're *almost* extinct. He told me that he only knew of a handful of others, most of them hiding over in Europe where there aren't as many hunters anymore."

Leaning back in his chair, he rubbed his face. A vampire. In Nowhere, Kansas. What were the chances?

"What's he doing here?" he asked, pulling out his phone and sending a text to Rick and the other Enforcers.

Nico: *There's a fucking vampire here. WTF*

"He didn't say, just that when Liam became alpha, he asked Finlay to become his second, and he accepted."

A vampire named *Finlay*.

Rick: *ARE YOU IN DANGER?*

Vanessa: *Are you serious???*

Marcus: *There haven't been any documented sightings in over a hundred years. Are you sure?*

Nico smiled down at his phone and quickly responded.

Nico: *I'm not in danger. He's the Second here. I haven't even laid eyes on him yet, but Voight is sure.*

He shoved his phone into his pocket before anyone else could respond. "Sorry. What's he like?"

She smiled. "Tall. Handsome. Smells a little like dirt. Did I mention handsome?"

He snorted and shook his head, pushing to his feet. "Very helpful. How long will you be staying?"

"I'm headed back to my daughter's pack tomorrow morning before word of you and I being in the same place together gets out."

Grimacing, he waited for her to stand, then extended his hand. "Thank you. Truly."

She inclined her head. "It was my pleasure, Nico."

His phone was vibrating in his pocket, but he didn't pull it out as he left the sitting room. He also didn't head upstairs to check on Keegan for himself or get some work done in the room he'd been given. It was too distracting being so close to Keegan, his scent of burning firewood so enticing Nico could barely sleep at night.

Instead, he went straight for the front door, stepping outside into the warm air and taking a deep breath for the first time all day. The surprise resurrection of vampires wasn't even enough to distract him from the aching pain in his chest whenever he thought about Keegan.

He sucked in a few more breaths of Keegan-free air and

reminded himself that he would survive. And at least now he knew Keegan was safe and would be happy and cared for with his family.

That was all Nico got, but it was still more than a lot of others ever knew.

Many never met their true mates, and even though he knew he'd be leaving his broken heart behind in that dumb cowboy-themed room, he also knew that he would be strong enough to survive without him. He had to be. His pack needed him now more than ever.

Striding across the wide porch and down the steps, he didn't have a plan on where he was going. He just needed to get away. He couldn't stay in the house any longer, hearing Keegan's heartbeat and scenting him in the hallway every time he went up to his room.

It was slowly killing him. He knew he'd have to go and talk to him before he actually left, but that wouldn't be for another day or so. Not until he was positive Keegan was on the mend.

The Silver Oak Pack was situated on a peninsula within the Silver Oak Lake. They weren't a large pack, and the tiny town down the road mostly consisted of the pack and a few humans who knew about them. Nico knew for a fact they hadn't grown in recent years, but he had a feeling that under the strong leadership of their new alpha, the pack would begin to thrive once more.

He looked around and sighed, not sure where to go. He was tired, not just physically either. The last week had been... a strain. The plan to rescue Keegan had come together quickly enough—with Marcus having the brilliant idea to use one of the councilmembers they actually trusted to get Keegan released.

It had been a bold plan and risky as hell.

If Beatrice or someone else in the coven had pushed back

against Voight too hard, they would have been fucked since they hadn't actually had the Council's full weight behind them.

While Marcus had contacted Voight where she'd been visiting with her daughter and grandkids while the Council was out of session, Nico's job had been to find a place that was neutral but safe territory. The last thing they'd wanted was to risk the La Fleurs following Keegan and Voight straight back to the Kincaid Pack.

Nico had thought about pushing it, insisting on bringing Keegan to the nearly impenetrable protection of the Kincaid Pack territory, but despite Keegan being his destined mate, he knew he didn't have the right to do that.

Keegan already had a family, a pup. Whatever may or may not have happened between them in their dreams, it didn't change the reality of the situation.

Nico wondered if it would be so hard to let Keegan go if he hadn't been spending so much time with him in his dreams. Considering the nighttime visits had stopped around the same time Keegan was texting a goodbye to Gabriel and then getting snatched by his mom, Nico was almost positive that the dreams he'd been having were real.

Everything they'd said to each other. Every look.

The way Keegan had called him silly that last time when he'd gotten jealous and grabbed his arm? *Real.*

He couldn't help but wonder why Keegan had done it. If he'd just stayed out of Nico's head, he wouldn't be dying inside at the idea of returning home soon without his mate.

Of never touching him, holding him, kissing him.

Claiming him.

The most cynical side of Nico, which he hadn't even known he'd *had* until he'd found out about Keegan's family, made him wonder if Keegan had known who he was to Nico and had used their connection to get Nico hooked on him, knowing he could use Nico to help him get away from his coven.

That all those dreams had just been him biding his time, but his mother had found out before he could enact whatever plan he'd been hatching.

Of course, the more rational part of Nico argued that in the six months Keegan had been visiting his dreams, he'd never once even mentioned his coven or being unhappy. He never asked Nico to do anything for him. He'd kept all the details about his personal life and family to himself.

No, his instincts were telling him that it was something else, even if his broken heart wanted to believe the worst to make the pain lessen.

As he reached the end of the road, he looked left and right at the houses lining the street in both directions. He started to turn left, but a high-pitched squeal followed by raucous laughter had him turning the other way before he'd even realized he'd changed his mind.

He needed the warmth and easy affection of pups more than ever, so he followed the sounds to a house down the street. The kids must have been in the backyard. Without hesitation, he walked down the side of the cheery yellow house with a bright red front door until he got to a gate leading into the fenced-in backyard.

He paused for a second, then let himself in, fairly confident he'd be welcome here. The Silver Oak Pack was small, and everyone probably knew who he was, if not what he was doing there. As soon as he stepped around the corner of the house, he saw several adults sitting on a covered patio, watching the pups—er, cubs—playing. They all turned and smiled brightly at him.

A middle-aged woman with striking red hair and the scent of a jaguar stood and took a few steps toward him. He could tell by her scent and the way she carried herself that she was at least a beta, if not another Enforcer. "Can I get you a drink, Enforcer Evans?"

He shook his head, then tipped it toward the kids playing some sort of ruthless version of tag that had them giggling nonstop. "Do you mind?"

The woman frowned in confusion for a second, but then a beautiful smile spread across her face, and she gestured toward the open space the cubs were playing in. "Not at all. Please let me know if you need anything."

He gave her a smile and a quick nod to the others before quickly stripping off his clothes and shifting into his wolf. There was only one other shifted person in the yard, an enormous tiger lounging near the back fence in the shade. He lifted his head and studied Nico for a second and then went back to relaxing.

As soon as he took a couple of steps toward the cubs, the first child noticed him and froze in place. She let out a shriek of delight and then raced toward him. His tail wagging, he moved farther into the yard, letting the kids crowd against him and run their hands over his head and sides. Most of them seemed like they'd never seen a wolf before, and he wondered just how isolated the old alpha had kept the pack.

There were so many small bodies and chattering voices that he didn't see her right away, but when a tiny boy with peanut butter smeared on his face stepped to the side, Nico stiffened at the sight of the beautiful little girl clutching the hand of a boy who was maybe eight. Her skin was a little lighter than Keegan's, and her curls weren't quite as tight, but her scent was familiar from the alpha's house.

And he'd recognize those eyes anywhere.

He almost turned and ran right then and there. He'd been doing so good at avoiding Keegan's daughter, wanting to spare himself the additional pain of seeing her and knowing she'd never be his to love and care for.

But the bright smile on her face and dimple in her cheek as she ran toward him as fast as her little legs could carry her wasn't something he could turn away from. The other kids were petting and grabbing at him, laughing and talking, but he barely noticed them anymore. His sole focus had narrowed to Keegan's daughter.

He wished he'd asked her name.

The boy holding her hand stopped a foot or so away, but she just slipped out of his hold and kept coming. Nico lowered his head so they were face-to-face, and she buried hers against the fur of his cheek, wrapping her arms around his neck tighter than he would have expected.

"Nice doggy," she said, and the boy behind her laughed.

"That's not a doggy, Rosie. That's a wolf."

Rosie.

Goddess, it fit her.

She rubbed her face against his again, and he couldn't stop the soft, sad sound that came out. This was the pup he would never have. He doubted he'd ever take another mate, knowing he had a fated one out there, so his chance of a family was gone.

"It's okay, wolfie," she said, rubbing her little hands over his face and ears. "Don't be sad."

One of the adults heard her—or scented his pain—and came over to gently guide the other kids away. When it was just him and her, he slowly lowered himself to the ground, and she followed, keeping herself pressed against him.

The longer she touched him, the more his heartache seemed to ease despite the fact her presence had initially made it so much worse. Something about her was helping him feel less like he was about to split apart and bleed out.

"There. That's better," she said, then pulled herself on top of him, giggling when he adjusted beneath her to keep her from falling.

She rubbed her face against his neck again after she was settled, and her innocent scent marking had the despair growing inside him once more, ready to burst forth in a howl at any moment.

He swallowed it down, deciding if that moment was all he would get, he would take it.

The memory of this moment—of her gentle touches and soft words—would be his and his alone, and he'd remember it for the rest of his life.

He was prepared to play with her all afternoon if that was what she wanted. To run or chase her or to carry her around like her noble steed. He waited for her to sit up and give him instructions or jump down and restart the game of tag.

Instead, her breaths grew slower, deeper, and her body became lax on top of him.

He settled in, not minding in the least, but he never shut his eyes, never even considered taking a nap of his own. Not while he had a pup to protect, even if she wasn't really his. Even if she never could be.

It didn't matter.

As long as he was with her, he would never let anything bad happen to her.

CHAPTER EIGHT

As soon as Keegan woke up, he knew someone was in the room with him, watching him. It was dark, the only light coming from a single lamp in the corner of the room. For a heartbeat, he was scared, unsure where he was or if he was safe.

Then his eyes landed on a framed picture of a man riding a bucking bull, and he melted back into the soft bed, letting out a quiet sigh. He was in Kansas. He was safe.

Nico had saved him.

"Are you okay?"

The deep voice was hushed but still so familiar it brought tears to his eyes. He blinked them away, chalking it up to being so tired still, and turned his head, needing to see *him* more than anything else in that moment.

Sitting in what looked like the most uncomfortable, spindly chair in the world was the giant Kincaid Pack Enforcer who'd been haunting his every thought. *Nico*. He ran his gaze over him greedily, trying to take in every single detail. He didn't know what had happened in New Orleans, if he was truly free of his mother and coven for good, but for that single moment, it didn't matter. They were finally together, in the same place, and he felt like he could breathe for the first time in years.

The longer he looked at Nico, the more he realized something was off. There was no sign of his easy smile, and dark circles were under his beautiful blue eyes as he watched Keegan with something that looked like apprehension. His dark hair was longer than the last time Keegan had seen him, the strands on the top falling over his forehead when he tipped his chin down and stared at his hands where they were fisted in his lap. His usual clean-shaven jaw had a bit of stubble, and his cheekbones seemed more pronounced.

But he was still the most handsome man Keegan had ever seen.

"You are here," he said, keeping his voice low too. It felt late, and he wasn't sure how many people were around the house trying to sleep.

Nico swallowed, keeping his eyes downcast. "I'm here. Jocelyn is with... Rosie." He paused, then cleared his throat and said, "She asked me to sit with you. How are you feeling?"

It'd be just like his sister to play matchmaker. The last time he'd woken up, he'd actually been able to stay awake more than five minutes and gotten to see Rosie and give her the longest hug of his life. He'd also confessed to Jocelyn about dream walking with Nico and how that had led to their mother suspecting him of betraying her. She'd teased him about Nico thinking they were married.

He shot upright—well, he tried, but it was more of a struggle than he would have liked, and Nico watched him closely, muscles tensed like he was a split second away from helping him.

Once he was braced against the hard headboard, he took

a deep breath and met Nico's haunted eyes. "I need to tell you something."

Swallowing, Nico stood, the small chair creaking in protest. "I already know about your family, Keegan."

Goddess, he looked... he looked like someone he loved had *died*.

He really thought Keegan had a family with someone else, that there was no chance that the two of them could ever be together. It would be a profound loss to any shifter, but especially to one like Nico. Being an Enforcer for such a large, powerful pack would make his wolf stronger too, his instincts more influential. The drive to be with his mate all these months must have been... unbelievably difficult to ignore.

And Keegan had planned on simply never seeing him again.

The guilt he was hit with nearly overpowered him. Being in the same room with Nico, feeling his energy and wolf just beneath the surface, was *intoxicating*. He felt so fucking foolish to think he could just give him up.

"Jocelyn is my sister," he said abruptly, needing to wipe away at least some of the pain on Nico's face. "Rosie's been living with her, but she's not... she's not my wife. I don't have one. I'm... single."

He grimaced at his awkwardness, his face heating at the way Nico stared at him without saying anything for a long moment. Finally—thank the goddess—Nico took a half step toward the bed, head tilted. "Your sister."

Keegan nodded. "Yes."

"Where's Rosie's mom?"

He shrugged. "New Orleans. I haven't spoken to her since coming here, but I doubt she's left. I'm sure she's keeping an eye on my mother and the elders. She's not a part of Rosie's life though."

Nico took another step forward. "She's not? You and she…"

Keegan smiled. "Best friends. Rosie wasn't planned, but she's the best thing to ever happen to me. I didn't want her anywhere near the La Fleurs though, so Gabe helped me get her to Jos. All Beatrice cares about is getting more power, more influence, and she'd see Rosie as just another tool to get it. That coven is fucking toxic, and I didn't want her growing up in that."

Nodding slowly, Nico looked away, but Keegan didn't push, wanting to give him space to think. It was killing him not to reach for him, but he knew he didn't have the right, not after what he'd planned to do. Nico didn't know yet, and while Keegan thought about just forgetting he'd ever been dumb enough to think the Council's coven was the answer, he didn't want his and Nico's… *anything* to start with a lie like that.

He just had to hope that Nico would see where he was coming from and understand.

"So I'm guessing those dreams were real, right?" Nico asked abruptly, still looking at the far wall, and a bad feeling began to grow in Keegan's stomach.

Licking his dry lips, he said, "Of course they were real."

Nico nodded, brows furrowing, and then he pinned Keegan with a hard look. The funny, chatty man he'd been getting to know for months was nowhere in sight. "Good to know. For a while, I thought I was going crazy. That it was my brain's way of making my wolf feel better after I missed out on the chance of knowing for sure about you. About us."

"Nico." Keegan had to swallow the lump in his throat before he could say anything else. Fuck. He'd messed up so damn bad. "I'm sorry I made you feel that way. I didn't… I didn't mean to do that."

Nico waved him off like it was no big deal, but his face

didn't change, frown firmly in place. "Were you ever going to tell me?"

"I didn't know you didn't understand what the dreams were," he said carefully, not sure what Nico was getting at.

"Not about that." He pointed toward the open doorway. "About her, your daughter. Or about your situation with your coven. Were you going to tell me about any of it?"

Keegan winced. "I—"

"Because I just thought you were shy or weren't sure about me. I thought I just needed to convince you that I could be a good mate," Nico asked. His words felt like a slap across the face, but his tone never changed, staying even and in control. He never raised his voice or used his size and power to try and intimidate Keegan. He had every right to be angry, but he just seemed hurt and in need of answers.

Answers Keegan was afraid to give, knowing it could possibly ruin everything between them before they had a chance to find their footing.

Keegan met his eyes and took a deep breath. "You need to understand. I—"

"Don't, Keegan. Just…" Nico squeezed his eyes shut and pinched the bridge of his nose. In a soft, broken voice, he said, "Just tell me the truth. Were you planning on telling me anything?"

Fuck. "I… No, probably not."

Nico tipped his head back and stared up at the dark ceiling for a long second, then let it drop forward to his chest and ran his fingers through his hair. "Can I ask why?

"Nico—"

"Is it because you didn't trust me? Because you could have asked me anything over the last six months, but you barely said a damn word. It was like pulling teeth to get you to share a single thing about yourself." Nico shook his head, then held his gaze. "What was the point of any of it? Why not... Why not just leave me alone?"

Keegan's heart broke at the catch in Nico's voice. "It's complicated."

"Explain it to me." His hard tone was so different, it was killing Keegan to know he did that. He'd hurt Nico so bad he'd hardened himself against Keegan to protect himself.

"I couldn't leave you alone," he whispered, glancing away when his eyes started to burn. "I tried. I knew I couldn't be who you needed me to be—that I couldn't give you the life you wanted—but I *couldn't* stay away. That night in the clearing, I knew who you were to me. I felt it. My magic recognized you."

Nico made a frustrated sound, and Keegan turned to look at him once more, wiping at his eyes quickly. "You don't even know what I want."

Keegan gave him a small, sad smile. "I knew you'd want me to be with you, but I couldn't just leave my coven. They —*she* wouldn't just let me leave. My mother... She wouldn't let me go, especially not to mate with a shifter."

"I could have helped you," Nico started to say, stepping closer to the bed. His calm façade was finally cracking, and there was the tiniest glow beginning to shine in his eyes. "We could have come up with a plan—"

Keegan shook his head. "I knew that if you knew about my mother and coven, you'd do something reckless like try and come steal me away." The way Nico clenched his jaw let Keegan know he wasn't wrong. "You would have gotten yourself killed."

"You don't know that. My pack is strong. And our coven might be smaller than yours, but they're strong too. We could have come up with a way to get you out of there."

"Maybe." Keegan glanced toward the open doorway again.

He didn't know where Jocelyn and Rosie were, but he'd guess nearby. "But it wasn't just about you and me."

Nico looked toward the hallway too, like he could see Rosie through the walls. Keegan was sure he could hear her heart, maybe even catch her scent. "We could have come up with a plan to get you both to safety."

"Maybe," he said again, "but I couldn't risk it, risk her. As much as I couldn't stay away from you, I couldn't put her safety in jeopardy either. So... I came up with my own plan."

Nico studied him, eyes narrowed. "I'm assuming your plan wasn't to get tortured by Beatrice."

Pressing his lips together, he looked down at his hands and ran them over the blanket. "No, that... that wasn't part of the plan. She found the ingredients for the dream walking spell and assumed I was meeting with one of her enemies behind her back."

Nico sucked in a breath. "She hurt you because of me?"

Keegan shook his head furiously. "No. She hurt me because she's... broken. Because she can't trust anyone anymore, not even her own son. It wasn't the first time, just the worst."

The bed dipped, and Keegan jerked his head up, surprised to find Nico kneeling on the edge of the bed. His eyes were glowing hotly, and when he spoke, the tips of his fangs were visible. "She hurt you before?"

Keegan was mesmerized by his beautiful, glowing eyes. Slowly, he reached up and traced the line of the scar on his face. "Yeah," he croaked, "she hurt me before. That's why I couldn't let her near Rosie."

Nico's eyes ran over the scar, his jaw tightening. He leaned closer, and Keegan got his first whiff of his scent—something that made him think of lush, green forests. Wild. Unpredictable.

When Nico's gaze landed on Keegan's lips, he thought

about just closing the distance between them and taking a taste. Stealing a moment that Nico wouldn't have given if he knew the full truth of Keegan's plan.

Nico planted a fist on the bed by Keegan's hip, his eyes going half-lidded, and Keegan gritted out the words he knew would change everything. "I approached the Council's coven about joining them."

Nico froze, eyes flaring wide, then he staggered back like Keegan had shoved him away. "What?"

"It was my one chance to keep Rosie safe," Keegan said, speaking in a rush to try and make Nico understand. "My mother wouldn't have let me leave to go to just any other coven—and she never would have allowed me to join a pack's coven. She would have stopped me from joining any coven she deemed inferior. But... the work that the Council's coven does—or is *supposed* to do—it's... it's a worthwhile cause. One that not even she could have been able to stop me from joining. She couldn't have even openly objected because it's considered an honor to be chosen to serve."

Nico shoved both hands into his hair and spun away from the bed. "You... Don't you know?" He turned back around, his face doing something complicated and heartbreaking. "Don't you know all the terrible things the Council has been doing? You saw Wendy. They did that, Keegan. They sent some fucked-up beast they cooked up with their witches after one of their own people. How could you think..."

Keegan struggled to get his legs over to the side of the bed, pushing aside the covers. "I know. Nico, I'm sorry. I didn't see another way. I needed to get away, and I needed to keep Rosie safe—"

"Everyone else be damned, right?"

Keegan flinched, pausing with his legs hanging over the edge of the mattress. "Please understand—"

Nico laughed, but it was a horrible sound. "Oh, I understand. You strung me along for months, lied to Gabriel about helping the pack, and all the while, you were planning on joining the *Council's* coven."

"No, not the whole time. I just... I only came up with the idea recently," he finished lamely.

"Oh, my mistake," Nico sneered, and it was worse than if he'd just yelled. "You just lied to Gabe and messed with my head while knowing you'd never actually help us or tell me what was going on."

Keegan felt like he couldn't catch his breath. He'd known Nico would be upset—angry even—but it was somehow so much worse to see it in person. A part of him wanted to fight back, to get angry too and throw it in Nico's face that he could never understand what it was like to have to put the needs of his child before himself, but he knew instinctively that would be the exact wrong thing to say. That it would cut a wound so deep they might not be able to come back from it.

When Keegan couldn't think of anything to say to make the situation better, Nico shook his head and took another step back, moving farther away from Keegan. The space between them seemed insurmountable even though it was less than five feet.

"It must have been so annoying to wake up and find out I was here too. That you'd have to actually face me after all this time." Nico said it so quietly, Keegan almost didn't hear him.

Horrified, he pushed to his feet. "No!"

Nico scoffed and rubbed at his eyes. "I really ruined your plans of avoiding me forever by playing hero, huh."

"Don't say that," he whispered. "I was wrong, and I'm sorry. Finally being in the same room with you is... Nico, it's the opposite of annoying."

Hand still over his eyes, Nico said, "You know what the

worst part for me is?"

Keegan's breath froze in his lungs, but Nico didn't seem to actually require a response. He dropped his hand and looked at him with such devastation Keegan's own chest hurt.

"If you would have taken the last six months to actually get to know me—the real me, not the reckless hothead you seem to think I am—you would have figured out pretty damn quick that you could have trusted me with"—he waved his hand around—"all of this."

"I'm sorry. All I could think of was protecting Rosie."

"I would have protected her too," Nico said fiercely, thumping his chest with his fist. "If you would have given me the chance, I would have protected you both. With everything I have—every resource, every fiber of my being. If you would have given me the chance, I would have gladly put my life on the line to keep her safe."

Heart beating faster than was probably healthy, Keegan stared at Nico. How could he have been so blind and so wrong? He'd let the pain and distrust of his mother paint his own view of others. Instead of giving Nico a chance—giving them a chance—he'd done what he always did and assumed he couldn't trust anyone but himself and the couple of people, like Gabriel, who'd proven they could be trusted over the course of *years*.

But even Gabriel Keegan had let into his life before Rosie. Since her birth... he'd closed himself completely off, not wanting to take the risk of trusting the wrong person.

And his sweet wolf was suffering the consequences.

"I..." He didn't even know what to say. His throat was tight and hot, and all he wanted to do was wrap his arms around Nico and hold him until the pain was gone. But that wasn't an option.

Sucking in a deep breath through his nose, Nico straightened his shoulders and pointed at the bedside table next to Keegan. "There's the journal. While you're here getting your strength back, Alpha Kincaid would greatly appreciate any translations you could provide regarding any prophesies in it."

"Nico—"

"Ericka, a Kincaid Pack beta, will be staying with you. She'll bring back anything you manage to translate. If you need to contact Rick, go through her."

"Where... where will you be?"

"I'm going home in the morning. It's too dangerous for us both to be here. This pack is too small, and it'll draw too much attention." Nico watched him, maybe waiting for Keegan to say something, but he couldn't. All he could do was stare back, terrified that this would be the last time he saw Nico. Swallowing, he turned away. "Goodbye, Keegan."

Nico only made it two steps before Keegan's body lurched forward without his say-so, the instinct to stop him from leaving too powerful to fight. But his body was still weak from what his mother had done, and he stumbled. He would have hit the ground if two strong hands hadn't caught him.

Gripping Nico's arms as tightly as he could, he pulled himself upright. "Don't go. Please. Don't just leave."

They were so close together Keegan could feel Nico's large chest expanding as he took in a deep breath, his eyes screwing shut.

"Nico, please. I'm sorry." He slid one hand up over Nico's shoulder all the way to his neck. As soon as his palm hit the warm, pulsing skin there, Nico's eyes flew open, and Keegan was suddenly moving, Nico's big hands holding him firmly as he carried him back to the bed.

He laid Keegan on the mattress and followed him down, pressing their bodies together and burying his face in

Keegan's neck with a groan and full-body shudder. When he rubbed his face against the thin skin of Keegan's throat, he shivered at the rasp from his stubble.

Neither of them said anything. There wasn't anything left to say.

Nico panted against him, rubbing his face and lips every once in a while, doing his best to thoroughly scent mark Keegan, and Keegan just wrapped his arms around him and let him do whatever he needed.

After several minutes, Nico started to slowly make his way up Keegan's neck to his jaw. Making a soft noise, he ran his nose up the line of Keegan's scar, the gentle touch almost too much. Keegan had to blink away tears, his arms tightening around Nico's shoulders.

Finally, after what felt like an eternity, Nico shifted over so his mouth was hovering right over Keegan's. He held his breath, waiting, wanting.

Nico dipped down, and Keegan let his eyes fall closed. He tipped his chin up and—

Nico was gone, slipping out of Keegan's hold with a low growl and darting across the room. Keegan raised his head, confused and frustrated, and found Nico standing in the doorway, eyes glowing once more and chest heaving.

They stared at each other, and then Nico turned and left.

Keegan dropped his head back onto the bed and groaned.

What the fuck had he done?

CHAPTER NINE

The dark sky and rolling thunder were the perfect match for Nico's mood as he drove toward the Medina farmhouse outside of town.

He'd gotten back to Michigan the night before and spent an hour with Rick, filling him in on any details he hadn't felt comfortable sharing over the phone. Then that had turned into an Enforcers meeting where everyone peppered him with questions about Voight and the vampire—even though he'd never actually seen the guy. His head had been throbbing by the time Rick had called an end to things, but then he'd made Nico stay back so he could ask him how he was doing in that gruff, caring way that usually made Nico's wolf want to tell him everything he wanted to know.

But Nico hadn't known what to say. It was obvious he'd returned without his mate, but he hadn't told them about Keegan's plan or that he'd met Rosie and fallen in love with her in a single afternoon of napping in the sun.

He'd just shrugged and forced a smile and said he'd be okay eventually. Rick hadn't looked convinced, but thankfully Kai had come looking for him, so Nico had been able to slip away while he was distracted by his mate.

When he'd gotten back to his house, José had been out with friends. Coming home to an empty house had stopped him in his tracks, feeling like the perfect horrible glimpse of his future. Never having a house full of magic and Rosie's laughter. Never having... Keegan.

So he'd done something he hadn't done since he was in his early twenties and gotten trashed on shifter wine, then passed out.

Of course, because his brain hated him, he'd dreamed about Keegan.

Not a magical dream walking kind, just a regular one. And he knew that because it had involved fewer clothes and more of Keegan telling him how much he loved being his mate and how he'd never leave him.

He'd woken up with a hangover and out of his mind with heartache.

His wolf felt... frantic. Had been scratching to be released since Nico had run away from Keegan's room back in Kansas. His wolf didn't give two shits that Keegan had lied to him and planned on betraying him. All his wolf cared about was that Nico had walked away from his mate, who'd smelled of pain and regret and... arousal.

He'd decided that he needed two things: to talk to his best friend and lots of coffee. But definitely not in that order.

After stopping at *Magic Beans* and grabbing himself the biggest cup of coffee they sold and an Earl Grey tea for Marcus, he'd headed out to the farmhouse where Marcus and his mate lived with other members of the Medina family.

It was hardly the first time Nico had been out to the farmhouse, considering that practically ever since Marcus and Robson had met, Nico had been working with Robson's brother Matteo to expand their family farm's operations.

Robson had been reluctant at first, thinking Nico's interest was charity or something, but Nico knew a good opportunity when he saw one. The pack was bursting at the seams with members looking for good jobs, and the local job market and economy were struggling to keep up.

Nico, after getting it okayed by Rick, had started working on getting a milk processing plant built and up and running. Thankfully, the paperwork for the plant had been far less complicated than the housing development, so things were well on their way. Plus, Robson's brother Teo was a wealth of information about dairy farming and knew a lot of other farmers in the area, helping Nico make connections with them so they could create their own dairy co-op for the processing plant.

Rick had also okayed doing upgrades to the Medina farm so they could take on more cows and hire workers to help out. Things were going so well with Teo that Nico wouldn't be surprised if they got brought into the fold of the pack since it was getting more and more difficult to hide things from him.

But that wasn't his decision to make.

Over the last half year he'd been making visits out to the farmhouse, he'd also realized that his best friend was avoiding him. It had taken him ages to realize it because he still saw Marcus at the manor plenty, and he'd just assumed his friend was enjoying his new mate and that was why they hadn't gone for as many runs together or he didn't seem to be around whenever Nico was at the house.

But then he'd made an unexpected visit about a month ago—needing Teo to sign some paperwork—and he'd witnessed Marcus *fleeing* his own home to avoid him.

He was done waiting around for Marcus to get his head out of his ass. He needed his friend and packmate, and if he had a problem with that...

Well, tough shit.

The rain was just starting to fall as he knocked on the front door. Robson answered a minute later, and Nico pushed past him as soon as he cracked it open, shaking his wet hair out of his eyes. He needed a haircut, but it was too far down on his to-do list to worry about anytime soon.

"You're back," Robson said and then looked out onto the front porch, like he was expecting someone else. He confirmed it a second later when he tentatively asked, "Are you by yourself?"

Nico grimaced. Not answering, he let his nose lead him to where Marcus was upstairs in his and Robson's bedroom. Marcus had been at the impromptu Enforcer meeting last night, though he hadn't said much, and he apparently hadn't had a chance to fill Robson in yet.

He ignored Robson grumbling behind him as he followed Nico up the stairs. "No, please, make yourself at home. Go on up to our bedroom."

"Thanks," he said as he pushed open the door to their room, ignoring the strong scent of their recent mating in the air, and focused on Marcus, where he was finishing making the bed.

He held out the tea and said without preamble, "Keegan was planning on joining the Council's coven to get away from his mother, even after... everything. Everything they've done and... even knowing about me." He took a deep breath. "And he's not married, but I don't know if I can trust him, so I left him behind in Kansas, and I may never talk to him again, and I could... I could really use my best friend right now."

Marcus stared at him without moving for several long moments, and then he stepped forward and accepted the insulated cup of tea. Gesturing toward a chair in the corner of the room, he asked, "Why did he need to join the Council's coven to get away from his mother?"

Nico moved a well-worn paperback off the seat and placed it on the table next to the chair before sinking down on it and slugging back some coffee. "You know about his coven, right?"

Marcus nodded. Before coming to the Kincaid Pack, Marcus had worked for years under the Council and knew more about them and shifter law than anyone else Nico had ever met in all of his travels. He'd also met quite a few different packs and covens, having been sent out by the Council to investigate certain incidents or look into complaints. His mentor, Mikel Gregson, had been the councilman to warn Rick about not trusting the Council.

Mikel had also been the one to get a message to Marcus through Wendy that had led to them finding the original Council charter, which stated that, per a powerful seer's prophesy, the Council would dissolve upon completion of one of her visions. That amendment to the charter had been removed from the digital archives that all packs had access to. Mikel had left the seer's journal for Marcus to find as well, but until Keegan translated it from Haitian Creole, they wouldn't know what the prophesy actually said.

Keegan had also been the one to find an injured Wendy and get her safely to the Kincaid Pack territory.

The same night Nico had locked eyes with him and his wolf had howled with joy, recognizing his mate even without catching his scent.

Nico rubbed his forehead and focused on his breathing, unable to even think about Keegan without feeling like his chest was splitting open. Marcus watched him with sad eyes but didn't try and offer empty words of comfort.

"I met Beatrice once," Marcus said, "not long after she took over the coven. She's a brilliant woman and extremely power-ful. And she's a true believer in the La Fleurs' mission to stay out of pack affairs and to only get involved when it is neces-sary to protect humans from shifters or other parahumans."

"Yeah, well, apparently she's gotten a bit power hungry over the years," Nico said and then told Marcus everything he had learned from Gabriel, Councilwoman Voight, and Keegan. When he got to the part where he was repeating what Voight had said about the condition Keegan had been in when she'd pulled him out of the warehouse his mother had been keeping him in, he had to stop for a minute.

Remembering how his ma—how Keegan had suffered, fighting her mind control for days and days while drugged and weakened by magic, it was hard to catch his breath.

Marcus didn't rush him, just sipping his tea and waiting him out. Nico knew Robson was lingering in the doorway, but they both ignored him. Robson was a trusted member of Rick's inner circle, his past tactical experience invaluable now that the pack was gearing up for what seemed like an inevitable battle.

Even if he wasn't—the fact that he was Marcus's mate and took such good care of Nico's friend meant he trusted the snarky human.

Once he could speak without his voice wavering, he finished telling Marcus what had happened in Kansas, glossing over the part about meeting and spending an after-noon with Rosie and nearly kissing Keegan.

Fuck. He couldn't even think about that almost kiss without his whole body heating up, followed by a wave of despair—he definitely couldn't talk about it.

"Do you think you'll be able to stay away from him?" Marcus finally asked after thinking for a little while. "Now that he isn't just the idea of your mate. You've met him, scented him…"

Nico had to clear his throat before he could answer. "I think once he's finished translating the journal, he'll disappear with his daughter, so it doesn't really matter what I want. I'll probably never hear from him again."

"I'm so sorry, Nico," Marcus said softly, his brows scrunching in sympathy. "I can't imagine what that feels like."

Nico shrugged and scrubbed out his face, his empty coffee cup long since discarded. "I'll get over it," he said hoarsely, though he wasn't sure if he was trying to convince himself or Marcus. "It's not like I don't have plenty of things to do to keep me busy."

The number of emails and phone calls he needed to return after being only semi-available for nearly a week was mind-blowing. He needed to recruit some betas to get some things off his plate once he didn't need the distraction to keep him from thinking about Keegan constantly.

Marcus nodded and then glanced at Robson. For some reason, the look on his face snagged Nico's attention, and he lifted his head to look at him more fully. There was that the faintest of blushes staining Marcus's pale skin.

"I know you already have a lot on your plate," Marcus said, voice too even, "but there's something I need to tell you."

"Is this something the reason you've been avoiding me?"

"Wasn't just you," Robson said, speaking up for the first time since Nico had barged into their bedroom.

That didn't actually make Nico feel better, but he's supposed it was something to know he hadn't been singled out.

Before Marcus could say anything, they heard the back door open and Teo come inside. He turned to his mate and said, "Your brother just came in. Can you keep him busy while we finish talking?"

Robson nodded and pushed off the doorjamb, but before

he left, he stepped over to the bed, cupped the back of Marcus's head, and planted a quick kiss on his mouth. It wasn't even anything showy, but it was still a reminder of something Nico wouldn't ever have, and he had to look away.

"Holler if you need me, cariño." Then Robson was gone, thundering down the stairs and calling a greeting to his brother.

Nico still couldn't quite meet Marcus's eyes, not trusting himself if he saw a sappy look on his face. "So what's going on?"

"It's the letter. The one Mikel left me."

When Jamie, Drake, and Gabriel had gone to Massachusetts to retrieve the charter and journal where Mikel had hid them, they'd also found a letter addressed to Marcus. As far as Nico knew, he'd never told anyone what was in it except that it wasn't anything to do with the Council or journal.

"Okay?"

"In it... he told me about the time he'd visited my family's pack, back when he was still the alpha of the coastal birds and before he was on the Council. He said he wasn't there very long, but... he'd met a woman while he was visiting."

Nico stared at him.

"He apparently tried to get her to leave with him, to become his alpha-mate, but she wouldn't go. She was already promised to another." Marcus's fingers twitched on his thighs, his eyes distant. "She was supposed to mate with the pack's alpha. Mikel explained that he didn't find out until much later that when she confessed to sleeping with him, the alpha—my old alpha—broke things off with her, refusing to take her as his mate."

Nico scrunched up his face. "Just because she had sex with somebody else before they were mated?"

Marcus shook his head. "No, because she was pregnant."

Nico blinked at him, stunned. "Are you saying what I think you're saying?"

Marcus's eyes were a little glassy as he dipped his head in a brief nod. "Apparently, Mikel Gregson was my real father. And that's why my alpha hated me growing up and sent me away when I was sixteen. My mom... I think she resented me for ruining her chances of being alpha-mate, and the man she did mate with, the one I thought was my father, didn't like me because he knew he wasn't her first choice."

"Holy shit, Marcus."

"Mikel said in the letter that he'd promised my mom he would never tell me, but... but he said he couldn't stand the idea of something happening to him and me never knowing."

"That's... I don't even know." Nico rose from his chair and stepped over to the bed, sitting right next to Marcus on the edge. "Are you okay?"

Marcus shrugged. "I've had a few months to adjust to the idea, but I still keep oscillating between anger that I never got to know him as my father and relief that I finally understand why I was so different from my old pack and why I was treated so poorly. But then that also makes me angry to think about how my old alpha's jealousy and hatred for Mikel affected my entire life and no one ever told me."

"Are you pissed he never said anything to you when you worked for him?" Nico snaked an arm behind Marcus, offering him the comfort he'd never let himself ask for, and some of the rigidness in Marcus's shoulders lessened.

He looked away from Nico, swallowing audibly and then nodding. "It's... difficult. I want to be angry with him for keeping it a secret, but then I think, he was probably killed trying to protect me and my pack, and then I feel bad for being angry."

He gave Marcus a squeeze. "You can be grateful for what

he's done for us as a pack and still be angry at him for what he took from you. You can be both. It's okay to be both. He lied to you even after meeting you and spending time with you."

Nico should know. He yearned for his mate and was furious with him all at the same time.

Marcus nodded and turned into Nico's body, burying his face into his shoulder. "I'm sorry I'm making this visit about me. That isn't why you came here."

Nico gave a half laugh, wrapping his other arm around Marcus. "We talked about me and my shit long enough. I can be sad about Keegan and for my best friend who's in pain all at the same time. I'm a complex guy like that."

Marcus laughed a little, and then they sat like that for a while, just taking comfort in having a packmate they loved and trusted so close, helping to share the burden of what was weighing each of them down.

Once some of the pain began to ebb out of Marcus's scent, Nico nudged him. "Let's go for a run. I haven't stretched my legs in ages."

Marcus sat up and stared at him, gesturing toward the window. It was a sheet of gray on the other side of the glass, the rain coming down so hard, but Nico just grinned at him.

"It's pouring," Marcus said, sounding scandalized that Nico would even suggest they go out in it.

He laughed as he stood and pulled Marcus with him, feeling a bit more like his old self. After everything he'd been through the last week—hell, even all the months of wondering if he was losing his mind and yet craving the dreams with Keegan—he doubted he'd ever be the same happy and carefree person he had been before Keegan had crashed into his life.

"You won't melt," he said, pulling his shirt off and

chucking it at Marcus's scowl, and then darting out of the room, knowing he'd follow.

He would always have this. His pack and his work and pups to play with, even if they weren't his. He would have Marcus and all his other friends that he could lean on when he needed to. He'd get through the pain of losing his mate.

He'd survive.

He might be a different person on the other side, but that was okay.

It had to be.

CHAPTER TEN

"You're wrong." Jocelyn had the audacity to laugh right in his face after she said that.

"No, I am not."

That just made her laugh harder. She collapsed back into the chair across from him, shaking her head. "Goddess, I forgot you were like this."

He looked up from the journal they were studying between them. They'd been given a small den to work out of by Alpha Amato and mostly been left alone, the pack going about their lives around them. He scowled at Jocelyn, tired and getting a headache. "Like what?"

"This," she said, waving a hand at him. "So stubborn. You've always been grumpy, but I forgot how hard you can dig in your heels and what an ass you can be when you think you're right."

He made an affronted noise. "I am not being—"

"Yes, you are," she interrupted. "It's been years since I've really seen this side of you, though, because you're usually on your best behavior in front of Rosie." Before he could come up with something to rebuke that with, she continued. "But now you're cranky as hell. And I get it. You're in pain, feeling weak and vulnerable. You're disconnected from a coven for the first time in your life, and so you're taking it all out on me. But I am telling you, that word means *kings*. Not royalty. Not in this context, Keegan."

Her voice had gotten sharper and sharper, and by the end, she was half risen out of her seat, glaring at him.

He wasn't the only one who could be stubborn.

He slammed the journal closed and pushed it across the table toward her. "This is useless. We can't even agree on a single word. How are we supposed to translate entire passages and know that they're accurate enough to provide information that will actually help the Kincaid Pack?"

"Ahem."

He whipped around and nearly groaned when he saw Kincaid's beta, Ericka, standing in the doorway behind them, her face sheepish and phone in her hand.

"So... I called Rick," she said, running a hand through her wild blonde curls.

Keegan really did groan then, slumping in his chair. He could just imagine how pissed off the big alpha was at their lack of progress. He had thought it would go faster if Jocelyn stayed since she had also learned Creole from their grann. And whereas he had been more fluent in speaking it, she had been better at reading it.

Or so she had claimed.

After the last week, he wasn't convinced either one of them was up to the job.

They'd done nothing but bicker for a week straight over everything, making very little progress in the prophesy regarding the Council's dissolution or the one that he had found near the back that seemed to be about some sort of royal family. Or, as Jocelyn kept trying to say, a family of kings, which to him meant the same damn thing.

She wasn't wrong about him feeling weak though. He hated it. It had been over a week since he'd been rescued, and yet he could still barely feel his magic. And he felt completely drained if he performed even the most basic of spells.

Physically, he was basically fine, though he still got headaches or some muscle fatigue if he pushed himself too hard during the day. For the most part though, he'd been good to go after those first few days of doing little more than sleeping. He'd gone for walks—and even a few runs—and played with Rosie and felt the same as he had before.

It was all... inside him. The well deep in his chest where his magic bubbled up from when he called on it felt... drained. Dry. Tapped out in a way he had never experienced before.

In a way that honestly fucking terrified him.

He hadn't said anything to Jocelyn, but part of him was worried he would never get it back. That in her attempts to break him, their mother had been successful in a way. That somehow, she had severed the connection between him and magic, and every time he used his powers now, it was draining what little he had left with no way to refill it. Eventually... he'd just run out.

He waved Ericka into the room, and Jocelyn watched, eyes wide, as Ericka set her phone on the table by the journal, speakerphone turned on.

"My beta tells me the two of you have been doing nothing but arguing for a week straight."

Rick's deep voice boomed out of the small speaker in the phone, and Jocelyn literally jumped in her chair before turning her startled eyes on him. He kept his focus on the pissed-off shifter on the other end of the line.

"Translations aren't an exact science."

"I understand that, witch, but it's been a week, and you haven't been able to translate a single page." There was an edge to his voice that made Keegan wonder if Rick knew what had happened between him and Nico. If he knew what Keegan's plan had been…

His face flushed as he ground his teeth together to stop himself from lashing out defensively.

"We're just a little rusty," Jocelyn offered tentatively.

Keegan expected Rick to bark at them that that wasn't a good enough reason, but the alpha sighed instead. "Be honest with me. No bullshit. Can you do this or not?"

Keegan met and held Jocelyn's eyes, the dark brown almost exactly the same as his and Rosie's. And their mother's. He swallowed. "I don't know. It's not even that my Creole is rusty. I mean, it's sort of that," he hastened to say when Jocelyn opened her mouth like she was going to contradict him. "I think the biggest issue we're running into is that it's not the same language."

"What do you mean?" Rick asked. Even Ericka took another step closer, looking curious.

"I mean, languages change. Quickly, actually. Think about how words or expressions change from one generation to the next. Things like slang—they make perfect sense to the group who use them, but outside that group, it's meaningless. Fuck," he said, rubbing his face, "the connotation of a word or phrase can be drastically different even within a single country, depending on where you live."

"Okay."

"Now add in the fact that Creole is basically a mishmash of multiple languages and that this version is over a hundred years old, and I don't know if anyone living *could* translate this accurately. I'm… I'm sorry."

Rick didn't say anything for a long time, and Ericka, who had been nothing but sweet to him and Rosie, wrapped her arms around her torso, her face pinching with worry.

He hadn't known all the details about what had been

happening with the Kincaid Pack—though he'd heard rumors. Especially the last year and with what had happened with the McAllister Pack. There had been a lot of chatter even among covens about how Rick had *erased* the pack after getting pissed at the alpha and the Council for refusing to side with him.

Now that Ericka had filled him in on more of the nuances of what had actually gone down between Rick, Alpha McAllister, and the Council, and then the fact that some of the council members were apparently working with some super-powerful witch or coven and had killed people, Keegan was so pissed at himself for having put off meeting with Gabriel for such stupid, selfish reasons. The Kincaid Pack had been holding on to hope for months that the answer to how to fight back against the Council was locked in the journal of a long-dead seer, assuming he'd be able to help them once he finally got it in his hands.

Shame filled him as he pushed the heels of his hands into his eyes.

"It's okay. Just do your best. Anything you can translate that you think might be even a little accurate, have Ericka send it to us, okay?" The disappointment in Rick's voice along with the quiet resignation felt like a punch to the gut.

"Yes, sir," he said softly, guilt thick in his throat.

He'd been so consumed with his own life and problems, and now Rick and his pack were paying the price.

Nico had been right to leave him behind.

He just screwed up everything around him.

He couldn't help comparing Rick's reaction to how his own mother would have acted if he'd failed like this. Beatrice didn't accept failure from anyone, not even her own son. *Especially* not her own son. He'd been on the receiving end of her disappointment more than once, and she'd done more than raise her voice to him.

Rick hadn't yelled at them. He hadn't even demanded they do better. He'd just quietly asked them to do the best they could. That was it.

Rick sighed once more, then said, "Any word about your mom coming after you?"

"No," Jocelyn answered for him, no doubt sensing his emotions. "We talked with a friend yesterday, and she said that Mom has been meeting with the coven elders and her inner circle a lot, but she hasn't made any sort of statement about Keegan. Rose Ellen said that word had gotten around —in large part thanks to her—about what Mom did to Keegan, and people aren't happy about it."

"Sounds like she's got her hands full."

"That's our thinking," Ericka added, speaking for the first time. "Gabriel's placed a number of hunters around the coven's territory, keeping their ears to the ground and eyes peeled, but it seems like Beatrice has accepted Keegan as a lost cause."

Keegan wasn't so sure, but the fact that she hadn't followed him immediately did make him feel a little better. He wouldn't put it past her to regroup, squash any disloyal voices, and then come after him in the future though.

As if reading his mind, Rick said, "If she changes her mind, we'll deal with it. Beatrice Toussaint doesn't fucking scare me. You hear me, Keegan?"

Swallowing, he said, "I hear you."

"Good. Get back to work. Ericka, take me off speak-erphone."

Keegan finally moved his hands and glanced up at the beta. She smiled apologetically at them, picking up her phone and quickly leaving the room.

"You know, the way you made him sound," Jocelyn said, leaning forward to flip through the journal pages but not stopping to look at any one passage, "I expected him to be meaner."

Keegan snorted. "To be fair, the only time I actually met him, I had just busted through the warding his witches had placed around his territory. Without permission. In the middle of the night. And with a half-dead friend of one of his Enforcers at my side."

She stared at him. "Yeah, okay, I can see why that might have made him less than hospitable toward you."

"He's a good alpha," Keegan admitted. "Nico wouldn't stay if he wasn't."

Jocelyn closed the journal again, raising her eyes to look at him. "Wow. Took a week, but you finally said his name."

Keegan looked away from her knowing gaze. "What's there to say?"

"Gee, I don't know. Maybe why some Enforcer, who—as far as I can tell—you'd never actually met until he rescued you, went to the effort of rescuing you in the first place. Especially when it consisted of calling in favors from several different people and packs and getting a councilwoman involved. That's a lot for someone to do who didn't actually know you even if Gabriel asked him for help." She watched him for a second. "He didn't know you, did he, Keegan?"

"He thought he did," Keegan said quietly, running his thumb over the scar on his face without meaning to. When her face darkened, he dropped his hand onto the table. "That night on Kincaid land, I didn't speak to him, but we had... a moment. A connection that snagged me and my magic and wouldn't let go even after I returned home."

She sucked in a breath. "Are you his...?"

"I think so. I started dream walking with him and got to know him. He tried to get to know me, but you know how hard that is." He said it self-deprecatingly, but it was painful to think about all those nights he'd strolled into Nico's mind without bothering to give him a chance to really know him.

She laughed softly. "People do say it's pretty difficult. Zeke complains all the time that even after three years of you visiting at least once a month, you barely say five words to him. If I hadn't grown up with you, I imagine I wouldn't know you as well as I do."

He didn't mean to be so closed off. It was just... what he was used to. It was what he'd had to do to survive, and now he didn't know how to change.

No, that wasn't true.

He'd never even *tried*.

"I didn't tell him about Rosie. That's why he made the assumption that you and I were together."

Jocelyn raised her eyebrows. "Did you think he wouldn't handle the news well?"

Keegan shook his head, knocking his knuckles on the table in front of him. "The opposite. I knew that if he knew all of the details about Rosie's birth and my inability to leave the La Fleurs, he would do something reckless to bring us all together so we could be a family."

The words tasted like a lie even as he repeated the argument he'd made to himself so many times. Detecting bullshit, Jocelyn narrowed her eyes.

"He didn't seem overly reckless to me."

He clasped his hands together and brought them up to press against his forehead, wishing more than anything he could go back six months and change... everything. So he and Nico could start over. "He's not. I... I fucked up."

"You know," Jocelyn said after a moment of weighted silence, "you act like you're so worldly, having traveled all over for the coven, but you don't really know what it's like to live in a pack."

"Your point?"

"My point is, you see packs when they're at their worst. You never get to see them at their best. And I think... I think some of that nonsense Mom and the elders spew about shifters being little better than mindless beasts got to you. At least a little. Like it sunk into your subconscious."

He bristled immediately. "I know they aren't—"

"No, I know, but you just told me that you assumed he'd react without thinking if he knew the truth about you and your situation. That"—she waved her hand at him—"has Mom's influence written all over it."

She was right. Nico had proved him wrong already. When Rose Ellen called Gabriel and told him she was worried about his safety, Nico hadn't lost his mind and run to New Orleans without a plan. He and his pack had come up with a risky but brilliant plan, and not once had Nico gone rogue, even when he found out for sure Keegan was being tortured.

"I think I ruined things," he admitted, swallowing. "You know my plan to get away by joining the Council's coven?"

"Oh god," she groaned. "You told him about that?"

Keegan nodded. "I had to. It felt... I needed to be honest with him, and understandably, he didn't take it well. I tried to explain it was the only way I'd seen to safely leave and be reunited with Rosie, but he didn't exactly see it that way."

"He might have if you'd explained things from the beginning instead of hiding it from him. How long have you been dream walking with him?"

He grimaced. "Almost since the very beginning. Half a year."

"Oh, Keegan." She sighed, shaking her head again. "You really hurt him."

Keegan flinched at the words. "I know I did. Don't you think I know that? Don't you think it kills me? He just *left*, Jos. I hurt him so badly he just left me here after finally being in the same room as me. Sharing the same space, breathing the same air. I might not be a shifter or have lived among a pack, but even I know that it had to have been excruciating for him to scent me and then... and then leave me."

He swiped at the wetness on his cheeks, not looking at his sister. If he'd been stronger, he would have chased after Nico that night. If he'd had his magic, he would have locked them in the room together until he could convince Nico that he really was sorry and that he'd make it up to him. That he'd rebuild the trust he'd so callously broken.

But it was probably for the best he hadn't been able to.

What did he really have to offer Nico?

"Well, what are you going to do about it?"

He thrust his hand at the journal, pointing at it angrily. "The only thing I can do. Try and translate this fucking journal to give him and his pack any kind of leverage they can use against the Council."

"No, I meant what are you going to do to make it up to him? To win him back."

"Jocelyn—"

"No, listen to me. You connected through a *glance*. He took on the La Fleur Coven for you. He brought me and Rosie here so we'd be there when you woke up, even when he thought I was your wife. That's not an infatuation. You are his true mate, and he would do anything for you. You need to be willing to do the same, or else it's not fair to him."

Her words sliced through him, cutting into the deep-seated fear he'd had since he'd met those beautiful blue eyes across the clearing and felt his whole world shift. How could he be enough for someone like that? He might have been a powerful witch, but he couldn't give a shifter the kind of mating they would really want. No human could.

And now, he might not even be a powerful witch anymore.

Sucking in a breath, he squeezed his eyes shut. Even if he went to Michigan, even if he begged Rick to let him into his pack and the man agreed, what did he really have to offer? Not just to Nico, but to the Kincaid Pack and coven. He wasn't even twenty-five, and the only thing he'd ever been good at—the only talent he'd ever had cultivated in him since the moment he was born—might have been ripped away.

He had nothing left to offer.

He realized he'd said that last part out loud when tears appeared in Jocelyn's eyes, her face falling. "Don't say that. You don't have to give him anything other than your love and trust. That's all he wants from you. He doesn't need the big bad witch. He just needs Keegan. The bad-tempered, foul-mouthed guy who can't cook but loves to eat. The guy who protected me from bullies and took the brunt of Mom's anger and disappointment even though I was older. The guy who would do anything for his daughter even if it meant sacrificing his own happiness."

He wanted to look away, the emotions building inside him feeling like they were too big to contain the longer he held her fierce eyes, but he couldn't. He was raw and broken and guilt-ridden, and her words were gently soothing his open wounds and putting him back together.

"Nico just needs the guy who was able to stand up against the leader of the damn La Fleur Coven for almost an entire week without giving her a single thing. That's not your magic, Kee—that's just you. That guy... he's worthy of Nico. He *deserves* someone like Nico. Someone who will love him and protect him even if he's being a stubborn ass."

He laughed wetly as hope began to spread in his belly for the first time in... goddess, he didn't know how long. Years? The only thing he'd lived for since Rosie was born was the idea of one day getting away from his mother and getting to raise her the way she deserved: feeling safe and loved. And when he'd met Nico's eyes all those months ago, he'd shut down any chance of them being together before he'd even let himself think about it. Instead, he'd just milked every second of their shared dreams, knowing it was all he'd get of his wolf.

But what if it wasn't. What if Jocelyn was right and it wasn't too late?

He'd fucked up, he'd admit that. He'd made assumptions about Nico and judged him based on the crap his mother spewed without actually giving them the chance to get to know one another. And he'd made it a million times worse by choosing the Council over Nico. He wasn't sure how he could even begin to make it up to him, but he knew he couldn't start half a country away.

He needed to get to his wolf as fast as he could. He needed to—

"Daddy." Rosie shuffled into the doorway, rubbing her eyes and squinting at him and Jocelyn.

"Sweetie, what are you doing up? It's late." He held his arms out, and the full weight of the love he felt for her hit him as she crawled up into his lap without hesitation.

"Couldn't sleep," she mumbled, rubbing her face against his chest as she curled into him.

"Did you have a bad dream?" He met Jocelyn's eyes over her head. At least one of Rosie's magical abilities that were starting to manifest was one she shared with her mom. They were both empaths. But Rosie was too little to know how to control the onslaught of other people's emotions yet, and Jocelyn had said she was having bad dreams lately, especially after they arrived in Kansas and she was kept away from Keegan.

"Mhm." She sighed as he wrapped his arms around her. "Want Wolfie."

He shot Jocelyn another look, but she appeared just as

confused as him. He'd never seen a stuffed wolf among her toys before—

He sucked in a breath when he realized there had been another wolf she might have run into recently. "Who's Wolfie, sweetie?"

"My wolf," she said with the perfect logic of a three-year-old. "He's sad, but I helped."

He's sad.

Swallowing, he tightened his arms around her. "Okay. We'll get your wolf back."

"Promise?" She sounded half-asleep, her little body slumping against him.

Jocelyn was watching him, her eyebrows raised as she slid the journal closer to him and gave him an encouraging nod.

"I promise."

CHAPTER ELEVEN

Nico didn't look up from the papers in front of him on his desk until Rick knocked and pushed open the door to his office, filling the space with his scent and presence immediately.

He'd heard him coming, of course, had been waiting for him all morning actually. He'd expected him to come get him at any moment, keeping him on edge and unable to get a single bit of work done. It was a good thing he'd already found one beta to help share his workload with because he wasn't sure how much he'd be getting done anytime soon.

"It's time?" he asked, shuffling his paperwork together and then pushing to his feet. His nonchalance wasn't fooling Rick, but Nico needed to pretend for himself that everything was normal.

Rick nodded, eyeing him carefully as he rounded his desk. Then he blew Nico's plan of faking it until he made it right out of the water. "Are you okay to do this?"

"Of course," he said, pasting on a smile he'd perfected in the last week.

Rick wasn't impressed with it. "Because I can get

someone else. Hell, I could even go alone, despite what all you mother hens around me think."

Nico wasn't touching that last part with a ten-foot pole. Rick liked to pretend he could still go wherever and do whatever he wanted, but that just wasn't true. Especially so close to the border of their territory where anyone with decent aim and a rifle could take a shot at him.

"It should be me," he said carefully, avoiding looking directly into Rick's eyes. "I'm the one who's met with all of the other witches who have applied to join our pack and coven. Tashmica and I have handled all the rest of them; I can handle this one too."

"Except none of the others were your fucking mate.," Rick said, no longer beating around the bush. One of his big hands landed on the side of Nico's neck, scenting him and calming him all at once.

"I wouldn't say Keegan is that either."

Rick snorted, shifting his hand to the back of Nico's neck and tugging him forward into a brief embrace, and then steered him out of his office and down the hallway like he was an errant pup who needed guidance. It should have been more annoying than it was, rather than an odd sort of comfort.

"You and I both know it doesn't work that way. The two of you can choose not to go through with the mating, but it doesn't change the fact that you're destined for one another." He gave Nico's neck an affectionate squeeze. "You were chosen for each other, and no matter what he's done or what you do, it doesn't change who he is to you. And I know that hurts right now."

The manor was buzzing with people going about their lives and jobs, and he felt like he had just been kicked in the face instead of having a simple truth told to him. A truth he had known his entire life. He remembered being a pup and his mom teaching him about mates. She had told him that true ones, fated ones, were the best kind. Most important, she'd said, not every shifter was blessed enough to have one, but when you were, you cherished them.

He had a feeling she would be ashamed of the way he had simply walked away from his, no matter his reasons or justifications. She would say that Keegan was his other half, and without him, he wasn't whole.

She'd also probably tell him to get his head out of his ass.

But he didn't know how. Didn't know if he *could.*

He swallowed, eyes downcast. "I keep thinking it'll get easier. Each day I wake up and I think, this is it. Today it won't feel like I'm suffocating."

"Nico." Rick paused, turning Nico to face him.

Shaking his head, he said, "I thought I was doing the right thing. I thought…"

"What?" Rick said, deep voice still gruff, even speaking so softly. "Talk to me, Nico."

He stared at his alpha, really looking at him. Rick had always been big, even to someone like Nico, who'd come from big, burly Midwestern stock. But as their pack had grown, so had Rick. Not in actual size, but he radiated power in a way that drew others to him. It was instinctual to seek out the strongest shifter in the area for protection and guidance.

But lately, he'd looked stressed and tired with shadows under his eyes and lines on his forehead. The weight of everything happening the last year was taking its toll.

In that moment though, with his focus entirely on Nico and his worry obvious, it was easy to see why he was such an amazing alpha. Snarly badassness aside—he just *cared* about his pack.

"In the moment, I thought I was right."

"About what?"

He hadn't told anyone but Marcus about Keegan's plan to join the Council's coven, so he wasn't sure what they thought the reason was for him returning with his mate. "Just, everything. He... lied about some things, and I thought I was right to think we couldn't make it work. I thought I couldn't ever trust him."

"But?" Rick gave his neck another squeeze.

"He had his reasons," Nico whispered. "I was hurt and angry, and I felt so damn betrayed. But... it wasn't like he did it with the intention of hurting me, you know?"

Rick's eyebrows quirked, and Nico thought he might ask for more details, but then he just said, "Unintentional or not, the pain happened. Being mates doesn't mean you won't ever fuck up. If you want to give him another chance, then give him another chance. He is coming here. That has to count for something."

"Maybe." He took a deep breath and then nodded. "Okay, sappy moment over. Let's do this."

Rick snorted, but he released his hold on Nico's neck and led the way out of the manor without another word.

Nico thought about what Rick said the whole way out to the SUV. He didn't know what would happen. He wasn't even sure if Keegan planned on staying. He hadn't spoken to him since he left, even though he'd thought about calling him a hundred times each day they'd been apart. Or jumping in a car and driving back to Kansas.

Or maybe hiring a skywriter to ask Keegan how he was doing.

And then two days ago, Keegan had tried to call him. Nico had been so surprised, he'd almost answered without thinking, but then he'd hesitated and ended up staring at his phone as it rang until it'd dumped into his voicemail. Keegan hadn't left a message.

Nico thought that would be the end of it.

Then he'd found out yesterday that right after he'd tried Nico, Keegan had called Rick directly and requested permission to come into Kincaid territory to apply to his coven.

When Rick tracked him down and told him, Nico had been shocked. And then skeptical.

The newly discovered pessimistic part of him couldn't help but wonder if Keegan was only bringing Rosie there to keep her safe, knowing that no matter how things stood between him and Keegan, Nico would still do everything in his power to protect both of them. And by joining the Kincaid Pack, he would have the entire pack standing between his daughter and his old coven.

Last night, as he'd lain in bed, unable to sleep, he'd let himself hope for just a moment that Keegan was coming for him. He'd reasoned that he could have gone to his sister's pack in Oregon, or anywhere else for that matter, now that he was healed up from what had happened with his mom. Nico was sure there wasn't a coven in the entire country— hell, the continent—that wouldn't gladly take him to help strengthen their numbers.

Yet he'd chosen to come to the Kincaid Pack, knowing the trouble they were and knowing the battle they were about to face. He was still bringing his sweet little girl here and choosing to stand with them.

The drive to the spot at the southern border where they were meeting the others seemed to take forever, and he was grateful that Rick didn't try and engage him in any more conversation. Or ask him again if he was okay.

He wasn't surprised to see Gabriel at the meeting spot too. And of course, Tashmica was there. She gave him a tentative smile as soon as he stepped out of the SUV. He wondered how long people would tiptoe around him. If nothing else, he hoped that no matter what happened between him and Keegan, they welcomed him and Rosie into the pack with open arms.

The small red rental car he'd left with Ericka in Kansas was parked on the side of the road about twenty yards ahead of them. As soon as he and Rick exited their SUV, it turned off, and Ericka jumped out, throwing everyone a smile and a wave before moving to the back of the car and opening the trunk. A second later, Keegan climbed out, and Nico couldn't take his eyes off him. He looked... really good. His brown skin was practically glowing with vitality, his black curls shining in the sun. And his *scent*.

Nico was so screwed.

He bit his lip, drinking in the sight of his mate. It was like he was a glass of water and Nico had been lost in the desert for weeks.

He watched as Keegan gave him a soft, tender smile, then turned and opened the back door. He leaned in, and a moment later, the tiny little ball of joy Nico had spent one glorious afternoon with tumbled out of the car. She shook off her dad's helping hands and booked it straight toward Nico.

Her curls were in pigtails that bounced as she ran, her pink sneakers lighting up with each step. "Wolfie!" she shrieked.

Nico's breath caught, and he took a step forward. She recognized him. How could she recognize him?

"Rosie, wait!" Keegan yelled, slamming the car doors shut.

Gabriel darted forward, hands out, and Nico snarled without thinking, but Rosie dodged him easily. "No, Gabe!"

Nico felt the warding magic flare up as she neared it, and he realized suddenly why Keegan and Gabriel had tried to stop her. Thank the goddess, she passed right through. He supposed she wasn't powerful enough yet to truly trigger it as a three-year-old.

He crouched, bracing himself just in time before she hit him at a full run. Her small body felt like perfection in his arms, and he breathed in her sweet scent, his eyes falling shut even as she launched into telling him about every single thing she and her dad had eaten during their trip to Michigan. Her words blurred together in her excitement, but he didn't care. He felt like he could breathe for the first time in over a week.

He stood, holding her in his arms, as she segued into telling him about the bugs she had found at the rest stop earlier that day and how mean her dad had been when he'd made her leave them behind.

He nodded along, settling her against his side and holding her easily with one arm. She was a tiny little thing and so adorable. He had a feeling she would be as beautiful as her father and aunt when she was older.

"I'm sorry."

Nico's head jerked up from where he was taking a whiff of Rosie's hair. He found Keegan staring at him, Gabriel stepping back from where he'd obviously just hugged him. Nico narrowed his eyes until the hunter made a face and took a step back, hands up.

"For her?"

He felt like he had to clarify, since technically there were a few things Keegan could be apologizing for. When he nodded, Nico just shook his head, giving her a bounce that made her giggle and hold on to him harder.

"You don't have to apologize for her." He cleared his throat and looked over at Tashmica, who was looking between them as she worried at her bottom lip with her teeth. "You ready to do this?"

She nodded, digging into the bag she was wearing across her body.

Keegan looked between them, then at Gabriel, his brows

furrowed. "Ready to do what? What do I have to do? Kneel and kiss the ring?"

Gabriel laughed, slapping a hand on Keegan's shoulder and leading him right up to the boundary warding. "Sounds vaguely familiar."

Rick rolled his eyes as he leaned against the front of the SUV and crossed his arms. "I don't wear a ring."

Ericka giggled where she was still pulling things out of the trunk of the car, and Nico hid his smile in Rosie's hair. She'd quieted down but wasn't fidgeting or anything, seeming completely fine just being held by Nico, and he was trying not to let his feelings run away from him.

Tashmica rolled her eyes and walked over to where Keegan and Gabriel were standing. "Nothing so medieval. We're going to ask you a few questions, and then I'll need to perform a couple of spells to make sure you're not hiding anything, test your power level, those sorts of things."

Tashmica almost sounded apologetic, and Nico knew it was because of him and who Keegan was to him. They'd done this a dozen times—some successful, some not—and she'd never acted sorry before. The process was in place to make sure the pack stayed safe, and Tashmica never apologized for taking care of the pack.

Keegan glanced around at all of them, his jaw tensing and fingers rubbing against his jeans.

Nico was about to ask what was wrong when Ericka stepped up next to Keegan, her bag over her shoulder, and placed a hand on his arm. "It's okay. You can tell them."

He narrowed his eyes on the beta, jealousy and possessiveness spiking through him. Not at the casual way she touched him—though he wasn't a huge fan of how many people seemed okay with just touching Keegan—but no, it was the way she knew what was bothering Keegan and Nico didn't.

It was irrational, but he couldn't help it.

Rosie laid her head against his shoulder, sighing softly, and her curls tickled at the underside of his chin. Her light, warm weight eased some of the tension in his body, his muscles loosening and the jealousy seeping away.

Keegan jolted, eyes wide. "Rosie, sweetie, don't do that without someone's permission."

"She didn't do anything." Nico frowned, glancing down at her in confusion.

"You felt bad things. I made you better," Rosie said, hugging him.

"She's an empath, or she will be," Keegan explained. "Her mother is one too."

"So she could... feel my feelings?" He smiled down at her, trying to ignore how proud he felt.

"She can feel others' emotions and also influence them if she's close enough sometimes. She doesn't have any real control over her abilities yet though." Keegan glanced at Tashmica and then Nico again. "She doesn't really understand what she's doing."

"That's amazing," Tashmica said, taking a step closer to him and Rosie. He had the insane urge to turn away from her, to protect Rosie even though he trusted Tash with his life. "How old is she?"

"Three," Keegan said.

"And her active powers are already beginning to show?"

Keegan nodded. "My sister and I were the same age. It comes from our mother's side of the family, I guess."

At that, Tashmica nodded like that made sense and turned back to Keegan, striding over to him. "I've read up on her lineage—well, and yours. Once we get this done, I'd love to pick your brain about that side of your family. If you're up for it?"

Keegan's smooth, smokey scent soured, but he nodded. "Sure, I'd be happy to."

"Great, maybe we could—"

"Tash," Rick interjected. She snapped her mouth shut, then mouthed an apology at him. He quirked a half smile before asking Keegan, "What was it you needed to tell us?"

Keegan sighed, turning to Nico and holding his eyes. "It's about my magic."

Nico's brows furrowed as he stared at him, arm tightening around Rosie unintentionally. "What about it? Still not quite fully recovered?"

"More like… hasn't recovered at all," Keegan said delicately, shooting a glance at Rick.

"What?" Nico walked right up to the border warding, running his eyes over Keegan's body more thoroughly, but he couldn't find a single thing that indicated Keegan wasn't fully healed.

"Yeah," Keegan said, voice hoarse as he finally dropped his gaze to his feet. "I think Beatrice might have actually broken something in me. So if you only want me around for my powers, you're going to be disappointed."

CHAPTER TWELVE

No one said anything for a long moment, but Keegan could feel their eyes on him. His skin prickled, and the hairs on the back of his neck stood up. He focused on keeping his breathing even and just hoped his scent was giving away everything he was feeling.

Admitting such a vulnerability was hard for him in general—he hadn't realized how much his magic was a part of his core identity until it was just *gone*—but to admit being nearly powerless to two shifters and a witch that didn't trust him and who possessed amazing abilities of their own had him a little nervous. He didn't think they would actually attack him or anything. If he did, he wouldn't have brought his daughter there, and he definitely wouldn't have let her get so far away from him.

Though, when she passed through the warding boundary and he realized he couldn't get to her, he'd had a moment of panic. But then he'd watched Nico lift her into his big arms and hold her against him gently, sniffing her and nodding as she jabbered at him, and his fear had melted away. He knew, down to his bones, Nico would never let anything happen to her.

It was funny, before Rosie sailed right through the warding, he would have said she had more magic in her than he did at that point, but it didn't seem to affect her at all, whereas he could *feel* the magic pushing at him, trying to repel him away from the pack's border.

He wasn't sure if that was a good sign or not. Maybe he had more magic left in him than he thought…

Ericka's squeezed his arm, offering silent support as the silence from the others stretched on into uncomfortable territory. He gave her a thankful smile, though it probably came off as more of a grimace based on her small huff of humor.

"Are you okay?" Gabriel finally asked. He kept his voice low, but Keegan didn't fool himself into thinking Nico and Rick hadn't heard.

He thought about just brushing off the question like he would have in the past. Even if it had just been him and Gabriel, but he was… he was trying to be better. If he really wanted to show Nico that he could be the man his wolf deserved, he needed to start right then and there.

Heart beating faster than was probably necessary for such a simple question, he held Gabriel's eyes and said honestly, "I don't know."

During the long drive from Kansas, he'd told Ericka about what had happened to him under his mother's oh-so-loving care and the subsequent discovery of how diminished his magic seemed to be. He'd even admitted to her, late the night before when they'd been stopped at a rest area so they could stretch their legs while Rosie was passed out in the back seat, about how he was worried that he didn't have anything to offer the Kincaid Pack and Rick would turn him away.

And Ericka, who had been nothing but sweet and kind and encouraging since the moment he'd met her, had laughed. It had burst out of her loudly like she couldn't help it, and then she'd slapped a hand over her mouth and apologized.

"I don't know how your coven worked—or how any coven other than ours works really," she'd said, sidling up next to him and bumping his shoulder with her own. Something she'd started doing since he'd told her he wanted to apply to join her pack, a subtle scent marking that had made his heart ache. "Do they have like specific rules about active powers or whatever? Because we aren't like that. Like at all. Rick and Tash won't care that your magic isn't what it used to be."

He'd licked his dry lips, remembering his mother's scorn for witches without active powers. "It was… an unwritten rule. You could technically be a member of the coven without them, but you'd never rise in the ranks."

Ericka had shaken her head in disgust, her mass of blonde curls swinging around her. "So dumb. Listen to me, Keegan. All we care about—all *Rick* cares about—is loyalty. Okay?"

He'd nodded, lump in his throat. He hadn't exactly proven himself to be the most loyal person, at least not in Nico's eyes. Would he ask Rick to turn him away?

Ericka had made a noise, then gripped his shoulders, turning him to face her head-on. Her voice more serious than he'd ever heard it, she'd said, "Forget the past. If you're loyal to Rick, he will be loyal to you. Forever. That's just how he works."

That had sounded… amazing.

After their talk, some of the tension in him had eased, and he'd let himself begin to imagine what it would be like to live in a pack like Ericka described. With a leader who didn't demand perfection, only loyalty.

But standing on the side of the deserted dirt road, staring at his mate who he had hurt and the frowning alpha who held Keegan's whole future in his hands, his nerves came back with a vengeance.

"Are you saying you don't have any magic?" Rick finally asked, his deep voice cutting across the open space between them and sinking into Keegan like claws and teeth.

He couldn't help but flinch. "I still have a little," he admitted, shrugging and doing his best to hold Rick's eyes. "But the couple of times I've tried to use it, it seems like..." He paused, not quite sure how to explain it. Finally, he turned toward Tashmica and said, "It's like my magic used to come from a rushing river, right? But now, there's a dam between me and the source, and all that's left is a small, finite pool of water. It's not getting refilled, and eventually... it'll go dry. That's what it feels like."

She frowned, her eyes sharpening as they ran over him from head to toe. "What did Amato's witches say?"

"I didn't tell them," he said, unable to help the defensive edge to his voice. "After I healed physically, they just assumed that my magic was coming back, and I let them make that assumption."

Nico grunted from where he stood just on the other side of the warding but didn't say anything. Keegan lifted his chin, despite the heat he felt rising to his face. He wouldn't apologize for hiding such a weakness from a pack he didn't know or trust.

"Well, without a closer examination, I can't say anything for certain," Tashmica said, eyes narrowed and staring at his chest like she could see inside of him. Which... maybe she could. He'd heard rumors about her and her powers, but no one he'd ever run into had known for certain what all of her abilities were. "Do you know what spell your mother used during her... interrogation?"

"Interrogation." Nico spat the word, his face creasing with anger. While Keegan liked how upset he was on his behalf, it just made him miss Nico's smiles even more.

Rosie reached up and ran a small hand down one of Nico's cheeks, but Keegan didn't feel her using her magic again. It still seemed to work to ease Nico's upset though, his face smoothing out until he gave her a soft smile and bumped his forehead against her temple. It was wolfish and affectionate and made Keegan's damn heart melt.

Goddess, how could he have ever thought he could live without this man?

Tashmica cleared her throat, drawing his attention back to her. He realized, when she did a terrible job suppressing her smirk, that he'd been making heart eyes at Nico in front of all of them. Next to him, Gabriel snickered, and even Ericka was grinning, looking down at her feet as she kicked at a stone.

Traitors, all of them.

"No, I don't know the spell that she used, but I could probably make an educated guess. I've seen her work on others before—though not to the same extreme."

"Well, let's get through the interview and whatnot, then we can do a more extensive examination back at the shop." She started to step forward, then paused and glanced back at Rick. "That is, if you're allowed to stay."

Swallowing, Keegan nodded. "I understand."

Ericka gave him one more shoulder bump and then stepped past him, heading for the SUV. She threw her bag in the back seat before starting to take off her clothes, tossing each article of clothing into the vehicle as well.

"Meet us back at the manor in a couple of hours," Rick said to her over his shoulder.

"Sure thing, boss man," she said with a cheerful smile. Once she was naked, she gave a big stretch and then began shifting into a large lioness, the process not taking more than ten seconds. Keegan knew the more powerful the shifter—and the stronger the pack—the faster they could change forms, but he'd never really paid that close of attention and absently wondered if Nico, as an Enforcer, was even faster.

She gave her whole body a shake, tail swishing behind her, then let out a roar that made the others grin. A second later, she took off sprinting toward some nearby trees.

Keegan watched her with a soft smile. "She said the first thing she was going to do as soon as we got here was go for a run."

Rick was staring at where she had disappeared, the corners of his mouth still turned up a little. "It can be tough being stuck in a place where you're not able to give yourself the one thing that should come most natural."

At his words, Keegan couldn't help but glance toward Nico, his breath catching in his chest when he realized his wolf was staring right at him. His face was serious, bright blue eyes intense. One of his big hands was rubbing a small circle on Rosie's narrow back, and it looked like she'd fallen asleep against him—or was well on her way, eyes closed and body slumping.

She'd been so excited to see Nico—her wolf, as she insisted on calling him even after Keegan explained, several times, that Nico wasn't just a wolf. He hadn't had the heart to tell her that he might not be hers either, thanks to Keegan fucking everything up.

Stepping forward, Tashmica dug into the satchel she was wearing and pulled out a small jar with a rubber stopper. The liquid inside was a murky yellow and glowed a little. "Hold out your hands, and we can get started."

She gave him an encouraging smile, and when he glanced at Gabriel, his friend clapped him on the shoulder and gave him a nod. Taking a breath, he made sure his hands were steady as fuck as he lifted them and held them out to her, palms up.

She eyed the tattoos on his palms curiously. "To focus your magic?"

"Yeah. All La Fleur witches get them."

"Interesting." She pulled the stopper out of the jar. "Ready?"

He couldn't help but glance at Nico, but he wasn't giving anything away, watching them with an unmoving face. Clearing his throat, he turned back to Tashmica and nodded. "Let's do this."

"She's fine," Nico said for the third time.

Keegan huffed, turning back around and slumping against his seat, arms crossed. "I don't like having her out of my sight."

"If you can't trust Rick to take care of her, I don't know that this pack is a good fit for you," Nico said carefully.

Keegan whipped his head around to stare at him. Nico was driving the SUV to the coven's shop, Tashmica ahead of them and Rick and Rosie behind in the little rental since it had a car seat for her. Gabriel had given Keegan one last hug, then headed toward his motorcycle, telling Keegan to come out to his place for dinner to meet his mates as soon as he could.

Which... it was still crazy to Keegan that the man who had asked Keegan to hide his scent to prevent shifters from having an advantage over him had broken the spell and was mated to not one but two shifters, the bite marks on either side of his neck an unshakeable testament to their bond.

The sight of them had sent a shiver down Keegan's spine and an aching pit of want to open up in his stomach.

But Nico's stiff, impersonal attitude since they'd gotten into the SUV was getting on his damn nerves.

"First of all," he said, doing his best to keep his voice as even as Nico had, "don't make it sound like I'm a terrible person for not trusting my daughter with some stranger I don't really know. Just because I trust Rick enough to ask to join his pack doesn't mean he gets carte blanche for everything else, especially when it comes to her."

Nico started to open his mouth, but Keegan wasn't fucking done, thank you.

"Second of all, it's not that I don't trust him to take care of her. I've missed so much of her life. Now that I get to be with her when she's not with me, it feels like my lungs have been ripped out of my chest and I can't fucking breathe."

He may have failed to keep his tone level, but he wasn't sorry for raising his voice. Rosie was his whole damn life, and he wouldn't apologize for worrying about her.

Nico didn't say anything for a minute, shooting Keegan a glance before focusing back on the road. The town of Meyerville was just coming into view when he sighed softly and said, "I'm sorry."

"You're sorry," Keegan repeated slowly.

"Yes. I shouldn't have said this might not be the pack for you or implied that I knew how you should act as her parent." Nico sighed, reaching up to run his fingers through his hair. It was still longer than Keegan remembered from last fall, but he had a feeling it'd be the perfect length to sink his hands into and hold on. "To be honest... I don't know why you're here, Keegan. Not really. And it's messing with my head."

Keegan stared at his strong profile, running his eyes over his pointed nose, full lips, and strong, square jaw. His wolf sure was a looker. His white skin had a nice tan, making Keegan think that he spent just as much time outdoors as he

146

did as a "paper wrangler," as Nico had put it during one of their shared dreams. He'd said it with a little laugh, like it was an inside joke, and his whole face had lit up. Keegan remembered wanting to be the one to make his face do that and then scolding himself for even thinking it.

But now… now he was going to have the chance to learn how to make Nico smile. At least, he hoped he was.

He wanted to make up for what he had done more than anything, but he was worried he might be too late.

After all of Tashmica's questions and tests, she declared him free of hidden threats and a viable candidate for the coven. Then she'd turned to Rick with her eyebrows raised, waiting for his verdict.

Keegan had held his breath as he waited for the big alpha to make his decision. In the end, he had simply turned to Nico and said, "It's up to you. I'll support whatever decision you make."

Keegan's heart had nearly fallen out of his chest when Nico had hesitated before saying carefully, "I think he should stay. No matter what's going on with his magic, his knowledge would be a valuable asset."

The words had been a bit of a kick to the gut, but nothing less than Keegan deserved.

He tried to come up with the words to express how he was feeling, what he was thinking, and how sorry he was. Nico's jaw tensed as he stared straight ahead.

"I came here for you. For us. I know I messed up," he croaked, emotions sticking in his throat, "and I know you may never be able to forgive me, but I'm still sorry. If there's even an inkling of a chance that you will forgive me, then I'm going to do whatever it fucking takes to win back your trust. I don't care how long it takes."

For the first time in his life, Keegan wished he was a shifter so he could know what Nico was feeling through his scent. As they reached the center of town and Nico still hadn't said anything, Keegan's stomach began to feel like it was full of lead. He tried to convince himself he hadn't made a mistake, that it was ridiculous to assume Nico would just forgive him and they could start over. He'd known he'd have to work to win him back.

He'd just been hoping for *something*. Some reaction or response that let Keegan know all wasn't lost.

Nico pulled into a parking spot right in front of the shop, *Wicca We Can*, next to Tashmica's vehicle. She wasn't in it, having already gone inside, he assumed. Out of the corner of his eye, Keegan saw the little red car carrying his daughter and driven by the pack's surly alpha continue past them.

He made himself stay focused on Nico and not watch them disappear from view. When Tashmica had said she wanted to examine his magic right away, she'd gently suggested Rosie not be there for the process. He hadn't liked the idea of them getting separated so fast, but he had a feeling Tashmica was right. Whatever she was planning on doing to him would probably be traumatic for his daughter to see.

Rick had offered to take her back to the manor with him, even going so far as to reassure him that his pups were there and would keep her busy. The reminder that other kids would be there had helped, and he'd nodded, giving Rosie a hug before buckling her back into her seat.

"A part of me understands why you did what you did," Nico said so suddenly Keegan jolted. He turned in his seat to fully face him, eyeing the way Nico's hands were squeezing the steering wheel. Nico had turned off the engine but was staring straight ahead at the shop, the silence between them thick with broken trust and unresolved anger. "The rest of me is having a hard time getting over it."

"Okay. I understand." Keegan would take a part of Nico

understanding—even if it was a tiny part of him. He'd take the foothold and use it to climb into Nico's life until Nico couldn't imagine them not being together anymore.

Maybe not the healthiest mindset, but he didn't really care all that much.

Nico gave his head a quick shake. "No, I don't think you do." He touched his chest, patting it. "This part of me, my wolf, he understands putting your pup first and doing whatever you felt like you had to do to keep her safe. That part of me even respects that you would sacrifice anything for her because he—I... I'd do the same."

Keegan held his breath, squeezing his hands into fists as he kept his eyes glued on Nico. "Okay. I—"

"But the other part of me," Nico continued, and Keegan snapped his mouth shut. "The man part... it isn't so black and white for me. I want to move past what happened and what you did, but... to that part of me, I keep coming back to the simple fact that you didn't choose me. Us. You planned on denying me and our mating."

"Nico," Keegan started to say, reaching for him, but his big, strong wolf flinched and dodged his touch, and Keegan froze.

"I don't know if that part of me can forgive you. Not yet, at least," Nico finished, reaching for the door handle. "I need some time."

"Okay," Keegan said softly, ignoring his burning eyes as Nico gave a clipped nod and then left the SUV. He just kept sitting there, staring at the seat Nico had been in, and tried to get his breathing and heart rate under control.

I don't know if that part of me can forgive you.

He squeezed his eyes shut and dropped his head to his chest, giving himself a single minute to feel his damn feelings. He reminded himself over and over that all hope wasn't lost, that Nico had asked for time.

Keegan could give him that. It would hurt to give him space when all he wanted was to eliminate all the space between them, but it was his own damn fault Nico was icing him out.

He'd broken something fragile between them, something he might not be able to repair no matter how much work he put in, and he needed to accept that.

Taking one more shaky breath, he straightened his shoulders and opened his eyes.

On second thought, fuck that.

He'd give Nico time, but he wasn't going to give up until he'd won over every single part of Nico. They were fated mates, perfect for each other in every way, and he wouldn't stop trying until he'd given Nico everything he deserved in a mate and then some.

He refused to accept anything less.

CHAPTER THIRTEEN

It took Keegan a few moments to get his game face on, doing his best to tuck away all of his squishy emotions before following Nico out of the car and into the small store. No matter how many revelations he'd had, what Tashmica was about to attempt on him was serious shit, and he needed to focus.

As soon as he stepped inside *Wicca We Can*, he felt a sense of peace and a feeling of rightness. He was at home here. The magic was so strong in the air he could feel it without trying, the buzz of it along his skin electrifying and soothing all at once. The scent of the candle burning on the table in the back next to the register tickled his nose, the herbs used in it ones he recognized as being powerful cleansers.

He didn't see Tashmica or Nico, but there was a familiar-looking young man behind the counter watching him. He recognized him from the night he had broken through the warding. He'd stood next to Tashmica, working with her to create a shielding spell strong enough that there was no way even he could have broken through it.

He hadn't said much, and then he'd disappeared with the

man they'd all called Doc and the woman Keegan had brought. Not for the first time, he wondered how Wendy was doing. He hoped he'd have a chance to see her for himself. Gabriel had let him know she'd survived, but a part of him had been shaken by the state she'd been in from the attack and wouldn't feel better until he actually saw her for himself.

As he made his way toward the back of the room, he couldn't help but run his eyes over all of the books and ingredients and other fun things stuffing the shelves full. He couldn't wait to dig in and see what hidden gems the coven had tucked away in the shop.

"This place is great," he said once he reached the counter and held his hand out. "I'm Keegan Toussaint."

"I remember." The guy's serious face broke into a small smile. "Damien."

He took Keegan's hand, a small zap of magic stinging his palm. Keegan raised his eyebrows as he shook out his hand. "Ow. That was rude."

Damian's light brown skin, a few shades lighter than his own, flushed immediately. He ducked his head and murmured, "Sorry, force of habit."

"You make it a habit to try and feel out other people's magic without permission?"

"When it's a witch I don't know." His voice was still soft, but there was an edge of steel to it, letting Keegan know Damien wasn't sure yet if he could be trusted.

Keegan couldn't decide if he wanted to take offense or respect the guy's protectiveness of his pack and coven. Honestly, he understood it. The only time Damien had met him, he'd been labeled a threat. He supposed in a way he *had* been a threat. He just hoped Damien—and the rest of the coven—gave him a chance to prove he could be trusted and would do his best to protect the pack right along with them.

The beads covering the doorway just to the right of the

counter broke apart, and Tashmica bustled through, clapping her hands when she saw him. "Ah, perfect. I've got everything set up back here. Damian, change the sign and set the warding, please. I'm going to need your help."

Damien nodded, quickly moving away to do as he was told without another word.

Keegan followed her through the beads into a back room stuffed so full of books he felt claustrophobic. Nico was standing in the corner of the small room, his wide shoulders touching both bookshelves on either side of him. He didn't look up from his phone, but Keegan knew he was aware that he'd entered the room, a hum of tension filling his big frame.

"Take a seat here, sweetie." Tashmica pointed at a chair at the table. There were even more stacks of books on it, and one of them was open and propped up with an arrangement of ingredients in front of it, along with a stone mortar and pestle.

He eyed the shelf closest to him as he sat, trying to pinpoint the thrum of energy he could feel. "You know some of these grimoires shouldn't be stored together, right?"

She made a face as she started to add ingredients into the stone bowl, glancing at the book in front of her. "I know. We have to cleanse the place at least once a week from the buildup of bad energy. We were supposed to be getting a new space—one for worship and storage as well as a new greenhouse for growing herbs—but that got put on hold with everything that happened last year. We make do though."

She shrugged like it wasn't a big deal, but Keegan could see Nico behind her, and his face did something complicated as he stared at her back. He glanced at Keegan, took a deep breath, then started typing something quickly into his phone.

Damien slipped into the room and came over to stand next to Tashmica. She pointed at something in the book, and Damien nodded, moving over to one of the shelves that had several spelled boxes on it. He opened one and withdrew a long, thin dagger with a black hilt and a ruby at the end. The athame was no doubt only used for specific spell work. Most covens Keegan had come across had several different ceremonial knives used for different spells, depending on the need.

"What the hell is that for?" Nico said, taking a step forward. "What exactly are you going to do to him?"

Tashmica tipped one of her hands back and forth as she continued mixing ingredients with the other. "Essentially, I'm going to crack him open and take a look inside to see what's going on."

"You're going to cut him open?" Nico sounded horrified.

At that, Tashmica finally looked up from what she was doing to throw him an incredulous look. "What? No, of course I'm not going to cut him open. Do I look like Dr. Bell to you? I just need some of his blood for the spell."

Keegan stood and met Damien around the table, holding one of his hands out over the mortar without needing to be asked. "It's fine, Nico. I know it'll hurt, but it'll be better to know what's going on, one way or the other."

Damien pricked his finger before Nico could respond, and Keegan didn't even flinch at the small pain, holding Nico's eyes to let him see he was fine.

Tashmica ignored them all, using the pestle to mix the few drops of blood he'd given with the rest of the ingredients. Once she was satisfied, she double-checked the book, then held her hand over the bowl and began the incantation.

Keegan stuck his finger in his mouth for a second before looking at the small cut and shaking out his hand. He sat back down and took a couple of deep breaths, trying to prepare himself for what was about to happen.

When he noticed Nico was beginning to look concerned again, he did his best to give him a reassuring smile and tried not to read too much into how Nico was acting. "It'll be okay. I've been through worse."

"That doesn't actually make me feel any better, Keegan," he snapped, then looked away, his jaw tight.

Of course it didn't. His sweet wolf. Even while still feeling hurt and betrayed, he was worried about Keegan and didn't want to watch him get hurt. He was about to suggest Nico not be there for the examination when Tashmica finished. The bowl glowed for a moment, and he felt a surge of magic in the air, the feeling so achingly familiar it took his breath away.

"Okay, Nico, can you hold Keegan? It'll be quicker and easier for everyone if he's not moving around too much."

"You mean thrashing in pain?" Nico said even as he stepped forward, coming up behind Keegan.

"Yes, that is exactly what I mean." She grimaced apologetically at Keegan. "Are you ready?"

He straightened his shoulders and shook out his hands. "Let's get this over with."

She nodded at Nico, and his big, warm hands came down on top of Keegan's shoulders, his grip strong and immovable. He couldn't help but take comfort from his hold and his warm presence behind Keegan. As if reading his mind, Nico rubbed his thumbs against Keegan's back.

Using her fingers, Tashmica scooped up the mixture from the bowl and leaned over him. She drew symbols on his forehead, throat, and the palms of each of his hands right over his tattoos.

"Try and stay as calm and relaxed as you can," she said softly, holding out her hand for Damien. He took it, and they both closed their eyes and took deep breaths.

Despite her advice, Keegan tensed as she raised her free hand and held it over the symbol she'd drawn on his forehead.

He squeezed his eyes shut and sent a quick prayer to the goddess.

As soon as she started chanting the spell, a searing hot pain sliced through him. It started at the points where she had marked him with the mixture, but it quickly spread throughout his whole body.

He clenched his teeth as he started to shake, feeling like his skin was being flayed off and his blood was boiling. He couldn't hear Tashmica anymore. He wasn't even sure if his eyes were closed still. His brain was so clouded with pain it was all he could feel.

That, and Nico's hands on him.

Panting, he pushed up into Nico's hold, grateful when he tightened his grip and forced him back down. He concentrated on the feeling of his hands, the way his long fingers dug in just under his collarbones and his thumbs on either side of his spine. It should have hurt, how hard Nico was holding him, but the pain of Tashmica digging inside him eclipsed everything else.

He focused so hard on Nico and his hands that he tapped into his magic without meaning to, and it reached out for Nico in tiny, weak wisps. It reached for the magic all shifters possessed, that Keegan could feel *pulsing* inside Nico, alive and whole and healthy. His wolf just beneath the surface of Nico's skin was glowing like a shining beacon, calling to Keegan's magic.

His magic chased it, desperately, wanting nothing more than to get a taste.

The pain in his body began to lessen—or at least, he noticed it less—as his whole consciousness turned toward the man behind him. He could feel all of Nico. The heat of his body, the soft vibration of his magic, the gentle huffs of his breath. The beat of his heart in perfect synchronicity with Keegan's.

The thin little wisps of Keegan's magic thickened as it danced around Nico's essence, turning to thick tendrils and sneaking out like ivy growing towards the sun. He tried to hold it in check, but it slipped away, and he lost control of it. Like a dropped ball of yarn, it unspooled from him faster than he could stop it. He sucked in a harsh gasp as it reached the center of Nico.

He could feel it—he could practically *see* it—the pulsing magic of his wolf, so warm and bright and inviting. Keegan wanted to latch his magic onto him, click their puzzle pieces together so they became one.

Before he could do it, before he could take something that hadn't been offered to him, he felt a sharp jerking in his chest right over his heart. He screamed and fought the hold on him as his magic recoiled in an instant, wrapping around him protectively.

For long minutes, all he could hear were his thundering heart and ragged breaths. He was shaking, twitching from head to toe, and the scent of ozone and smoke was thick in the air.

"Keegan? Can you hear me?" A feminine voice was calling to him, but he shook his head, not wanting to respond. He felt raw and fractured, exposed in a way that terrified him.

Then the scent of trees just after dawn filled his nose, and he began to relax automatically. He was safe. He knew the person who belonged to that scent, and they'd keep him safe. He was sure of it. "Keegan, sweetheart. Open your eyes. Please."

He couldn't deny that voice, not when it sounded so sad and scared.

It took more effort than he thought it should, but he finally peeled his eyes open and looked around. Oh, that's right. He knew where he was.

Looking at Tashmica, he rasped out, "Did it work?"

She nodded, lips pressed together. "It worked. The good news is that your connection to magic isn't broken."

His eyes felt so heavy, he could barely keep them open. "Bad... news?"

"The bad news is... I can't tell you if you'll ever get back what you lost. I don't know if you'll ever be as powerful as you were before. There's just... no way to know. We'll have to wait and see."

Well, fuck.

"Are you sure you're okay to do this?" Tashmica asked, throwing another worried look at him as her fingers drummed on the steering wheel of her car. "I can turn back around, and we can go back to my house. I'll even have someone bring Rosie over. You should still be resting."

Keegan gave her his best smile, which probably wasn't that great considering how exhausted he felt. He was almost as tired as he had been when he'd woken up in Kansas. "I'm fine. It's just a meeting."

She huffed, letting him know she didn't believe him, but that was okay. He needed to prove to Rick and the others— and himself—that even if his magic never returned to where it had been before, he still had value.

He needed to believe it himself.

He turned to look back out the passenger-side window, watching the blossoming trees go by. They were on their way to the manor for a meeting with Rick and his Enforcers, and Keegan couldn't help but be apprehensive about seeing Nico again after what had happened the day before.

When he'd woken up that morning, Tashmica had been there, and she'd explained that he'd passed out after the exam, so they'd brought him to her house to rest. He'd looked around, hoping to see Nico lurking in the shadows of the bedroom, but Tashmica had cleared her throat delicately and then told him it was just the two of them there.

He'd been disappointed, and then he'd been worried as he'd realized that Rosie had spent her first night in their new home all by herself.

"She's fine," Tash had assured him, helping him lie back down. "She had a sleepover with her new friend Callie. You'll see her shortly."

She'd wanted him to stay in bed at least another day, but when she'd told him that Rick wanted to talk to him as soon as he was able, he'd pushed himself back up despite his protesting body and told her he'd be ready in half an hour.

She'd called him stubborn and pigheaded, but she'd still made him breakfast.

As they'd eaten, he'd found the nerve to ask about Nico, and Tashmica had told him plainly that he'd looked pretty shaken after the spell. He'd carried Keegan to the SUV and then into Tash's house, and then he'd apparently made some excuse about needing to get back to the manor and left.

Keegan wasn't sure what part of the spell had freaked him out the most, but he had a feeling that Nico had been able to sense the way Keegan's magic had tried to latch onto him. He wasn't sure what it might have felt like for him. But he had a feeling it might have seemed like Keegan had been trying to steal Nico's magic.

But that couldn't be further from the truth.

If he'd been trying to steal magic, he would have gone for someone with a hell of a lot more than Nico had. There had been two extremely powerful witches in the room that he could have tried to siphon off if that had been his intent.

Of course, choosing the more powerful one would have been a toss-up. Damien hadn't said much and kept his head down the whole time Keegan was there, but even with his own diminished powers, he could sense immense magic inside him. There was a raging fire in Damien, just waiting to be let out.

And he had to know it. He'd been well trained.

The fact that he had tested Keegan's magic when they'd shaken hands was proof of that. It was an old-school trick, something few modern covens taught anymore. And it made Keegan very curious about where Damian might have come from before moving to the Kincaid Pack.

But no, when his magic had reached for Nico, it hadn't been because he was desperate for more power. It was because, just like Nico's wolf recognized him, so did his magic recognize Nico's wolf. They were two sides to the same coin. His magic had been exposed and felt threatened and reached out to the one person it had known would protect them both.

He just didn't think Nico understood that. It had probably felt... invasive. Then he'd run off while Keegan was unconscious, so he hadn't had a chance to try and explain.

Tashmica didn't try and talk to him the rest of the way to the manor, which thankfully didn't take that long. When the large mansion came into view, he couldn't help but raise his brows, wondering if Rick was trying to compensate for something.

As they passed through the gated entrance, he could feel that it was humming with magic. When he exited the car after Tashmica parked on the wide, looping driveway, he could still feel it in the air. It was saturated in the very soil that the manor had been built on.

Smart. The place was a fortress. One even his old coven would have a hard time getting to.

He looked over at Tashmica. He could tell a lot of it was from her. It had her signature on it. Sort of like how shifters could identify a person by their scent, witches could identify others by the feel of their magic if they knew how. There were other signatures mixed in with hers, though hers was the most prominent. He assumed the others belonged to the rest of the coven. He wondered when he'd get a chance to meet them and what they would think of him. Some of them may have even heard of him before, but he couldn't help but think they'd be disappointed.

Tashmica had gently told him this morning that they had no reason to believe his magic wouldn't eventually grow back to what it was before his mother fucked with him, but he wasn't so sure.

His whole body ached still, even after all the sleep he'd gotten, and he felt even more drained, like it had taken what little magic he had left to survive what Tash had done to him. He told himself it wasn't true, that she was sure he still had a connection to magic and wouldn't run out. A part of him couldn't help but wonder if that would have been better—if he'd eventually run out, at least he'd be able to mourn the loss and move on. But stuck with a tiny fraction of what he'd had before?

Accepting such a loss of his abilities would be even more difficult.

Tashmica didn't knock or hesitate at the front door, walking straight up to it and pulling it open. She stepped aside and waited for him to go through first, offering him a smile when he passed her.

There was a shifter just inside the door, standing off to the side behind what looked like a hostess podium from a restaurant, but Keegan didn't get a chance to do more than glance at the man before he heard a familiar shriek of "Daddy!" and then the slapping footsteps of his daughter.

She and another girl, maybe a little older, came careening out of a nearby room, hands clasped together and faces smudged with whatever they'd had for breakfast.

Not too far behind them was a young woman with long, straight hair. She was maybe sixteen or seventeen and had the exasperated look of an older sibling. "Callie, you know better. You can't just go running because you hear the front door open."

When his daughter reached him, he picked her up and gave her a tight hug, breathing in her familiar scent. "Did you make a friend, sweetie?"

Rosie nodded. "We sleeped in the same room!"

"Slept," he corrected absently, tucking some of her curls behind her ear. "I'm sorry I wasn't here."

"That's okay, Daddy. Wolfie was." She grinned and threw her arms around him, squeezing the breath right out of him.

Nico had stayed with her?

Tashmica pointed at the young woman. "This is Saman-tha, and that's Callie. The alpha-mate's siblings."

Keegan nodded. He'd heard all about Rick's mate, Kai, from Ericka and how his two youngest siblings had become more like his and Rick's pups since their parents had been abusive pieces of shit and then been killed by whoever was helping the Council. The Blood Oath that had been used to ensure their silence had sounded horrifying and fascinating. It was the kind of old-world blood magic he rarely came across. Someone very powerful who knew their shit had to have been the one to mark Kai's parents like that.

As they stood there making introductions and small talk, the two girls excitedly telling him all about their night together and morning so far, Keegan could feel the house's energy, a comforting background noise. On the second floor, he spotted people moving from one side of the house to the other, and down the hallway off to the right, he caught snatches of chatter and activity. And there was something delicious-smelling in the air that was distracting him.

As much as the place felt like a fortress on the outside, it was a home on the inside.

A couple of men walked into the entrance hall, and he recognized them from the night in the clearing. The tall redhead was Marcus Rivera, the one Wendy had been trying to reach when he found her. The other was the giant second-in-command, Bennett Young.

Bennett smiled at him and Rosie as they neared their group, and Marcus gave a small nod, saying, "We're headed up to the library."

"Okay," Tashmica said. "Samantha, do you mind watching Rosie a little longer so Keegan can come talk to us?"

Samantha shook her head, giving Keegan a shy smile. "I don't mind. She's much more well-behaved than this one."

"Hey," Callie protested with a huff, crossing her little arms over her chest like a certain alpha he knew.

Rosie giggled and gave Keegan one more hug. Just as he was about to pass her off, the door opened behind him, and she began to vibrate with excitement.

"Nico!" she yelled, trying to squirm out of his arms.

Keegan held on to her—barely—and turned to find his wayward mate had slipped in behind them. He looked tired but not freaked-out as he looked at Keegan, so he hoped that was a good sign.

He gave Rosie a genuine smile. "Hi, sweet girl. Are you behaving for Samantha?"

She nodded furiously. "Callie has a puppy!"

Keegan grimaced, wondering if he would be badgered into getting her one too.

Nico chuckled as he stepped closer. "Yeah, she does. Why don't you two go play with Loki?"

He moved like he was going to grab Rosie to hand her to Samantha or maybe just touch her and scent mark her, but when his eyes locked with Keegan's, he stopped. There was a wariness in his eyes Keegan didn't like.

Clearing his throat, he turned to Samantha and offered his wiggly child. "Thank you. I really appreciate you keeping an eye on her."

She smiled and nodded, grabbing Callie's hand with her free one and taking the girls farther into the house.

Marcus stepped over next to Nico and scented the air. "You smell like magic."

Nico glanced at Keegan, but all he said was "I've been around a lot of witches lately. Is Rick ready for us?"

Marcus didn't seem convinced, but he nodded, him, Bennett, and Tashmica heading up the stairs. Nico hesitated, looking between them and Keegan, then sighed.

"Come on. Rick doesn't like to be kept waiting."

Keegan frowned after him, watching his mate just walk away from him when they had some serious things to discuss. Just as Nico hit the landing and started up to the third floor, Keegan narrowed his eyes and muttered, "Well, he's just shit out of luck."

CHAPTER FOURTEEN

Nico paused at Keegan's growled words, turning to him with raised eyebrows as he stomped up after him.

Even before he'd opened the manor door, he'd known Keegan was on the other side, and it hadn't been from catching his smoky scent on the air. He had a feeling that after what had happened the day before, he would always be able to tell when his mate was near, even if they never did a traditional bonding.

He wasn't exactly sure what had happened between them in the back room of *Wicca We Can*, but something inside of Keegan had reached out and grabbed onto Nico. It felt like it had left an imprint on his very being, marking him as Keegan's.

His wolf had liked it, but it had scared him too. It had been... intimate in a way he'd never experienced or heard of, and it had been horrible to watch Keegan in so much pain. The best he'd been able to figure was that Keegan's magic had gotten tangled up with his wolf, leaving something more permanent than scent behind.

And he wasn't proud of the fact that he'd taken off after

bringing Keegan to Tashmica's, not even waiting for him to wake up.

He'd just been too freaked-out.

Keegan's face was set in serious lines, his jaw so tight a muscle flickered beneath his scar. His dark eyes were determined, his scent full of outrage and worry. Nico's wolf stirred, wanting to soothe his mate, even as he watched him march up to Nico with admiration.

Keegan was always beautiful, but he was a sight to behold all worked up.

Nico opened his mouth, though he wasn't even sure what he was going to say, but Keegan grabbed his wrist and tugged on him, pulling him the rest of the way up the stairs and then in the opposite direction the others had gone, away from the library.

"You and I need to have a conversation."

Nico's wolf rumbled inside him at his mate's tone, and he was a little ashamed of the urge he had to... to... *mount* Keegan and show him who was in control. As much as he listened to and trusted his wolf, he'd thought he was above that sort of behavior. Not to mention, he didn't think Keegan would appreciate Nico's wolf trying to hump him into submission.

Voice remarkably even, he said, "We're expected in a meeting with Rick."

"I don't give a shit. I'm not going to spend however long dancing around each other and pretending like we aren't who we are to each other." He glanced up and down the hallway he'd dragged them to. "Can you please pick a damn room for us to have a private conversation in?"

He waved his hand around, more agitated than Nico had ever seen him. It was eye-opening to see this side of Keegan. He was usually so in control of himself, barely giving anything away. At least, that was how he'd been in their dreams, and even to an extent in Kansas, despite being weakened from his mother's handiwork still.

He was also surprised at the foul mouth his mate seemed to have developed. Was this the real Keegan? The one he'd kept hidden from Nico for all those months?

He had to admit... he and his wolf didn't hate it.

He tugged Keegan to the right since the hallway to the left led to Rick and Kai's private quarters. He didn't think his alpha would appreciate them invading his den, even if he and his mate weren't in it. He found an empty bedroom, opened the door, let Keegan go in ahead of him, and then closed it behind them. He leaned back against it, not trusting himself to get any farther into a room with a bed and his mate.

"You know they can still hear us, right?"

Keegan rolled his eyes. "Oh really? Is that how shifters' abilities work?"

His sarcasm lit Nico up like a damn firework, his wolf prowling just below the surface, wanting to lunge forward. "Maybe we should do this later."

When he had his damn libido under control and there wasn't a bed less than ten feet behind Keegan.

"We should do this now. Especially considering you weren't there when I woke up earlier and just now you tried to run away from me. We need to have this conversation before things get even more strained between us."

"I didn't run away," he said stiffly, but they both knew he was lying.

As powerful as a wolf as he was—with a strong connection between him and his alpha and his packmates—and despite all the things he had seen and experienced in his travels, he had never come across anything like what Keegan had done. He wasn't even sure if Keegan was aware of it. He had been so out of it, writhing in pain and screaming until he'd gone hoarse, as Tash had burrowed inside of him.

Ignoring his denial, Keegan planted his hands on his hips and met Nico's gaze head-on. "Okay, so about what happened at the shop. I wasn't trying to steal your magic or anything."

That answered the question about whether he'd been aware of what had happened between them. Nico furrowed his brows. "Okay. That's good to know, I guess, though that hadn't even crossed my mind."

"Oh." Keegan took a half of a step back, dropping his arms and rocking onto his heels. "Why were you so freaked-out then? You looked fucking scared of me downstairs." Before Nico could answer, he ran a hand over his curls and sighed. "Not that I blame you. I can't imagine what it must have felt like for you when my magic touched yours."

"Is that what happened? All I knew was that something in you reached out for something in me, and it was... like nothing I've ever experienced." He licked his lips, watching Keegan frown at him in concern. "I can still feel it, like I have a piece of you inside me."

"And you don't like it?" Keegan asked softly, some of the stiffness in his shoulders relaxing. "I didn't mean to leave anything behind. I didn't do any of it on purpose."

Nico looked away, fighting down the urge to close the distance between them and just... touch Keegan. Anywhere. Everywhere. "I didn't say that. I... I like it. I probably like it too much."

The way Keegan's scent changed, sweetening and deepening as he made a soft, surprised sound, had Nico's claws extending. He squeezed his eyes shut to hide the glow.

Even without his sight, he heard Keegan take a step forward, his scent filling the space between them so completely, Nico could have swum in it. His body heated, blood pumping fast and thick, as his fangs bit into his lip.

He needed to end this conversation and get out of the room before he did something they both weren't ready for.

"Do you know why my magic reached out for you and your wolf?"

Nico sucked in a breath and forced his eyes open, meeting Keegan's dark gaze. His mate's lips parted, like he was surprised to see Nico's wolf eyes, and then he sucked his lower lip into his mouth, and that was...

He shook his head—as much in answer to Keegan's question as to try and clear the thoughts filling his mind. Thoughts like *mine* and *claim*.

"The same reason it reached out for you that night when I brought Wendy."

Nico jerked his head back in surprise. He'd known that Keegan had felt a connection with him that night, something that had made him dream walk with Nico for months, but he hadn't realized he'd been as affected as Nico that night. "It did?"

Keegan laughed. "Oh yeah. I'm pretty sure Tashmica felt it too. I had it close to the surface in case I needed to defend myself, and as soon as we locked eyes, it fucking lunged for you. It happened so fast I couldn't stop it. It was all I could do to pull it back."

Nico put a hand on his chest, rubbing softly. "That's how my wolf felt. It was the hardest thing I'd ever done to just stand there and let you walk away." He grimaced and added, "Though I've since had to do something even more difficult."

Dark eyes locked on Nico, Keegan asked, "Something more difficult?"

Nico huffed and rubbed at his face, feeling more in control of himself now that he was thinking about how painful leaving Keegan had been. How devastated he'd been to learn his mate had chosen a path that didn't lead to him. "Oh yeah. Turns out walking away after talking to you and breathing in your scent and spending time with your daughter—" His voice broke, and he had to clear his throat. "It was a hundred times more difficult."

"Nico," Keegan said softly, pain and sorrow souring his scent. "I really am sorry for everything. For not telling you about Rosie and my mother and my plan. I'm sorry for not being strong enough to stay away from you and for letting you walk away from me in Kansas. I'm so fucking sorry for letting you think for even a *second* that you weren't what I wanted."

Nico's heart sped up as he straightened off the door.

"I'm sorry I hurt you so badly, but I'm not sorry for those stolen moments in those dreams." Keegan swiped viciously at his wet eyes. "I can't be sorry for that. I thought that was all I'd ever get, and I was selfish, but I'm not sorry. I thought... I thought I had to choose between you and Rosie, and it *killed* me."

Nico's stomach tightened, his own eyes burning. "Keegan—"

"I know I fucked up. I was so scared of putting her life in danger, not to mention yours and my own, and I should have just... I should have listened to my stupid heart that was screaming at me to trust you. I hurt you, and then I scared you yesterday, and I'm so damn sorry. My magic was just so exposed it reached for you out of reflex." Keegan scrubbed at his damp face and took a shaky breath. "I know you said you need time, and I'm not trying to pressure you or anything. I just... I need you to understand I didn't not choose you. I thought I couldn't have you."

"Why?" Nico asked, halving the distance between them.

"Because I thought it was too dangerous—"

Smiling, Nico shook his head. "No, why was it a reflex for your magic to reach for me?"

Keegan frowned. "Because it's me—a part of me—so it knows what I know."

"And what's that?"

"That you would keep us safe."

He said it like it was obvious, like Nico was being deliberately dense and it was just a given that when Keegan and his magic had been at their most vulnerable, they would turn to him to protect them.

Something inside Nico snapped, and he was reaching for Keegan before he even realized it. He cupped the sides of his face and closed the last of the distance between them. He leaned down as Keegan tipped his head back, gripping at his wrists. Gently, he traced the scar on Keegan's face with his thumb, promising himself he'd never let anything hurt his mate ever again.

"I've dreamed about this moment for so long. Of finally having you in my hands. Of tasting you."

Keegan nodded weakly within his hold, his eyes fluttering shut. "You have me, Nico. Fucking fuck, just kiss me already. *Please*."

His wolf howling in triumph, Nico leaned down the last few inches and sealed their mouths together. The taste of Keegan exploded on his tongue, burning into his memory, along with the way his scent surged in the air around them, smoky and sweet, and the way his nimble fingers grasped at Nico's arms as he pushed up onto his tiptoes to get them even closer.

He'd remember that moment until the day he took his last breath.

Nico was lost to him, everything else forgotten as his whole reason for being narrowed down to his mouth moving over Keegan's over and over. He nipped at Keegan's full lower lip, then delved his tongue inside when he moaned.

Nothing else mattered but Keegan.

He let go of his face so he could wrap his arms around him, and then he lifted Keegan into the air, holding him against him and walking farther into the room towards the unmade bed.

Keegan wrapped his arms and legs around him, making a muffled noise of surprise but not pulling away even for a second, trusting Nico to hold him and support him. To protect him.

Just as they reached the end of the bed and he started to bend down, lowering Keegan toward the mattress, a loud knock startled him. His wolf surged to the surface, not wanting anyone to come between him and his mate.

He turned his head and snarled through his fangs, "What?"

"We're all waiting on you two," Bennett said with more than a little humor in his voice. "Rick's getting impatient, man."

Right. The meeting. In the library.

"Fuck," Keegan said, dropping his head back.

Nico couldn't agree more.

"We'll be right there," Nico said, then lowered Keegan the rest of the way to the bed and let his face drop into the crook of his neck. He groaned as he ran his tongue up the length, saturating Keegan with his scent.

Keegan sucked in a breath. "You should probably stop that if I have to go stand in front of all of your friends in a minute."

Nico just grumbled, continuing to nuzzle into the fragrant skin and absently grinding his half-hard cock down against Keegan's. "Give me another minute," he said, sucking in huge lungfuls of his scent.

Keegan nodded, his fingers sinking into Nico's hair and gently carding through the strands, soothing him and his riled-up wolf. "Whatever you need."

It probably took Nico longer than it should have to get himself and his wolf under control, but when he was finally able to put some distance between him and Keegan without losing his mind, he straightened their clothes and promised Keegan they would finish their conversation later. Then he grabbed his hand and dragged him back down the hallway to the library.

The glare Rick was sending him when he walked in probably should have had him cowering. But that'd never been his style. And he couldn't exactly be upset about kissing his mate for the first time.

Just the reminder had him smiling widely. He shrugged and chuckled. "Sorry about that. You know how it is though."

Rick rolled his eyes, a few people in the room trying to cover their laughs with coughs, but he gestured toward an open chair to his left without any further reprimands. Nico led the way over and then sat, patting the arm of the chair in invitation and smiling at Keegan.

His mate raised an eyebrow but perched on it. If Nico had done what he really wanted, he would have pulled Keegan right into his lap, but he figured that would be too distracting for both of them since he definitely wouldn't have been able to keep his mouth or hands off him.

Goddess, all that bullshit he had spouted in the car about not being sure if he could forgive Keegan had gone up in flames the second Keegan told him that he and his magic trusted Nico to keep them safe. Nico hadn't even realized that was what he'd really been worried about, the thing that had been holding him back.

As much as Keegan keeping secrets from him had sucked, he realized it was the fact that it felt like his mate hadn't thought he could take care of him—to keep him and Rosie safe from his mother and coven—that had been hurting him the most.

Protecting his mate and pup was a fundamental part of him and the most important job he would ever have. Thinking that Keegan thought he couldn't do it had gutted him and left him bleeding on the floor.

Quickly, he went around the room and put names to faces since Keegan had met, or at least seen, all of the Enforcers the night he'd brought Wendy through the warding. After that was done, Nico sat back and pulled out his phone, prepared to jot down any necessary notes or to-dos.

"Do you have the preliminary translation?" Rick asked, not beating around the bush at all.

Keegan sighed and reached into the back pocket of his jeans, pulling out a folded-up piece of paper. "I do, but it's gibberish. I'm sorry." He passed it over to Rick anyway. "I did have one other idea though."

Rick raised his eyebrows and then glanced at the page, grimacing. "Yeah, this is useless. What's your idea?"

Keegan sat up a little straighter. "I summon my grann's spirit and have her help me translate it."

There was some murmuring around the room, and Nico leaned forward, bumping his arm against Keegan's leg. "Can you do that?"

"Yes." Keegan made a face. "I'll need some help, but yeah, I can do it. It's a complex spell but not impossible."

Rick was watching Tashmica, and Nico realized she was frowning on the other side of the room. "You don't like the idea."

She tilted her head, voice cautious. "That kind of magic… If something goes wrong, it can go *very* wrong. Like, zombie apocalypse wrong."

Keegan snorted at that, and Nico bit his lip, keeping his head down to hide his amusement. "Yeah, maybe if you're an amateur, which neither of us are." He pushed to his feet, seemingly unable to sit still. "This is our only hope of translating this prophesy."

"Why don't we just summon the spirit of the woman who wrote it? The seer?" Fiona asked.

Keegan turned and stared at her. "Um, maybe because none of us would be able to communicate with her? I can't translate her journal, but you think I could have a clear enough conversation with her that we'd get reliable information?"

"Watch it," Rick said, and Nico bristled, not liking him talking to his mate that way.

Keegan didn't even seem to notice. Beginning to pace, he waved a hand at Rick in acknowledgment. "Also, there's no telling whether she would actually help us even if we could somehow communicate with her. We have no personal connection to her, and we have no way of convincing her that we're not the bad guys trying to usurp her vision since we don't know what the prophesy actually says. We can't know that she would support us."

"We have Jessica," Marcus said. "That's a personal connection."

"Who?" Keegan asked, spinning toward Nico.

Before he could answer, Tashmica was slicing her hand through the air. "Absolutely not. Putting the spirit of Angeline Pierre-Louis in the same room as her reincarnated self is a recipe for disaster. We don't know her or what she'd do—it could put Jess in real danger if she decided to try and hijack her body."

"Shit, seriously?" Nico asked, and Tash nodded, looking grim.

"When can you perform the spell to ask your grandmother for help?" Rick asked, cutting through the chatter and bringing them back on point.

"Soon." Keegan screwed up his face in thought. "A friend of mine was able to get the stuff I had hidden in New Orleans—spell books and whatnot—to Voight before she left, so I have the spell I need. The ingredients... That might prove difficult if I'm remembering correctly."

"We have a very well-stocked store, as you may recall," Tashmica said, almost sounding offended.

"Do you have mandrake root that was harvested under the light of a full moon?"

Everyone turned to stare at her, and she sighed. "Okay, no, we don't have that, but probably everything else."

Keegan nodded. "I know where we can get some, but it'll take a couple of days to get here, and then the spell itself needs to be said under a full moon."

Rick sighed, long and hard, and pinched the bridge of his nose. "So until then, we can do nothing but wait as far as the prophesy goes."

"Unfortunately. If you have other plans you want to move forward with, I'd understand," Keegan said, moving back over to where Nico was sitting and leaning against the arm of his chair.

Rick nodded and turned to Drake, where he was standing behind one of the couches, leaning his good shoulder against the wall. "Any of the hunters have any luck tracking one of those beasts?"

Drake shook his head. "Gabriel took a team himself and went back to where that hunter Aiden said Trevor was attacked, but they couldn't find any trace of it. None of the other teams that we've sent out have been able to find anything either."

"These are the things that attacked Wendy, right?" Keegan asked, glancing down at Nico

He nodded. "A few attacked Drake and his mates when

they were retrieving that journal. We've been trying to track some of them down."

"We thought," Tashmica said, "that if we could get our hands on one, study the magic used to make it, we could maybe figure out who was creating them, and that's probably the same person or group who's helping the council—"

"—come after you guys, yeah," Keegan finished, nodding. "It's not a bad plan. Did you try using any residual magic left on Wendy? Follow it back to the source."

Tashmica recrossed her legs, sighing. "We couldn't find any. By the time we thought about trying to track the beast down, she had been healed as well as she could be using a combination of medicine and magic, and that seemed to erase any traces."

Keegan rubbed at his jaw, thinking. Nico noticed he wasn't the only shifter in the room not saying anything, just looking between the witches and waiting to see if they could be of use.

"What about the spot where she was attacked?" Keegan finally said. "You go back there?"

Nico raised his eyebrows, turning to Tashmica.

She sat up straight, eyes wide. "No, no we didn't. I didn't even think about that. She didn't remember any people being there, just that beast, so it stands to reason nobody came along to clean up afterward. They left her for dead, and she just managed to get away."

"She didn't get too far before I found her. So even if she can't remember the exact spot, I bet with a couple of trackers, we could find where it happened."

"The scent would be long gone," Nico felt compelled to point out.

"Not shifter trackers," Keegan said, smiling at Nico like he was the silliest man he'd ever met. But maybe also like that wasn't a bad thing? "Witches."

"Even after all the rain and snow and everything else, they would be able to track her path?" Rick asked, dubious.

Keegan shrugged. "I could at my full strength. You just have to know the right spells."

Nico felt a small surge of pride that Rick didn't look to Tash to confirm that, like he had at the beginning of the meeting regarding the summoning spell. It was small, but it felt like Keegan was already finding his place within the pack.

"Alright," Rick said, pushing to his feet. "Until you can perform the spell to summon your grandmother, your focus needs to be helping to locate where Wendy was attacked and seeing if you can find any residual magic to track back to one of those damn beasts."

Keegan nodded, rubbing his hands together and looking downright excited. "Hell yeah, I can do that."

More than one person smiled at his enthusiasm, and Nico was definitely one of them.

"As for the rest of us," Rick continued, turning to his Enforcers. "We'll continue to prepare the pack as well as contacting allies to secure help if we need it. No slacking on training. But above all else, continue to keep each other safe."

CHAPTER FIFTEEN

I t took three days before Nico was able to be alone with his mate again.

Which was, quite frankly, ridiculous.

After their meeting in the library, he'd been pulled one way and Keegan another. By the time he'd found him again, over an hour later, he and Rosie were both sleeping on the couch, Rosie sprawled across his chest and Keegan's arms around her protectively. They were in the family room, some cartoon Nico didn't recognize playing on the large TV. He'd covered them with a blanket, arranged for them to have a room to stay in at the manor, and then gotten back to work.

It had been hard to pin him down over the next couple of days as Keegan had worked with the coven to track down where Wendy had been attacked and then visit the location to see if they could follow the magic. Nico had gone with them, him and Colt and a couple of betas as backup since the witches were busy concentrating on spells and not able to keep a close eye out for danger.

It had been an interesting experience. Nice even, in a way. Nico had never really gotten to experience Keegan in his element before. And while he hadn't been the one performing the magic, he'd been the one instructing and guiding the others. He may have been young, but it was obvious how much knowledge he had.

They'd been successful too, finding some trace of magic that Nico hadn't seen or sensed but Keegan and the other witches had been excited about. They'd knelt right there in the dirt, pulled out a large map, and performed a spell so they could use the map to follow the path of the beast rather than track it on foot. Keegan said it would be a slow process, but he was encouraged.

Finishing his work for the day, Nico finally decided that his best option was to bribe Samantha into babysitting Rosie for them and then taking his mate out on a proper date. She'd agreed, even teased him a little, and he'd been practically floating on his way to the room Keegan had been given.

Except he wasn't there.

Or anywhere in the manor.

He pulled out his phone and sent his missing mate a text.

Nico: *Where are you? I wanted to ask you something.*

Keegan: *Rosie and I are at WWC. Not sure when I'll be back. Urgent?*

He sighed and said no, disappointment flooding him. Keegan had been spending a lot of time at the shop, working with the others on the map or hunting down ingredients for his summoning spell. Nico understood, but it was frustrating when he wanted to spend some time with Keegan.

Hell, maybe even kiss him again.

He was about to shove his phone away and head home when he realized what Keegan had said. Worried, he quickly shot off another message.

Nico: *Wait, why is Rosie with you? Is she okay?*

He would have heard if something had happened, right? Surely someone would have told him. And she'd seemed completely fine the day before. He'd played with her for hours outside, blowing off his growing stack of papers, and then let her nap on him again in wolf form. She'd been her normal sweet and silly self the whole time.

Maybe Keegan just liked having her there with him. Nico wasn't sure at what age Keegan had started learning from his parents, but he figured if his powers had started around the same age as Rosie's were, it made sense that it would seem normal to him to bring her along to the shop.

Keegan: *Had a little incident with Callie—emotional, not physical and she's fine now. T & D are making her an amulet to help block emotions and prevent her from influencing others unintentionally.*

Even with Keegan's assurance that Rosie was okay, Nico had to tamp down the urge to get to *Wicca We Can* as fast he could to check her over himself. He almost left it at that, not wanting to overstep, but a thought was niggling at him, and he couldn't resist.

Nico: *How will she learn to control her empath abilities then?*

When Keegan didn't answer immediately, Nico convinced himself he was upset because Nico had no right to try and tell him how to parent his child—a child with abilities Nico didn't understand. It was just that... Pups learned how to use their enhanced abilities by *using* them, not by blocking them out.

He was just sitting down to dinner with Rick and some of the other Enforcers when his phone finally went off. He ignored the way Vanessa laughed at him when he nearly dropped it trying to get it out of his pocket.

Keegan: *LOL don't worry, papa wolf, she'll learn. It's just too overwhelming right now while she's so little. She's gotta learn to regulate herself first, then we can focus on other people's BS spewing at her.*

He stared at his phone, unbreathing.

Papa wolf.

"You okay, Nico?" Kai asked when he just sat there without moving for a few minutes.

Raising his head finally, he grinned. "Perfect."

🐾

When he walked into his house, still preoccupied with Keegan's teasing and thinking he could use a run, he almost didn't notice José coming down the stairs. He did a double take when he did though, surprised that the beta was wearing a button-up with dark jeans and his hair styled in a loose pompadour.

He whistled, kicking off his shoes. "Wow. Got a hot date?"

José grinned as he grabbed his jacket. "Hell yeah, I do. Don't wait up, roomie."

And then he was gone.

Nico looked around his quiet house with a frown. He wanted to be going out on a hot date. Hell, he'd take a cold date with Rosie there as a chaperone at that point. He just wanted to spend time with his mate.

He flipped through channels on his television for a little while, then poked around his streaming services, but nothing was jumping out at him. When he got to the third bookshelf without anything looking even remotely interesting, he decided he'd been right about going for a run.

He felt restless, even though he'd been running multiple times in the last week. It was like his wolf was just itching to get out all the time.

As soon as he shifted, he sprinted into the woods behind his house and howled.

He was elated when several others answered his call. That was the beauty of such a large pack: he never had to run alone if he didn't want to. He took off toward the others and joined them, enjoying just running and playing with his packmates for a while.

It was fully dark when he returned to his house, and he wasn't sure how many hours had passed, but he felt better. He was exhausted, if nothing else, so he hoped he'd be able to sleep and not just lie awake all night, wishing he was with Keegan.

As he stepped out of the shower, he paused, head cocked to the side as he tried to figure out what the noise had been that he'd heard. A second later, somebody knocked on his front door. Frowning, he threw a towel around his waist, in case it was one of his human neighbors, and headed down the stairs.

Halfway down, he caught the tantalizing scent of woodsmoke and nearly tripped over his own feet. He hurried the rest of the way down and shot forward, nearly ripping the door off its hinges as he opened it.

Keegan smiled up at him, eyes dancing with amusement. "Hey, you. Heard you were looking for me."

Nico nodded absently as he inhaled through his nose, taking his mate's scent deep into his lungs. His wolf was too close to the surface after his long run. It was all he could do not to grab Keegan, drag him inside, and mount him.

He reminded himself that one heated kiss didn't mean that was what Keegan wanted. Nico needed to go slow. His mate was human, even if he was a witch, so he was sure it would take him longer to come around to the idea of being claimed by Nico.

"Can I come in?" Keegan asked, chuckling.

Nico stumbled back out of the way, a little embarrassed that he hadn't said anything and had just been standing there sniffing at Keegan like a pup whose balls had just dropped. "Of course, yeah. Come in."

Keegan stepped past him, and Nico didn't think it was an

accident that he happened to brush the back of his hand against the front of Nico's towel right over where his dick was tenting it a little. He had to shut his eyes and take a breath through his mouth, shuddering, as he tried to regain control of himself.

"I met Marcus's mate tonight."

It took a minute for Nico's brain to start churning and for Keegan's sentence to make sense. He closed the door and leaned against it. Keegan was standing in his living room, gazing around at his furniture and bookshelves.

Nico had to clear his throat before he could answer. "Robson? I hadn't realized you hadn't met him yet."

Keegan nodded, half turned away. "I hadn't. I also didn't realize he was human."

Nico shrugged, finally feeling like he was getting his footing, though he wasn't sure why they were talking about Robson. "It was a bit of a shock for Marcus, but they're a good fit."

Humming, Keegan leaned over to look at one of his books more closely. "I talked to Gabriel yesterday. It was the first time we'd had a chance to be alone since I got here."

Nico still wasn't sure what he was getting at, but he smiled and played along. "That must have been nice, being able to catch up with him."

"It was. We were at his house when his mates got home, Drake and Jamie. I'd met Drake before, obviously, and I'd seen Jamie around the manor, but I hadn't put together who they were to Gabe."

"Okay," Nico said slowly, then just waited. He was sure Keegan would clarify why meeting certain members of the pack was important.

Keegan made a slow turn of the room, running his hand along the back of the couch and a chair, then turned on a nearby lamp with nothing more than a flick of his fingers.

Nico lifted his brows. "You're using your magic."

Keegan gave him a soft smile that warmed his insides. He'd grown to love Keegan's sharp tongue and foul mouth over the last few days, but nothing got his blood pumping quite like a glimpse of his sweet side.

"I can feel it growing," he admitted in a hushed voice. "At first, I wasn't sure, but I realized earlier today that it really was coming back. I think just being a part of a pack as strong and as vibrant as this one is feeding my magic in a way I've never experienced before. I'm curious to see if my powers get back to what they were before or maybe even grow bigger."

"Tashmica told me once being a part of a pack is like being hooked up to an endless supply of power that she can tap into if she needs it."

Keegan nodded. "That's true. Though if you funnel too much power through a single conduit or person, it can burn straight through you. Like plugging a lamp into a power plant."

Tash had said something similar to him, but he tried not to think about it. The idea of his mate or one of his friends tapping into the magic that coursed through the pack bonds and using too much too quickly chilled him to his bones.

"I noticed Marcus has a bonding mark. And Jamie and Drake each have two as well."

Nico's shoulders straightened as heat flushed through him. He should have expected Keegan to have questions, having not lived within a pack before. Keegan probably wasn't used to seeing human and shifter matings. And as far as Nico knew, the spell Damien had created that allowed human mates to return a bonding bite was unique and not something he would have found outside their pack.

"That's true," Nico said carefully. "Is that something you might be interested in?"

Keegan kept walking around the room until he was right

back in front of Nico, mere inches away. Nico became very aware of the fact that he was still only wearing a towel.

Reaching up, Keegan ran a finger down the side of Nico's neck, the touch light, and yet it sparked against his skin like a jolt of static electricity. The trail left behind was heating, spreading the warmth through his veins.

Keegan stopped right over the spot where a bonding bite would go. "Do you mean would I be interested in leaving a visible mark right here so that everyone would know you're taken. That you are mine."

"And you would be mine," Nico murmured, his fangs poking down a little and his eyesight sharpening.

Keegan smirked up at him. "Yeah, you might say I'd be interested in that."

"I came to find you today to ask you out on a date," Nico said, his voice low and rumbling.

Keegan huffed out a soft laugh, trailing his finger over Nico's collarbones and then down between his pecs. "Goddess, it's weird to think after all this time, we really haven't been out on a date, have we? Everything we've been through, all of our dream walks, you rescuing me…"

Nico swallowed. "I thought we could use the chance to get to know each other a little better. You never shared much in the dreams."

Keegan grimaced, dropping his eyes away for a moment. "I know. I'm sorry. I thought it would make it harder if you knew more about me."

Nico didn't want to think about that, about his plan to leave and never see Nico again. "What do you say? Can I take you out for dinner tomorrow?"

Keegan shook his head. "Tashmica and I need to do ingredient prep for the spell to summon my grann. Some of them have to be prepared in a very specific way at a specific time. I'm sorry. What about lunch?"

Nico growled in frustration. "I have a meeting at lunchtime."

Keegan laughed. "Breakfast?"

"Doesn't seem very romantic," Nico muttered. "Though Mama's does serve some really good french toast."

"You silly wolf." Keegan pushed up onto his toes and brushed his lips against Nico's. "You don't have to romance me. You've already got me."

Mama's was busy.

Apparently, it was the place to be for breakfast on random Thursdays. Nico didn't mind, though, as long as no one came over and tried to talk business with him or ask him for help with something. He was officially off the clock.

He wanted to do exactly what he'd told Keegan the night before and get to know his mate. Despite what Keegan had said about Nico already having him—which, just thinking about the way he'd whispered the words against Nico's lips, then slipped past him and through the door before Nico could stop him—he wanted more than his magic recognizing Nico's wolf.

He was selfish. He wanted his witch's love, and he wouldn't stop wooing him until he got it.

He slid into a booth, placing the bouquet of orchids he'd brought onto the vinyl next to him. He was watching the door when the server came over, and he ordered coffee for both of them. Right after the guy had come back to drop off the mugs and fill them, the door to the diner opened, and Nico's whole body lit up with happiness.

He watched as Keegan looked around, a slight frown between his brows until he found Nico, and then his face softened. He'd noticed it only did that when Keegan looked at Rosie… and now Nico.

Relaxing back into the booth, he couldn't take his eyes off Keegan as he made his way through the crowd. He was wearing a long-sleeved tan thermal that looked amazing with his dark skin and tight jeans that appeared to have been painted on.

Nico couldn't help but wonder if he'd worn them for him.

"Morning," Keegan said, slipping into the other side of the booth.

"Good morning." He was just picking up his bouquet when their server back over with their menus, letting them know he'd be back in a few minutes.

Keegan nodded and then peered into his coffee mug and grimaced. "Do you have tea?"

The server nodded. "We sure do. I'll be right back."

"You don't like coffee?" Nico asked, trying to hide his horror

Keegan pushed the mug in front of him across the table so it was closer to Nico. "Hell no. Don't tell me you're one of those people who think that coffee is life."

"That's because it is."

Keegan sat back as the server returned, one side of his mouth quirked up. He murmured a quiet thank-you, and the server said he'd be back for their order in a bit. Nico watched, fascinated, as Keegan flipped through the tea bags in the container the server had brought. Once he picked one, he put it in the empty mug and then poured hot water over it from a carafe. All of his movements were quick and deft.

Nico was pretty sure he could watch his hands do anything and be fascinated by them. The tattoos added to his allure, but it was the easy grace he seemed to do everything with that Nico really found appealing.

"Why are you staring at me like that?" Keegan asked once he finished preparing his leaf water.

"I just like watching you."

Keegan lifted his head and stared at him, a vulnerable sort of light in his eyes as he ran his tongue over his bottom lip. Finally, he said softly, "I like when you watch me."

Grinning, Nico finally picked up his bouquet and handed them to Keegan, the scent of orchids filling the air. "These are for you."

"Oh," Keegan said, sounding surprised. "Um, thank you."

Nico frowned. "Don't you like flowers? You took me to that solarium during one of our dream walks."

Keegan sniffled in response, and Nico's head jerked back in horror.

Had he made his mate cry?

"You don't have to take them if you don't—"

Keegan threw his elbow over his face just in time, his sneeze loud in their little enclosed space. A couple of people around them said, "Bless you."

Keegan shoved the bouquet back at Nico, eyes watering.

"Are you okay?" Nico asked, accepting the flowers.

"Allergic," he croaked.

"But what about—"

Keegan sneezed twice more.

"Oh hell." Nico looked around and saw a server coming their way, a large tub half full of dirty dishes in their arms. As soon as the guy was close enough, Nico chucked to the bouquet inside the tub. "Throw these away for me, please."

The guy looked at them, eyebrows raised, but just nodded and kept going. Keegan tore a napkin out of the dispenser on the table and blew his nose.

"I'm sorry. I had no idea," Nico said, feeling helpless.

"It was a sweet gesture." Keegan's voice was thicker than normal, and he sniffled again.

"I just thought since you liked that greenhouse…"

Keegan chuckled. "The one full of hard-to-find spell ingredients and deadly plants?"

"Oh." That made more sense, he supposed.

"I appreciate the thought though."

Niko smiled weakly. Not a great start for his plan to woo Keegan into loving him, but he wouldn't give up.

Just as their server appeared next to their table with a peppy, "Y'all decided?" Keegan sneezed again, startling the kid.

Nico wished he could start the whole day over.

CHAPTER SIXTEEN

"Y ou didn't!"

"What was I supposed to do? The guy looked me right in the eye and said, 'What are you going to do about it, witch?'" Keegan smirked.

"So you cursed him into being a toad?" Nico cackled, drawing the eyes of the few people in the diner with them. But Keegan barely noticed, unable to look away.

"It's a classic for a reason, and it was temporary." He loved watching Nico laugh, his whole face lighting up with joy and blue eyes sparkling. He was... breathtaking.

And not because of allergy-induced wheezing this time.

It was their third date in five days, and Keegan couldn't remember ever being so damn happy. For their second date, Nico had brought Rosie and a picnic basket to *Wicca We Can* and dragged him away for a lunch at the park, and then spent two hours playing with her and feeding Keegan bites of food and smiling in that way that made Keegan want to rip his clothes off.

Honestly, if his daughter hadn't been five feet away, he

probably would have sucked Nico's dick right then and there.

For their third date, he'd tried to take Keegan to a fancy restaurant the next town over, but Keegan had nixed that idea. Mama's was perfectly fine for him, and he liked staying close to the pack and Rosie, just in case. As happy as he was, he couldn't let himself forget that there were still threats out there. He'd chatted with Rose Ellen earlier that day, and she'd said things were getting... weird in New Orleans. His mother had locked herself away in her house and hadn't been seen in days.

As long as she didn't start heading north, he didn't care what she got up to.

While they were eating dinner, Nico had asked him about some of the jobs he'd done for his old coven, and he'd enjoyed sharing so openly about himself. He'd told some of the funnier stories, not wanting to put a damper on their good time with any of the fucked-up stuff he'd seen. Plus, a lot of those stories shouldn't be shared in such a public setting.

It was still nice, just being himself and having Nico smile at him like he *liked* everything he saw.

They'd been sitting in a booth—the same one they'd shared their perfectly disastrous breakfast in, and Keegan was beginning to think of it as *their* booth—for close to two hours, having long since finished their food. Their server, a huge guy named Cole, who'd welcomed Nico with a grin and a back-slapping hug, had checked on them a couple of times but otherwise given them their space.

Still smiling, Nico reached across the table and snagged one of Keegan's hands, a move he'd started doing more and more and Keegan definitely didn't hate it. "When can we do this again?"

Keegan laughed. "We're still technically doing this now."

"You know what I mean." Nico dropped his eyes to Keegan's lips before snapping them back up. It happened so quickly, Keegan would have missed it if he wasn't paying such close attention to his mate. "I like spending time with you."

Keegan ran his tongue over his bottom lip, studying Nico. Other than the super-intense but quick make-out and scenting session at the manor over a week ago and the brief press of lips Keegan had given him when they'd made their breakfast date, Nico had been pretty damn stingy with his kisses. It was the one dark spot on their growing relationship.

Keegan had thought after their breakfast together, they might at least fool around some, but between his lingering stuffiness—the opposite of sexy—and Nico's meeting, it hadn't seemed like the most opportune time.

And it wasn't like he could climb his mate like a tree in front of his daughter.

So he had high hopes for the after-dinner activities, but Nico's question had him wondering if they weren't on the same page. Did Nico not want to get naked with him?

The thought sent a wave of trepidation through him, but he put on a smile when Nico started to lose his own, obviously scenting something from Keegan. "I like spending time with you too."

And he did.

He just wanted some of that time to be of the more horizontal variety.

Smiling, Nico got Cole's attention and handed over some cash before he even saw the bill, telling him to keep the change. He stood and held a hand out to Keegan, pulling him from the booth and then leading him outside, fingers loosely entwined.

Maybe Keegan was wrong. Maybe just wanted to take things slow for some reason.

In a way, it was kind of nice. He'd never been pursued like this, and it made his stomach get all fluttery when he thought about how someone like Nico seemed to genuinely like spending time with him. The few people he'd hooked up with in the past had either been like Rosie's mom, where they'd just fallen into bed at some point but were mostly still just friends. Or they'd been random people he'd met on jobs that he hadn't cared about and who hadn't cared about him.

This was different.

And as he thought about it while they walked to Nico's SUV, he realized that if they'd jumped into bed or Nico had wanted to bite him right away, a part of him would have always felt like it was just Nico's wolf that wanted him, his instincts telling him that they were a good match, who cares if they actually liked each other.

It was reassuring, in a way, to have spent time getting to know Nico. As much as he wanted to throw himself down on the nearest flat surface and beg Nico to claim him, getting the chance to win Nico over in a traditional way eased some of the worries he didn't let himself think about too much.

Like how if they hadn't been fated mates, Nico never would have even noticed him.

But the longer they went without Nico making any kind of move toward the claiming portion of their mating, the more opportunities Keegan would have to fuck up and drive Nico away again.

He swallowed down the lump that formed in his throat at the thought. "Maybe I can take you out next time," he said instead, glancing up at Nico and getting lost in his smile all over again. His handsome face looked striking in the light from the setting sun, and Keegan couldn't look away. "What, um, what kind of movies do you like?"

Nico, apparently unaware of the way he was ramping up Keegan's libido with every grin, led him across the street to where they'd parked. "I like actions and comedies. Not a big fan of horror or anything too violent."

"I think I could probably find something to fit the bill."

Nico squeezed his hand, then asked, "How's Rosie settling in? She seems happy whenever I see her, but I want to make sure she really is. Does she need anything?"

The warm way he asked and the way he looked at Keegan like the answer truly mattered melted his heart even further. Even if Nico hadn't taken him on a single date or spent any time alone with Keegan, he was pretty sure he'd still be falling in love with him just from the way he treated Rosie.

Oh fuck. He was falling in love with Nico.

"She loves it here," he said quickly, trying to distract Nico from noticing how his heart was suddenly beating faster. "She and Callie and some of the other pups around the manor are thick as thieves. They're constantly playing outside or trying to con Beth out of cookies."

Nico laughed. "Oh, Beth's pretty used to that. She's been fending Rick off for years."

Keegan could believe it. The older woman was always so nice and cheerful whenever he popped into the kitchen. He'd learned that she'd been Rick's housekeeper since he'd taken over as alpha, her daughter, Vanessa, one of his Enforcers.

"She misses her cousins though," Keegan admitted. "And my sister, who's been like a mother to her most of her life."

Nico made a soft sound. "They can visit anytime they want. Though with things the way they are right now…"

Keegan nodded, not needing him to finish the sentence. "Once we figure out what's in that journal and how to stop the Council so that things can go back to normal, I'll be sure to invite her and her family for a visit."

Nico was smiling in a way that made him look younger as

he pulled open the passenger-side door for Keegan. He looked almost... bashful.

"What's that look?"

He shook his head. "It's nothing. I just like that you're planning for the future here."

Keegan stopped, one foot inside the vehicle, and reached up to gently cup the side of Nico's face. "*You* are my future, baby."

The endearment just slipped out, but based on the soft rumbling sound emanating from Nico's chest, he liked it. Or maybe he just liked being called Keegan's future.

Either way, the deep sound was sparking the low hum of arousal Keegan had been feeling the entire time they were in the diner, stoking it into a crackling fire that threatened to burn him alive. He let his fingers trail down Nico's chest as he climbed into the SUV, not missing the way his nostrils flared as he sucked in a deep breath.

"Would you like to come to my house for a while before heading back to the manor?" Nico asked, still standing in the doorway and staring at Keegan with an intensity he'd missed the last few days.

He ran his teeth over his bottom lip, nodding.

The drive to Nico's was blessedly short, the silence between them thick with anticipation and a tension so delicious Keegan could barely stand it. Nico shot him glances every chance he got, running his eyes over Keegan's body before turning back to the road and tightening his hands on the steering wheel.

Keegan? He never looked away.

He stared at his mate the entire drive. He was an ensnared prey, and he hoped he'd never get away. He wanted his hands and mouth on Nico more than anything. In that moment, he'd give just about anything to have it.

When Nico pulled up in front of his house, he paused, a

look of uncertainty passing over his face, but before he could second-guess, Keegan undid his seat belt and jumped out.

He hurried up the sidewalk to the front door, throwing a glance over his shoulder to make sure Nico was following. His heart leapt in his chest at the way Nico was striding after him, head down slightly and eyes glowing.

He was stalking after Keegan like he had only one thing on his mind.

Thank the goddess.

Keegan glanced around as nonchalantly as he could as he reached the porch, but he didn't see any other vehicles.

"José's not here," Nico said, catching up to him and plastering himself to Keegan's back. He gasped at the wonderful heat of Nico's body and the way his hands rubbed over his chest and stomach. "He's still with Kai. Apparently, he really likes him and keeps requesting José."

That made Keegan smile even as Nico reached around him to unlock the front door. He'd only met the young beta a couple of times, but he reminded him a little of Nico. He always had a quick smile and laugh. So it was easy for Keegan to see why the alpha-mate would like having him around as his shadow anytime he left the manor.

Keegan also understood why Rick had insisted on his family having extra protection every time they went anywhere. If he and Rosie weren't staying at the manor, he wouldn't have felt nearly as comfortable leaving her at home with a babysitter. But while they're there, not only was the alpha almost always there working but also any number of Enforcers and betas, as well as the alpha of the Keshena Pack and dozens of her packmates. Keegan had only seen her in passing since he'd been staying there. She and her pack liked to stay out of the way, as Tashmica had told him.

The manor was full to bursting with powerful shifters. And even when Rosie was at daycare with Callie and Henry, there were multiple betas stationed inside and around the building.

Rick wasn't taking any chances with his pups.

As soon as they were inside the house, Nico crowded Keegan up against the door and caged him in, nuzzling against the side of his face. Against his scar.

Keegan sucked in a breath, catching the forest scent he associated with Nico. It was wild and comforting all at the same time. When he smoothed his palms up Nico's wide chest, he growled and pressed even closer.

"You are temptation personified," Nico snarled.

He wasn't sure if that was good or bad.

"I want to taste you," Keegan said, pressing a kiss against the hinge of Nico's jaw and smiling at the foul word Nico whispered.

He wasn't ashamed of what he wanted, and he felt like he'd waited long enough. Nico was the other half of his whole. The person who had been made just for him. He'd been blessed with a strong, powerful, and *kind* mate, and he couldn't hold back anymore.

He gripped the back of Nico's neck with both hands, using his thumbs on his jaw to guide his face over so it was right in front of Keegan's.

They were so close together he couldn't actually see Nico's features that well, but he didn't need to. He'd had Nico's face memorized months ago. He'd spent hours and hours staring at him during their dream walks, listening to him talk and laugh and feeling himself relax more and more each time they were together. Knowing he was making it more difficult for himself but unable to stay away.

Growing up like he had, his mother constantly berating him and expecting more, expecting perfection, he'd learned at a young age to close himself off. He'd never been good enough for her, and it hurt far less if he didn't let himself feel anything. So he'd protect himself, hiding behind his stone wall because it was the only place he'd felt safe.

But then Nico had come along with his sweet smiles and earnest affection and chiseled away until it had started to crack.

Seeing daylight through his protective wall for the first time in years had been terrifying, and he'd nearly ruined everything.

He knew it would take a while for Nico to trust him again, but he was okay with that. He was willing to earn it. And until then, he would do his best to show Nico how much he meant to him by being the best kind of mate he could be. He'd show Nico how perfect they would be.

He shuddered, brushing his lips against Nico's and ignoring the stinging in his eyes. He couldn't wait to be a family with Nico. To finally have what he'd always wanted, what he'd always craved.

Safety.

Love.

A *home*.

He could never gain another ounce of magic back and still be ecstatic as long as he and Rosie got to have Nico.

"You're ruining my plan," Nico rumbled, leaning down to press his face into Keegan's throat.

He tipped his head back, baring it for him. His whole body tingled at the soft growl Nico released at the submissive gesture. Oh yes, his wolf liked that.

"What plan is that?" He was already breathless, but he didn't care. He sank his fingers into Nico's hair, holding on to him, and shut his eyes.

Nico gently kissed and licked at the thin skin of his throat, making him shiver and moan. "My plan to woo you. To help you see it's not just my wolf that wants you."

Keegan stilled, giving Nico's hair a yank to pull his face

back so he could study him. "That's why you've been holding back? Why you got me the flowers and have been holding my hand but not fucking kissing me?"

Nico grinned, his fangs peeking out. Keegan's cock twitched at the sight, and he nearly lost his train of thought. "You say that like it's a bad thing. I know the flowers were a bust, but I thought I'd been doing a pretty good job otherwise."

Keegan shook his head. "You silly wolf. You don't have to... to woo me. I need to woo you! I'm the one who broke your trust. Who let you think you weren't everything I needed."

Nico stared at him, his glowing eyes intense. "You're used to being alone. To not having anyone to depend on but yourself."

Keegan wasn't sure where that came from, but he nodded slowly, tracing one of Nico's eyebrows with his thumb. "When I was little, I had Jocelyn. But even before she left, as we got older, my mother isolated us from each other in ways I didn't even recognize until after she was gone. It wasn't until she took in Rosie and we began talking regularly for the first time in years that I saw the true extent I had let her come between us. I barely knew Jos at that point."

Nico made a soft noise, turning his face into Keegan's hand and nuzzling against his palm. "And your work for your coven, you did that alone too, right?"

"Usually." Keegan nodded. "That's how we're trained to work. We're taught not to trust anyone and to simply follow the evidence wherever it leads. Then we're supposed to do what's for the best of humans—though my orders were sometimes more about what was best for the coven."

"Now, you're part of a pack, and you have to learn to trust others and rely on them to work as a team to come up with answers."

Keegan smiled. "Which can be difficult for me, yes. But I think I'm doing pretty good so far."

"Agreed." Nico returned his smile, his teeth back to normal and his eyes losing some of their glow, but he was still looking at Keegan like he was his whole world. "But that's also how our mating should be."

"Involving the rest of the pack?" Keegan teased, even though his heart was ramping up and his fingers were a little shaky where they still framed Nico's beautiful face.

Nico shook his head, then pressed a kiss to each of Keegan's palms. "It's not just about lust and instincts. At least that's not how I want it to be. I want us to choose each other, to want and need each other. To rely on each other. If one of us stumbles, I want us both to know that the other will catch them. I want to raise Rosie to believe in that so that she knows her pack is her greatest gift and weapon."

His pulse was thundering in his ears. "I want that too. I want... all of that."

Nico leaned down and pressed a soft kiss to Keegan's lips. "Okay, good. So we don't have to rush this." He raised his head and held Keegan's gaze. "I'm not going anywhere."

Keegan shuddered at the words, squeezing his eyes shut and pushing his face into Nico's chest, holding him as tightly as he could. He was still afraid of that. Afraid that if they didn't complete their mating quickly, something would happen and Nico would walk away from him again.

He didn't think he'd survive it a second time.

Nico held him as he caught his breath, his hands rubbing up and down Keegan's back slowly as he pressed his face into his hair.

Swallowing, Keegan said, "What if I don't need more time..."

Nico chuckled, his arms tightening. "Let's take some more anyway. Just to be sure. And when we're both ready,

I'm going to claim you so thoroughly, so completely, it will erase any lingering doubts you might still have."

Okay, that sounded like something he absolutely didn't want to wait for.

But he would.

For Nico.

"Can we at least do some more kissing? Or are we going full-on prude until this thorough claiming occurs?" Keegan said, voice muffled against Nico's chest.

He felt more than heard Nico's chuckle. "Kissing is okay."

"What about some over-the-clothes action? Is that on the table?"

Nico's laugh that time boomed through the whole house and settled deep in Keegan's heart.

CHAPTER SEVENTEEN

"He's good with them, isn't he?"

Keegan startled, having not heard Kai walk out of the manor. He's been completely absorbed watching Nico and Rosie play with some of the other young kids from the manor. Callie was getting pushed on the swings by Samantha, and Henry was in the sandbox with a couple of other little ones, a Keshena Pack member supervising close by.

Nico was in his wolf form, and Rosie was rolling around with him in the grass, shrieking with delight and laughing every time Nico pretended to growl at her. Other kids would come over and join them off and on, but his two goofballs had been playing together for nearly an hour. Keegan's heart had melted into a pool of goo in his stomach, filling him with a sense of happiness and warmth he hoped he'd never get used to.

"The kids?" Keegan asked, smiling. "Yeah, he is. Rosie just adores him. She told me the other night, as I was getting her ready for bed, that it wasn't fair that she had to sleep with just her teddy bear and not her wolf."

Kai laughed. "Oh my god, that's so cute."

"It was." Keegan smiled over at the pair again. It had also been a reminder that something was missing. As much as he adored Nico for wanting to take things slowly and make sure they were on the same page, when he was lying all alone in his bed at night, he couldn't help but imagine what it would be like if Nico were there next to him. Or under him. Or on top of him.

Goddess, he was horny.

Kai lowered himself onto a chair next to him, snickering. "Is everything okay? You seem a little... frustrated."

Keegan covered his face with one of his hands, shaking his head in embarrassment. "Oh fuck. Is it that obvious?"

Kai made a muffled sort of sound that made him raise his head, and he realized the alpha-mate was doing his best not to laugh at him. Keegan couldn't help but chuckle himself.

"I wouldn't say it's obvious," Kai said, but Keegan wasn't sure he believed him.

He thought he'd been catching a few side-eyes around the manor the last few days as his sexual frustration had grown. He peeked over at Nico and Rosie, but it didn't seem like he was listening to them. Keegan had noticed that when he was in his shifted form, Nico tended to focus on one thing at a time. While Keegan was sure that he was always listening and ready for threats, he had an easier time ignoring other conversations and unnecessary input from his senses than he did as a human.

Keegan wasn't sure how much he should share with Kai though. Not just because it was embarrassing that his own mate was cockblocking him, but because he wasn't sure if Nico would appreciate him telling Kai about their sex life. Or lack thereof.

His hesitation must have been obvious because Kai held up both hands. "You don't have to tell me anything you're not comfortable with. I mostly came over because I saw you sitting out here by yourself, and I realized it was the perfect time for us to chat. I haven't really had a chance to get to know you between all the time you've spent working with the coven and taking care of your daughter and the general chaos around here. So I just wanted to check in with you."

Kai's smile was open, his green eyes still sparkling with humor, and Keegan was hit with the realization that they were probably around the same age. It wasn't that he looked old or anything, but as alpha-mate, he simply radiated power and authority.

Keegan had to admit that it felt nice having someone ask how he was doing just for the sake of wanting to know. Kai barely knew him yet and still seemed genuinely curious about his well-being. It was just one more way his life had changed for the better since he'd joined the pack, but it was also a reminder that other than Nico, and maybe Tashmica, he hadn't exactly gone out of his way to make friends.

Even Ericka, who he'd bonded with in Kansas and on their long drive to Michigan, he hadn't really seen much of since they'd been back. He was used to doing things a certain way—Nico had been right about that—but he knew that if he didn't make an effort now, it would be harder to come back from later. And he didn't want that. He didn't want to be isolated anymore.

He felt like he'd been living on the fringes of his own life for years. He wanted the connections, the deep pack bonds Nico and the others talked about so easily, like they were just a given. While he felt the strength of the pack—especially as it healed his fractured magic—he knew that not everyone probably felt it as strongly as the Enforcers and their loved ones did. Just like any other kind of relationship, it took work on both sides to keep the bond strong.

Good thing he wasn't afraid of hard work.

Taking a breath and one last peek over at Nico, who had

flopped on his side in the grass with Rosie sprawled on top of him and both seemingly half-asleep. He leaned a little closer to Kai and said quietly, "You could probably say that I'm frustrated, yes."

Kai scooted his chair over so he was next to Keegan and darted a glance over to Nico as well. "You two aren't…"

Keegan shook his head. "We decided we'd take things slow."

"Slow can be good," Kai said slowly. "But it's been over two weeks since you got here. That's like… a year for a shifter."

Keegan laughed. It was a slight exaggeration—but only slightly. He knew a lot of shifter pairings who had mated within days of meeting each other, especially when they were fated like him and Nico. But thanks to their tumultuous beginning, it seemed like Nico was hesitant to dive in. Keegan couldn't blame him. In fact, when Nico had laid out his reasons, they had made perfect sense.

They'd choose each other instead of letting their instincts control them.

Sweet, right?

Except another week had passed, and they'd spent *hours* together. Eating meals, snuggled up on the couch, playing with Rosie, talking. Keegan had never felt more connected to another person in his life.

And yet the furthest they'd gone was a couple of make-out sessions that ended as soon as things got too heated.

Considering what a strong, virile wolf his mate was, Keegan was more than a little surprised that it seemed like he was the one who was cracking. He'd been half tempted to try dream walking with Nico again, to see if he could coax him into something more that way. But he'd scrapped that plan immediately. He wanted their first time to be real so that he'd be able to feel and taste him.

"Have you told him that you're ready to... move things along?" Kai asked quietly, mindful of the others out in the yard.

"Not exactly."

"Maybe that's what he's waiting on."

Keegan cocked his head and thought about it. After their date when he'd tried to put the moves on Nico, he'd done his best to be respectful of the pace his wolf had set, but was that what was stopping Nico? He was waiting for Keegan to say he was ready?

He was pretty damn sure he was. He couldn't picture his life without Nico. Didn't want to, in fact. Hell, even José seemed to be waiting on them. He'd pulled Keegan aside the other day to let him know he'd swap places with him and Rosie whenever they were ready to move into Nico's. Keegan had felt bad for a second, thinking he was kicking José out of his home, but he'd just laughed and said not to worry about it. That it would make his job of keeping an eye on Kai easier actually.

Not to mention, each day as his magic grew stronger, it yearned for Nico more and more. If Keegan wasn't careful, it would try and slip out of his grasp and reach for Nico, wanting nothing more than to wrap around Nico and never let go.

Considering Keegan felt the same way, he couldn't exactly be upset about it.

"You might be right," he finally said, nodding to himself. "After the summons tonight, I'll make sure he knows."

Kai grinned and pulled something from behind his back. Keegan hadn't even noticed he'd brought something outside with him. He held a small thermos out to Keegan and winked. "I think your chances are good that you'll get lucky. Tashmica dropped this off for you a little while ago."

Keegan took it, holding it in front of them. "Is this the tea that I've heard so much about?"

"Damien's special blend of mating magic? Yes, indeed." Kai snickered. "Just be careful. I've heard this stuff is potent as hell. That's why Tashmica steeps it herself now. Robson and Marcus apparently left it a little too long, and Robson got a bit... stoned."

Keegan snorted, trying to picture the snarky human high on magical tea. "She could have just given it to me tonight."

Kai shrugged, pushing to his feet. "She was here to see Rick about something else and asked if I'd discreetly slip it to you. I don't think she wanted to try and give it to you in front of a room full of shifters."

Okay, yeah. He didn't want that either. He wasn't ashamed of his mate or their sex life or anything, but there were certain things other people didn't need to know. "That's probably good thinking."

He stared down at the thermos, hoping he'd be using the tea sooner rather than later.

"Did Kai remember to give you my gift?" Tashmica asked, laughing when he shushed her.

"Yes, he gave it to me. But if you're going to talk about it in front of everyone, I don't know why you couldn't have just brought it to me yourself."

She waved a hand, double-checking the piece of paper in her hand before spraying one more line on the floor. "I was here earlier with Jess to talk to Rick, and I wasn't sure *exactly* when you would need it. Just that you would."

Keegan felt his face getting hot, and he turned away from her. He knew that Tashmica had premonitions, but it made him more than a little uncomfortable thinking about her seeing him and Nico using the tea. Or, more accurately, what they'd be doing after Keegan drank it.

"There. How does that look?" She stood and stepped away from the sigil she'd just finished painting on the floor.

Keegan carefully checked it against the one in the book he was holding, making sure every single line was in the correct place, and then nodded, moving to the next step of the spell.

"Perfect. You know, I'm sort of surprised Rick said you could spray-paint this on the floor of his Great Hall," he said absently, turning the page to go over the list of ingredients needed, even though he'd already done that half a dozen times and knew they had everything.

Tashmica hummed, tapping her chin with one finger. "You know, I probably should have asked."

As if summoned by their conversation, the big alpha stormed into the room, face set in a stern scowl as he stared at the fresh black paint on his previously unblemished wooden floor. "What the fuck?"

"We're just about ready to get started," Tash said, hurrying away.

Rick turned his frown on him, and Keegan shrugged. "The paint might come off?"

Rolling his eyes and huffing, Rick stomped away, joining his mate and a few others where they waited on the other side of the room. Keegan turned to find Tashmica and Damien standing a few feet behind him, doing their best not to laugh.

"That wasn't very nice," he said.

"Oh, he'll get over it."

"I meant leaving me to fend for myself when you were the one who did the actual painting!"

Tash waved him off, then gestured Damien forward. "Go ahead."

Carrying the jar with the meticulously combined spell

ingredients, Damien poured some of the mixture at each of the indicated spots that coordinated with the cardinal directions and then some directly in the center of the sigil.

Keegan and Tashmica placed the tall, white candles between the ingredients and then lit each one. Keegan picked up his discarded book once more, triple-checking that they had everything prepared the correct way.

"Okay," he said, "I think we're ready."

He set the spell book on the table next to the journal and the empty pad of paper that would hopefully soon contain the translated prophesies.

Right on time, Nico strolled in carrying Rosie, who looked like she was barely awake. It was definitely past her bedtime, the full moon nearly at its zenith, but Keegan knew this would probably be the only chance she'd have to meet her great grandmother. He just hoped she'd remember.

Nico gave him an encouraging smile, soothing Rosie as she whined a little and reached for him.

He looked at Tash and Damien, and they both nodded, faces set. Taking one more deep breath, Keegan called Jessica over so she could help them.

The spell could be said by one person, but it was strongest if it was said by four, each standing at one of the cardinal directions. He took the south position, Tashmica the north, Damien the west, and Jess the east. The rest of the people in the Great Hall grew silent as the four of them closed their eyes, channeled their magic, and began chanting the spell.

Keegan assumed it would take a while. He had never performed the spell nor seen it done before, but it was powerful magic to pull a spirit from the other side and force them to manifest.

The sigils on his palms had just begun to heat as he funneled his magic toward them and out to the others when he felt her. Or what he thought was her. It felt like invisible fingers brushing against the back of his neck.

A moment later, there was a surge of magic in the air, the sigil crackling on the floor with the amount of power they were pushing into it.

And then he heard her voice for the first time in almost a decade, her accent and cadence exactly the same. "My sweet boy, you're all grown up."

Tears running down his face, he opened his eyes and looked into the translucent face of his dear grann. "Hi."

His throat was dry, and he wanted to rush forward to wrap her in a hug, but he knew her form wouldn't allow that. But it was still so, so good to see her. He wished Jocelyn was there, knowing she missed their grann just as much as he did.

Her shoulders were a little stooped, her face wrinkled, but she smiled at him just as brightly as she always had. She raised one of her hands as she stepped to the edge of the sigil right in front of him, and he felt the staticky feeling of her again as she stroked his cheek.

When she glanced past him, her eyes widened, and she covered her mouth. He felt Nico step up next to him, Rosie still in his arms and ducking her head down with sudden shyness.

"Who is this beautiful little girl?"

"This is Roselyn, but we call her Rosie. She's your great-granddaughter."

"She is perfect." His grann just looked at Rosie for several long moments, a soft smile on her face, and then she glanced up at Nico and smirked. "And who is the handsome man holding your sweet daughter?"

Keegan laughed. She was just like he remembered. Not the last year when she'd been so sick, withering away from the cancer until she was barely able to open her eyes or hold a conversation. From before that, when he was young and she was so full of life, always teasing him gently and loving him fiercely.

"This is my mate, Nico."

Nico gazed down at him with adoring eyes.

"He takes good care of you?" his grann asked without looking away from Nico, like she wasn't sure if he was up to the job.

"He does. He saved my life," Keegan answered honestly. Then he looked up into Nico's brilliant blue eyes and whispered, "I love him."

CHAPTER EIGHTEEN

After spending nearly two hours just watching Keegan and his grandmother flip through the journal together, going back and forth mostly in Creole, Nico decided he should take the sleeping pup in his arms up to bed.

The others in the room had been coming and going, taking bathroom breaks or getting a snack. Rick had taken a phone call a little while ago, and Kai had gone up to check on Callie and Henry. But everyone kept coming back, an uneasy feeling to the whole room as they all just waited, hoping they'd finally get something of value to use against the Council.

He touched a hand to Keegan's back and waited until he turned to look at him before saying, "I'm going to take Rosie upstairs, but I'll be right back."

The soft, *loving* smile Keegan gave him and his daughter heated Nico's blood and soothed his anxious wolf. "Okay, we're going to get started translating the actual prophesies in here. Apparently, most of it is just general journal entries about her life and a woman she was sleeping with."

Nico snorted. "Okay. Be back in a sec."

He couldn't resist pressing a quick kiss to the corner of Keegan's mouth or his arrogant grin when he pulled away and Keegan chased him for just a second, eyes still closed. He heard a couple of people cough to cover their laughter, and a couple more not even bothering, but he ignored them. He rubbed the back of his fingers down the front of Keegan's throat, then left the room, arms secure around his—around *Keegan's* daughter.

He stared down at her sleeping face as he took the stairs slowly, not wanting to jostle her too much, though she hadn't stirred in over an hour.

She was beginning to feel like his.

It was a dangerous thought. He tried not to let himself imagine he was Rosie's parent. That she was his to nurture and protect and to guide through all of the ups and downs of life. Him and Keegan, side by side.

It wasn't that he thought Keegan was going to change his mind. Mostly. But until his teeth were in his mate's neck, his knot in his ass, and they were locked together in the most intimate and primal of ways, he wouldn't let himself picture them as a family. Because there was a tiny part of him that *was* still afraid Keegan would choose Rosie over their mating for some reason and walk away. It wouldn't be silenced.

No matter how many kisses they'd shared. Or late-night conversations. Or how much he had covered Keegan in his scent.

Until they were tied together, he couldn't help but worry.

But then Keegan had said he loved him.

Right in front of everyone, even his dead grandmother. He hadn't tried to take it back or act like he'd meant something else by it. He'd smiled up at Nico, completely at ease, then turned to his grandmother and gotten to work.

If Keegan loved him, that had to mean he was ready for them to complete their mating.

He was almost positive.

And that… that was good. Stopping himself when Keegan was pressed against him, kissing him and touching him and cursing under his breath, was becoming more and more difficult.

He'd begun to think he should have jumped at the chance to claim Keegan a week ago, lingering doubts and hesitations be damned. But then Keegan would look at him sometimes, his face open and vulnerable in a way it normally wasn't, and Nico knew he'd been right to wait.

They both needed to be sure and to know that they were choosing one another.

He reached the pair of rooms Keegan and Rosie had been given and let himself into hers, carefully juggling her as he opened the door. Keegan had tried to turn down the second room, insisting he and Rosie could share since space was at a premium in the manor, but Rick had rolled his eyes and made a comment about knowing how hard it was to find time with your mate with pups around. Then he'd just walked away, conversation over.

Nico had been grateful. When they were ready to take things further, they would still be near enough to Rosie that if she needed them, they would be there in just a second.

Gently, he lowered her onto her bed and then stared down at her sweet face. Her curls were wild around her head. She looked so tiny in the bed, even though it was just a twin. On either side, there were removable barriers sticking up to protect her from falling out, but he still carefully tucked her covers in around her, a need inside driving him to make sure she was safe and secure.

He brushed her hair out of her face with the back of his fingers and started to pull away, and that's when she finally stirred. Softly, he said, "You're okay, sweet girl. Go back to sleep."

"Okay," she mumbled. "Night, Papa."

Papa.

He'd never heard her call Keegan that. His breath froze in his lungs as he stared at her as she fell back asleep, her little nose wrinkling for a second before burrowing farther into her pillow.

She always called Keegan Daddy.

Keegan had jokingly called him papa wolf that one time, but that wasn't... he wasn't...

Was he Papa?

Eyes stinging, he backed out of the room, making sure her moon night-light was on before closing the door. He took a deep breath to steady himself, then pulled out his phone to shoot Samantha a text, asking her to keep an ear out while he and Keegan were still downstairs.

She had wanted to stay with Kai and Jess as moral support but had finally agreed to watch the pups. It was late, but he wasn't surprised when she texted him back an okay right away.

Heading back downstairs, he decided he'd talk to Keegan tomorrow about what Rosie had said and ask his mate if he was ready to bond with him. He bit his lip, remembering again how Keegan had said he loved him and Rosie had called him Papa.

How had he gotten so damn lucky?

As he neared the Great Hall, he was surprised to hear Keegan's raised voice. He didn't sound angry, more frustrated. "That can't be it. There has to be something else."

He slipped into the room and made eye contact with Marcus, who was frowning and leaning back against Robson. The open display of affection wasn't as weird as it had been when he'd first mated with the former deputy, but the fact that he seemed to need Robson's support had Nico worried. What had he just walked back into?

"I'm telling you, it is," Keegan's grandmother said, her own voice a little testy. "Everything else on this page is just speculation about whether she and her lover should go on some vacation."

The whole room was tense, but nobody was saying anything. Huffing, Nico walked over and stopped next to Keegan. "What did I miss?"

"Apparently, the prophesy we were all pinning our hopes on is a single fucking line."

His grandmother muttered something in Creole, and Nico suspected it was over Keegan's language, but he barely noticed. His stomach had plummeted. "One line?"

"Yup," Keegan said, sounding disgusted as he rubbed at his forehead.

"What is it?"

Keegan picked up the pad he'd been jotting notes down on and recited, "Upon my rebirth, the Council will succumb to the decay within."

Nico glanced at the translucent spirit hovering over Keegan's head. "You're sure there's nothing else?"

She grimaced. "I'm sorry, but no. Not for that prophesy. If there was more information, she didn't write it down here. She might not have written it down anywhere for fear it would fall into the wrong hands."

"Maybe there's something in the prophesy about her reincarnation," Tashmica said, face scrunched up. "There's a translated copy back at the shop. I hadn't looked at it in years before a couple of months ago, but I haven't really dug into it yet."

She very obviously didn't look at Jess, but the young witch huffed. "We're just going to ignore the fact that my mere *presence* might be the reason the Council falls apart? I mean, I know they've done a pretty shit job lately, but isn't anyone else worried about what will happen if they're just *gone*?"

"I doubt it's just your presence," Keegan's grandmother said slowly, looking deep in thought. "I'm sure there's more to it. She just didn't write it down here."

"So... what?" Nico said. "Succumb to the decay within sounds like they'll destroy themselves... but why try and kill Jess then? It has to mean something that the prophesy involves Angeline's reincarnation, right? That's, like, the trigger somehow?"

The spirit shrugged. "I really couldn't say. You *could* try summoning her and asking."

"You'd have to be here," Keegan said, sounding tired. "I could barely make heads or tails of the journal; I wouldn't want to bet on being able to understand her."

His grandmother sighed, and even though Nico was close enough to have felt it if she had been real, the fact that he didn't was a weird sensation. "I doubt she would answer the summons. You'd need a lot more magic to bring her forth, and..."

When she didn't continue, Rick stepped forward. "And what?"

"I just don't know if it'd be a good idea to have her anywhere near her reincarnate self."

Rick exchanged a look with Tashmica, and Jessica seemed to catch it, her tone sharp when she asked, "What's that supposed to mean?"

"I mean, you would be vulnerable to possession. It would be quite easy, actually."

"Their spirits would recognize each other," Keegan said, crossing his arms and frowning down at the journal. "But a person can't live with two souls, especially not two as powerful as Jess and this Angeline. I wouldn't want to risk her losing that battle."

"Yeah, no," Jess said, voice shaky.

"Whatever she saw," Keegan said, tapping the journal with his pen, "I don't think we'll ever really know. We're going to have to just make a plan and hope for the best."

His grandmother nodded. "Unfortunately, I agree. Let's finish the rest of these, and then we'll have to say goodbye, I'm afraid."

Keegan swallowed, his brows furrowing, but he started flipping back to one of the marked pages at the front. His scent was sad but determined, and Nico had to squeeze his fists to stop himself from reaching out to comfort him. Seeing his grandmother after all these years and losing her again would be hard on his mate, harder even than he'd thought Nico suspected.

"No, let's start with the last one," she said, pointing at something on the notepad. "The one about the fourth king and the seal."

Rick's head shot up, and Nico jolted. Fourth king? That couldn't...

"What did you say?" Rick snapped, eyes glowing.

Keegan looked at him, eyebrows raised. "The last prophesy in the journal is about a fourth of four kings, I guess? I thought it was about four royals, but it's four kings." He glanced around the room as everyone stared at him in horror. "What's wrong? There's no such thing as shifter royalty. And nowhere on this side of the world is there a place with four kings. I don't see how—"

Voice breaking, Kai said, "My last name is King."

Keegan stared at him, scent souring with apprehension, and then he quickly flipped the pages of the journal to the last one marked. "Fuck. Yeah. Okay, um, let's start with this one."

As their group began to disperse a couple of hours later, Keegan and his grandmother were still finishing the last of the seer's visions, but none of them seemed to involve anyone currently alive. At least, not as far as they could tell.

Some were very specific, but most were frustratingly vague. It made Nico think that Angeline would just jot down the general idea when she saw it rather than all of the details out of habit, and not because she worried about it falling into the wrong hands.

Either way, they all felt pretty shitty, considering the Council prophesy hadn't really told them anything, and then they'd found out Angeline seemed to think baby Henry would destroy the world.

Unless there was another group of four kings somewhere...

Rick had left not long after that prophesy had been translated, guiding a crying Kai out of the room and murmuring to him that he would never let anything happen to their son. For the first time in his life, Nico had felt like he had an inkling of how they might feel. He couldn't imagine hearing something like that about Rosie, and he'd only known her a few weeks.

Kai had been there when Henry was born. Had protected him from their abusive parents and cared for him like he was his own. And from the day he'd mated with Kai, Rick had loved Samantha, Callie, and Henry like they were his flesh and blood.

Nico walked out of the Great Hall next to Marcus, Robson on his other side. Neither had said much of anything all night, but Marcus's scent betrayed him like usual. His face might not have shown a thing, but he was filling the hallway with his grief.

Gently, Nico laid a hand on the back of his friend's neck and squeezed when he shuddered. "You okay?"

Marcus didn't say anything, didn't even act like he'd heard him, so Nico pulled him to a halt. Robson stopped too, but he didn't interfere, his own scent full of worry.

Finally, Marcus shook his head. "I thought there would be more. Why would Mikel... He went to a lot of effort to get us that journal, and for what?"

"He might not have actually known what was in it," Nico pointed out. "Unless he found somebody who knew Creole better than Keegan and his sister, he might not have been able to have it translated. He could have just known that it was the volume that contained the information about her vision regarding how the Council would end."

"Maybe," Marcus said. "I remember that phone call Rick got right before he died though, and he told him not to trust the Council and that he had to come see him to tell him something. I just assumed it was about the charter and vision."

Nico sighed. "It might have been, or he might have found out there was a prophesy in there about a King and realized what it could mean, thanks to the whole mess with Kai's parents. He might have thought it could be about Rick's mate or one of his siblings."

"Or maybe he knew who was working with the Council to come after us," Robson said, his voice low. "My understanding is that things were already in motion when he was killed. That witch Agnes and her friends had already disappeared, and Kai's parents had been killed by that spell when Tash tried to make them talk."

Nico nodded. "That's true."

"So maybe he found out which coven is involved then, the ones jerking Alistair Kincaid's chain and really calling the shots. Kincaid might be the face of it," Robson said, "but I think he might just be a puppet, and we need to find the puppeteer."

Marcus looked at his mate, eyes glassy. "That might have been what got Mikel killed."

"Come here, cariño." Robson held his arms open, and Marcus fell against his chest.

Nico brushed his hand over Marcus's back, then turned away, leaving him in Robson's capable hands. He didn't think they'd ever truly know what Mikel Gregson had wanted to tell Rick that had gotten him killed, but Nico still suspected he might have found out about the Fourth King prophesy. The letter to Marcus confessing his true parentage just seemed like too much of a coincidence. If he'd been feeling guilt and shame over hiding who he really was to Marcus, would he risk his life to help Rick and his mate?

No matter what, the knowledge Mikel had had been enough to get him killed. Drake had nearly lost his life in an attempt to kill Jess. Wendy had almost died fleeing the Council's headquarters.

Whoever was coming after them, they wouldn't stop until they got what they wanted.

Or until they were stopped.

Permanently.

CHAPTER NINETEEN

L ate the next afternoon, Nico was still thinking about the prophesy that seemed to be about Henry. Keegan had written out several copies and handed them out, but Nico had it memorized at that point.

When the last of the four Kings accepts his birthright, the final lock will fail and the seal will be broken. Creatures long forgotten will roam the earth once again, bringing the damnation of the Underworld with them. The one who opens the door, must be the one who closes it with the blood sacrifice. Until the Sacrifice is made, darkness will reign.

It reminded him of a story he'd heard when he was roaming the country. He was staying with a tiny pack in North Dakota, and they had been mostly traditionalists with very few human amenities, but he could remember they would sit around the campfire in the evenings and tell stories about myths and legends. The history of shifters, how packs came to be, how packs fell.

He'd stayed for nearly a month just to listen to those stories, and there had been one a particular elder had loved to tell about how there used to be monsters in the world, but long ago, they had been sealed away. He'd said that it had taken the life forces of a vampire, a shifter, a seer, and a witch to seal the door.

The story had gone that through their deaths, the world had been saved, but the world had forgotten about their sacrifice. Had forgotten that most of the creatures had ever truly existed and weren't just bedtime stories to scare children. He'd insisted that the door holding the creatures at bay would be reopened one day *because* the lesson had been forgotten. That parahumans would unlock the seal and unleash hell on Earth once more.

Nico had thought it was just a story used to explain why the pack lived "the old ways" and rebuffed any offer of advancement or change. And he hadn't given it much credence or thought about it in years.

But if Angeline Pierre-Louis was as powerful a seer as they were led to believe, he was beginning to wonder if parts of that story might have been true. Having been passed down who knew how many generations, it would stand to reason that there would be exaggerations and missing information. And the fact that vampires—who everyone had been led to believe were extinct—were returning when they were specifically mentioned in the story had Nico worried.

But little Henry growing up to be the equivalent of the shifter antichrist?

A soft knock on his office door jolted him out of his thoughts, and he looked up as Keegan walked in. His automatic smile drifted away when he caught his mate's scent: sad and frustrated.

Keegan had been disappointed like the rest of them about the lack of information regarding how to defeat the Council, but Nico knew it had also been hard for him to have gotten a little bit of time with his grandmother and then to have lost her again. He'd offered to take the day off and spend it with him, but Keegan had wanted to keep busy and had gone to *Wicca We Can* to work with Tashmica. They were still trying to follow the magical trail of the beast who'd attacked Wendy but hadn't had much luck recently. Nico was beginning to think the one they were tracking was one of the ones Gabriel and his mates had already killed.

"Hey," he said softly, scooting his chair back from his desk. "Come here."

Keegan shut the door behind him and then padded quietly across the room and around Nico's desk. He started to stand, intent on hugging his mate to try and make him feel better, but paused when Keegan made a sound and touched his shoulder, halting him. A second later, he was climbing into Nico's lap, clutching at his shirt.

The salt of his tears tickled Nico's nose, and real fear raced through him as he wrapped his arms around Keegan protectively. His heart was beginning to race. Keegan didn't usually lose his composure like this. He did his best to keep his voice calm as he asked, "Are you okay? Is Rosie okay?"

Face buried in Nico's throat, Keegan nodded and mumbled against his skin, "She's fine. I'm fine too. It's just…"

He didn't finish, but his fingers dug in a little harder. Nico swept his hands up and down his back, trying to soothe him. "It's been a hard few days."

"I hate feeling so helpless."

"Hey, if anyone *ever* has been the opposite of helpless, it's you. You are the strongest man I know."

"My magic is still a fraction of what it was," Keegan argued, sighing into Nico's skin and sending goose bumps down his arms.

Nico chuckled. "I didn't mean your magic. I meant you."

Keegan stilled against him, seeming to be holding his breath.

Smiling to himself, Nico said, "You are strong and

resilient. Compassionate and kind. A little bit of a potty mouth, but a terrific father and a good friend. Not to mention a lov—"

His words got cut off by Keegan's lips, the kiss almost violent in its desperation. Nico didn't fight it though. He rode the waves, giving everything of himself to his mate just as he always would.

Why had he been holding back from this?

Fuck being scared. Keegan wouldn't leave him.

He had belonged to Keegan since the moment their eyes had met in that clearing. There had never been a chance for him to protect his heart.

Luckily, he didn't need to.

Still, he would give everything he had, every part of himself, to his mate whenever and wherever he needed it. Keegan pressed closer, wrapping his arms around Nico's neck and sweeping his tongue inside Nico's mouth.

He couldn't help the soft rumble of his wolf in his chest. Having Keegan in his lap, squirming on his hard cock, was just about all he could take. Especially after all the months of not knowing if they would ever really meet, and then the weeks since Keegan had arrived while they'd slowly gotten to know each other and learned to trust one another.

He felt like he'd been edging himself for years at that point.

If he didn't slow them down, there was a good chance he would come in his pants. He tried to ease his mouth away, but Keegan followed him with a whine.

"No. Don't. I need you," Keegan mumbled against his lips.

Hearing those words from his mate was like throwing gasoline on a fire. With a rough growl, he surged up from his chair, blindly sweeping at the top of his desk and knocking his phone and papers out of the way. Then he lowered Keegan onto the cleared surface, his wolf howling with happiness when his mate's legs wrapped tightly around his waist.

Keegan sank his fingers into Nico's hair and finally let them break apart to catch their breath. He licked his damp, swollen lips and stared up at Nico, his face open in a way it usually wasn't. Warm affection unfurled in Nico's chest as he leaned down and nuzzled against Keegan's cheek, bracing himself on his arms on either side of him.

"I need you," Keegan said again, and Nico's hips flexed in response, pushing his hard cock against Keegan's own reflexively.

"You have me."

"No, I need your knot and your teeth," Keegan said, his voice thready even as he arched up off the desk, pressing himself as close to Nico as he could get.

Nico wanted nothing more than to say yes, but he needed to be sure Keegan understood the only thing Nico needed was *him*. His poor mate was still raw from the night before, had admitted to feeling helpless, and the last thing Nico wanted was to have him make a rash decision and do something he wasn't ready for. Their mating should only happen when he was sure. "I'm here. You have me. Even if we were to never exchange those things, you are still my mate. I will be by your side always. I can wait until—"

Keegan surged up, biting at his lips and ravaging his mouth until Nico was dizzy from his taste and scent. Arousal pumped through his system so fast and furiously he wasn't sure how he hadn't collapsed on the floor.

"I am ready," Keegan said as soon as their lips separated. "I don't know what's going to happen. I don't know what's coming for our pack, our family, but I know I have never felt safe until I was in your arms. I have never felt wanted until I felt your body pressed against mine. And I have never felt loved until I saw your smile. I am ready, Nico. I love you."

For a moment, Nico couldn't say or do anything, and then he dove back down, licking inside Keegan's mouth for a quick taste before pressing kisses down his chin and across his jaw. When he reached his scar, he paused and laid softer, gentler kisses against that faint line, an unspoken promise he would never let something like that happen to Keegan ever again.

When Keegan shuddered against him, fingers digging into his scalp, he knew he understood. Satisfied, he moved down to his neck and sucked in a deep breath of his scent, then ran his tongue up the side of his throat.

"I love you too," he murmured against the thin skin there. "I think I loved you before I even met you. You are my whole reason for existing, the breath in my lungs, the blood in my veins. You are my whole heart."

"Nico," Keegan whispered, a thousand emotions thrumming in that one word.

"I love Rosie too. I know you don't need me to help you raise her to be a strong and powerful witch, but it would be my honor to be her dad too."

When the scent of salt hit his nose again, he lifted his head and was concerned at the tears running down from the corners of Keegan's eyes. He gave his head a slight shake and asked, "How are you so perfect?"

Nico snorted. "I'm not perfect. I'm just perfect for you."

"Come here." He tugged Nico back down, sealing their mouths together in a slower but no less passionate kiss. Nico let himself get lost in it. The sensation of Keegan's lips and tongue, his hands in his hair, his body thrumming with magic beneath him, and the way his thighs tightened every time Nico gave a small thrust against him.

It felt like hours later before he finally resurfaced. "We should probably go somewhere else," he panted as he nuzzled into Keegan's neck some more.

"Definitely. Unless we want to give everybody in the manor a show."

"Not this time," Nico said and gave a small nip to the skin beneath his mouth.

Keegan sucked in a breath. "We should probably have a conversation about that."

"But not right now."

"No, not right now. Right now, we should go to your house—oh, after we take a detour to my room. But then we should go to your house, and you should shove your knot in me, baby."

Nico groaned, grinding down against him. "Rosie?"

"Still at daycare. I'll text Samantha and ask her to watch her when they get home."

"Yeah, but tell her we'll come get her later. I don't want her staying here without us."

Keegan's scent deepened, his heart picking up just a little more. If Nico hadn't been pressed so close to him, he might not have even noticed. He lifted his head and met Keegan's eyes. "Are you okay?"

Keegan nodded. "More than. I gotta say, it's a real turn-on how great you are with her."

Nico cocked his head and stood up, finally put some space between them. Even though he hated it. "Seriously?"

"Oh, yeah," Keegan said, nodding as he pushed himself up onto his elbows and ran his teeth over his bottom lip.

Nico wasn't sure if he'd ever be able to work at his desk again. Not now that the image of Keegan sprawled on top of it, the firm line of his erection clear in his jeans, was burned in his mind. "I suppose that's good to know."

Keegan smiled. "Then again, I think everything you do turns me on. Every time I look at you, all I can think about is you touching me and kissing me and fucking m—"

"Careful, mate," Nico growled. "Or we won't be going anywhere for a while."

Keegan tipped his head back and laughed.

It was the most beautiful sight Nico had ever seen.

🐾

"Goddess, that took fucking forever," Keegan snarled as he slammed Nico's front door shut behind him.

Nico did his best not to laugh, but when Keegan turned toward him and caught a look at his face, he was busted.

"Oh, was that funny to you?" Keegan asked, shaking the thermos in his hand at Nico. "I swear, half the pack was at the manor, and every single one of them had a question for you. It was like some pack-wide conspiracy to give me blue balls."

Nico couldn't hold in his laughter anymore. "It wasn't that bad."

They'd bumped into a couple of people on their way out that he'd had to stop and talk to, and yes, that had delayed them, but only about half an hour. Keegan had even slipped away to go and ask Samantha about keeping an eye on Rosie for them for most of the time.

"I swear that woman from the finance council knew," Keegan grumbled as he stomped up the stairs. "She kept looking at me and smiling. Did you fuck her or something?"

There was an edge of jealousy to his voice that pleased Nico and his wolf as he slowly followed him up the steps. "Terran? No, I never fucked her. She's just new to the finance council and has questions."

"Well, that hardly excuses her—"

Keegan's words cut off when Nico darted forward, plastered himself to his back, and wrapped his arms around his waist. "I don't want to talk about Terran anymore," Nico murmured in his ear. "I need inside you, mate."

"Fuck, baby." Keegan curled his arm up, sinking his fingers into Nico's hair as he tipped his head to the side, giving him even more access to the fragrant skin of his throat. "I need that too."

Nico shuffled Keegan into his bedroom and closed the door behind him even though he knew they wouldn't be disturbed. He'd texted José, letting him know to steer clear for a while, and he'd said he'd just stay at his girlfriend's for the night.

"Need to drink that tea?" Nico said as he slipped his fingers underneath the hem of Keegan's T-shirt, running his fingers over the warm skin he found there.

Keegan nodded and lifted the thermos, twisting off the top with shaky fingers. "It's actually a really clever spell."

"Absolutely."

"I asked Damien about it, and the way he uses the magic of the parahuman partner as the final ingredient is brilliant."

"Uh-huh." Nico was barely listening as he stepped back and stripped off his shirt, then reached down to unbutton his jeans as he watched Keegan make a face at the smell of the tea before tipping the thermos up and swallowing the whole thing down.

"Fuck. That is terrible."

He was kicking off his pants by the time Keegan turned to him, mouth open like he was going to say something, then snapping it shut as his eyes went from the top of Nico's head to his feet. Making a face, he glanced into the empty thermos. "What's wrong?"

"I'm wondering if there's a hallucinogenic in here because there's no way you're this fucking perfe—"

Nico growled and tackled Keegan, careful not to let him hit the bed too hard. "Told you, I'm not perfect."

"Just perfect for me," Keegan said, smiling up at him.

"Made for you." He buried his face in Keegan's neck, lightly biting at the spot he'd soon sink his teeth into. Keegan quivered beneath him, hands gripping at Nico's back. "You're wearing too many clothes."

Keegan laughed and pushed at his shoulders to separate them. "You're the one who got all impatient."

He had, but he could also rectify the problem easily enough. Sitting up on his knees, he grabbed the bottom of Keegan's shirt and tugged it up and off him, then went to work on his jeans. Keegan tried to help but only got in the way, and Nico snarled at him.

"Okay, fine." Keegan let his arms flop to the sides as Nico pulled his pants and underwear off his muscular legs. "You do the heavy lifting. Might be a good idea since that tea is already working. I'm getting kind of... floaty."

Nico paused, half-stretched over his bed where he'd been about to grab the lube, and turned to study his mate. "I thought Tashmica was supposed to make it not as strong?"

Keegan shrugged and then stretched, rubbing himself against Nico's comforter. "Maybe Robson was even worse and this is the toned-down version?"

"Maybe your magic is interfering with it." Nico sat up on his knees, lube in hand and cock already half-hard against his thigh. "Should we stop and ask Damien—"

"Fuck that," Keegan said, scrambling up to kneel in front of Nico. He grabbed his shoulders and scowled at him. "I'm not unable to consent here—we're doing this."

Nico's mouth twitched up. "Well, if you're sure."

Rolling his eyes, Keegan flopped back on the bed, arms and legs outstretched. "Ravish me, wolf."

"With pleasure."

He dropped down on top of Keegan, stealing his mouth in a hot kiss, and ran his hands over his well-defined biceps all the way up his arms to his hands, then threaded their fingers together, palms touching. For long, slow minutes, he did nothing but hold his mate's hands and kiss him, his cock swelling between them. Keegan's woodsmoke scent was all around him, soaking into his skin and his bed, and he kept making tiny, hungry noises against Nico's mouth.

It was driving him crazy.

When he finally had to catch his breath, he decided the first order of business was to taste every inch of his mate.

And that was exactly what he did.

He started with his left hand, tugging it up to his mouth and licking at the black tattoo on his palm, then tracing the lines on top of his fingers with the tip of his tongue before sucking each one into his mouth. Then he made his way up the inside of his wrist, the ditch of his elbow, and then his armpit, where he buried his nose and hummed for a second.

Then he went down the other side of his arm until he reached his hand again and kissed his palm once more.

"Nico," Keegan said, his legs moving restlessly back and forth and long, thin cock weeping already. "Fucking fuck."

Nico's grin was downright feral as he switched to Keegan's other hand and repeated the whole process again. By the time he'd returned to kiss Keegan's palm again, his mate's hips were pushing up off the bed.

"Touch me," Keegan begged, grasping at Nico's shoulders and trying to push him down between his legs. Nico let him, then kept going until he reached his feet and did the same thing to each leg as he'd done to his arms.

He discovered his mate was sensitive on the back of his thighs, the inside of his left wrist, and the bottoms of his feet were ticklish.

He also discovered his mate's foul mouth could really get him going. He was rock hard as Keegan cursed a blue streak at him, even as he turned over onto his stomach after

Nico finished with his chest and abs. As soon as he was facedown, Keegan pushed his cock against the bed and moaned.

"Not yet. I'm almost done," Nico said, holding his hips in place as he kissed and licked his way across Keegan's shoulders and then down his back, smirking and licking the same spot on his low back again when his mate's right leg twitched.

"Nico, I swear to the goddess, I will *murder* you if yo—oh *fuck!*"

Nico grinned and ran his tongue over his mate's hole again, fingers digging into his cheeks as he held him apart. He spent a long time learning every way he could make Keegan twitch and moan and sigh. But his favorite was probably the way Keegan yelled when Nico pushed his tongue inside him for the first time.

"Oh fuck. Nico, baby, please. Put your fucking cock in me." Keegan bucked under him, rubbing his dick against the bed and pushing back to get Nico's tongue deeper despite his begging.

He could spend hours worshiping his mate like that—and planned to in the very near future—but his own cock wouldn't be ignored any longer. Pressing a kiss to Keegan's softened hole, he dug up the lube again and slicked his fingers, not wasting any time before pushing one inside.

Keegan's head thrashed. "I won't break. Faster."

Nico gritted his teeth, carefully working a second finger in and groaning at how tight Keegan felt. How was he ever going to take Nico's damn knot?

A lot slower than Keegan would have liked, Nico worked his fingers in and out, stretching and loosening him. When he finally sank a third finger in him, Keegan groaned and nodded against the bed, his eyes squeezed shut. Sweat was dotting his forehead and glistening along his back, and Nico couldn't resist leaning forward and running his tongue up his spine.

Keegan jolted like Nico had electrocuted him. "*Shit*. Every inch of me is sensitive after your special treatment. I've never been so fucking hard in my life."

"I'm almost done," he assured him, nuzzling into Keegan's smooth skin between his shoulder blades as he gave his fingers a twist and finally brushed against his poor, neglected prostate.

Keegan spasmed around him, his body tightening. "Fuck. Okay, enough."

He nearly elbowed Nico in the face as he forced him back and turned over, his face flushed and teeth sunk into his bottom lip. Nico ran his eyes over him in appreciation as he slicked up his cock, the base of his shaft already sensitive and a little swollen.

"Ready?" he asked, his voice little more than a rumble.

"Are you kidding?" Keegan grabbed the back of his thighs and pulled his legs up, opening himself for Nico. Despite his snappish words, his face was soft, and Nico couldn't resist leaning down and giving him a deep, thorough kiss as he pushed the wide head of his cock against his hole.

"I love you," he murmured against Keegan's mouth, pushing a little harder and finally breaching him for the first time.

Keegan cried out, letting go of his legs to grab onto Nico instead, his lips turning frantic. "Love you too. So fucking much. Make me yours."

Nico snarled at the words. A wave of possessiveness surging and washing over him, he shoved the rest of the way into his mate's body. The sound Keegan made would stay with him for the rest of his life. He was still so fucking tight and so hot; he was burning Nico alive.

"You are mine," he grunted, pulling partway out and then

driving forward again to hear Keegan's breath catch on a moan. "And I'm yours."

Keegan nodded, the side of his face rubbing against Nico's and his fingers digging into his shoulders. He reached down between them, giving himself a squeeze, and then started stroking his shaft to Nico's thrusts. "Call me yours again."

Groaning, Nico pushed his face into Keegan's throat and pounded into him. "Mine. My mate. My heart. All mine."

Keegan's hand sped up, his knuckles bumping against Nico's stomach, and then he tensed for a second, and Nico raised his head, not wanting to miss watching his mate's face as he came for him the first time. His hole clenched down on him so hard, Nico grunted, driving in as deep as he could, and then Keegan was arching under him, his head thrown back as he yelled.

His hot come splattered against Nico, and he could *taste* his scent. That was it, that was all Nico could handle. He drove in and out of Keegan's rippling body a couple of times, then buried himself as deep as possible as his knot started to expand and his come began to fill Keegan.

Keegan was panting, staring up at him with dazed eyes. When he saw Nico's fangs as he strained above him, lost in the feeling of utter perfection that was filling his mate for the first time, he turned his head to the side and bared his neck.

Nico didn't think, didn't hesitate.

With a bone-deep growl, he lunged and sank his teeth into Keegan's skin, then jolted when his own neck was pierced, the pain sharp but brief.

And then the world exploded around them.

All Nico could see was purple as something big and powerful began to fill him up from the inside and then spilled out into Keegan. And then came back to him. Back and forth, the force cycled between them through their sparkling new bond, driving Nico's ecstasy higher and higher.

Almost as fast as it started, it began to fade. The almost overwhelming feeling of pure power settled in him, but it didn't completely disappear. Licking over his teeth marks in Keegan's neck, he made a soft, questioning noise and turned to nuzzle into his throat.

"My magic is back," Keegan said, voice hoarse and astonished.

Nico lifted up to see his face. "Was that what that feeling was when we bonded?"

"I think so. Did you notice the light show?" Keegan reached up and caressed Nico's face, then down to his already healed bonding bite mark.

"The purple stuff?"

"Yeah, that was... that was my magic, I think." Keegan tried to move, then groaned when he didn't get anywhere, thanks to Nico's knot still swollen inside him.

Nico moaned, squeezing his eyes shut. "It's gonna be longer than a couple minutes."

"Right." Keegan laughed. "I forgot. Anyway, look."

He raised one of his hands, and Nico watched, astonished, as purple tendrils of something began to grow around his fingers. When he pointed at a pair of socks that hadn't quite made it into the hamper, the light darted forward and the socks lifted, landing with the rest of Nico's dirty clothes.

"Holy shit," Nico breathed. "Has it ever looked like that before?"

"No." Keegan shook his head. "But it's... bigger now. Filling me and you to the brim. I've never seen magic manifest like that before. I wonder if it'll last."

Nico settled down on Keegan to wait for his knot to deflate. "I don't see why not. Maybe it's a side effect of the tea?"

"I don't think so," Keegan said softly. Nico's eyes were half-closed, but he could still see the glowing purple light and smiled against Keegan's neck, realizing his mate was playing with his magic behind Nico's back. "I think it's just from you. From being connected to so much magic."

"It's beautiful," Nico mumbled, wondering if he could take a nap and then convince his mate to go again before they went to pick up Rosie.

"Yeah?"

"Just not as beautiful as you."

"Such a sap." But Keegan's scent was full of affection, and he wrapped his arms around Nico, holding him as he ran his fingers through his hair.

It was… perfect.

CHAPTER TWENTY

"Oh, fuck yes," Keegan grunted, shuttling his cock in and out of Nico's perfect mouth. He was so close, and Nico knew it, his damn eyes nearly twinkling as he stared up at Keegan from where he knelt on the floor in front of him.

Keegan darted a glance at the beaded doorway that led to the front of *Wicca We Can*. Damien was helping another member of the coven, but he could finish at any moment, and then he'd probably come and see what was keeping him. Biting his lip at the idea of getting caught, Keegan pushed forward, sinking all the way inside Nico's warm, wet heat and groaning deep in his chest at the way Nico just took him. He opened all the way up for him like it was nothing, like he'd been made to suck Keegan's brain out through his cock.

After a few more quick thrusts, that was exactly what he did. Keegan had to shove his own fist in his mouth to keep from crying out, his back arching as he shot off. His magic surged in his veins, passing to Nico through their bond and then coming back again in an endless loop, feeding and strengthening his magic until it felt like it would burst through his skin. As he came back down from his orgasm, it finally began to wane, settling into the warm current constantly flowing between them.

"Don't know if I'll ever get used to that feeling," Nico murmured into the junction of Keegan's hip and thigh.

"Me either," he panted, running his fingers through Nico's hair and gently petting him.

Luckily, his mate's ears were able to give them enough of a heads up that by the time Damien did come looking for him, he had his pants righted, and Nico'd rearranged himself so his erection wasn't so noticeable. Though the look on Damien's face when he skidded to a stop just inside the back room made him think they weren't fooling him at all. But of course, Damien was too nice to actually say anything.

He cleared his throat and asked softly, "Did you find the book you were looking for?"

Keegan glanced around, finally finding the grimoire on the table, where he'd tossed it as soon as Nico had backed him up against the bookshelf. "Yep, right here. Where's Tashmica today?"

It was an obvious change of subject, and the slight pause and glance at Nico before Damien answered made heat suffuse Keegan's face. "I'm not sure. She had a phone call a little while ago and left in a hurry."

That got Nico's attention, and he looked up from where he'd been studying the map showing their lack of progress in tracking down the beast that attacked Wendy. Keegan was pretty sure it was one of the ones that had gone after Gabriel, Drake, and Jamie, and that's why the trail had gone so cold. The thing was dead, and the magic source they'd been trying to track down had disappeared.

"Did she seem upset?" Nico asked. "Like something had happened?"

It was easy to tell from Damien's face that he didn't want

to answer—whether because he didn't know or because he didn't want to betray Tash's confidence, Keegan couldn't say. Finally, he just said, "I'm not sure."

Nico nodded absently, pulling out his phone and checking it as Keegan thanked Damien once more for the book and led him out of the shop. Their SUV was waiting for them right out front where they'd left it. Keegan smiled at a family walking past, vaguely recognizing the parents.

As they passed him and Nico, a warm feeling settled in his stomach as he realized he was settling in and becoming familiar with the pack and the town. It was starting to feel like home in a way New Orleans hadn't since his grann died.

"I don't have any missed emails or calls," Nico said as they climbed into the vehicle.

"Maybe it was personal," Keegan offered.

"Maybe."

Or maybe something had finally happened. There hadn't been any word from the Council or Keegan's old coven, and despite his training to always be on guard, he'd let himself get comfortable. Relax even. It was easy to forget at times how much danger was lurking outside the pack when he was so well insulated within it.

He flexed his fingers around the steering wheel as Nico continued to work on his phone. At least he had his magic back—and then some. The free-flow tap of Nico's power meant that if his mother or the Council came for them, he was confident for the first time in his life that he could come out on top. Especially with Tashmica and the others at his back and the strength of the pack fueling them.

He wished he would have realized sooner how much power a well-bonded pack could supply their coven with. He couldn't help but wonder if he would have fled to Nico months ago instead of coming up with his silly plan of seeking refuge with the Council's coven.

When Nico huffed at something on his phone before quickly typing out a response, Keegan smiled to himself. Even if it took him a little longer to arrive, he was still grateful to be there at his mate's side. Rosie was blossoming under the attention she had lavished on her every day at the manor and at daycare, and Keegan was... well, the attention his mate gave him every night had him blossoming in an entirely different way.

"Mate," Nico growled, without looking up from his cell, "what are you thinking about over there?"

"You."

The enormous smile Nico gave him at his quick response loosed a herd of butterflies inside him. Goddess, he didn't know how he'd gotten so lucky, but he'd do his damnedest to be worthy of Nico's smiles every single day.

He stiffened as he turned onto the driveway leading to the manor. Before they even pulled through the gates, he could tell something was off. There was a buzz of tension and magic in the air.

Fuck. Something *had* happened.

Tashmica's and Doc's vehicles were parked haphazardly right in front of the steps leading up to the front door, and the sight of them made Keegan's gut clench, his magic reaching out for Nico automatically for comfort.

But his mate was just as worried as he was, eyes narrowed on the cars. "What the hell..."

As soon as they stepped inside the manor, Keegan froze. Rick was standing at the bottom of the steps right in front of him, arms crossed over his wide chest and face serious. It was obvious he had been waiting for them.

Heart sinking, Keegan glanced around the entrance hall. "What happened? Is anyone hurt?"

"The pack is fine," Rick reassured him, taking a step

forward. "As is your sister and Rosie's mom. Gabriel's already checked on them."

Keegan's eyes narrowed. "Who isn't okay then?"

Nico's hand slipped into his, holding firmly. It was only then that he realized he was trembling, fear and adrenaline coursing through him.

"It's your mom," Rick said carefully.

"What did she do?" The worst-case scenarios started spinning through him. His mother and the rest of his old coven charging through the warding around the territory. Her finding out about Rosie and trying to take her. Members of the pack he'd come to care about so much dying as they tried to protect—

"She's here, Keegan," Rick said, snapping him out of his spiral. "She's upstairs."

Keegan sucked in a breath, face going numb. "You let her in?"

Kai came hurrying down the steps, Henry in his arms. He stopped next to Rick and wrapped an arm around his waist, but his sad eyes were locked on Keegan. "She's hurt. Really badly. You need to go and see her right away."

He stared at Kai, his brain not quite processing what he was saying. Then he turned to Nico, but he didn't have to say anything, his mate knowing what he needed. He gave their clasped hands a squeeze and nodded.

Feeling like he was walking through quicksand, Keegan silently ascended the stairs, Nico right at his side. When he reached the top, he paused, not sure where to go, and Nico gently guided him to the left and down a hallway until they reached a room with the door partially open.

Keegan stared at it, not sure what he was about to see but feeling like he needed to prepare himself. Somehow.

Slowly, he raised his hand and pushed the door the rest of the way open.

Holy. Shit.

He hadn't been prepared for *that.*

The person lying on the bed beneath the covers barely resembled the woman he knew. The woman who had raised him, who had scarred his face, who had tortured him, and who had terrorized him for years. The bones of her face, wrists, and hands were clearly visible under her ashy skin, her black hair streaked with white.

There was a strange sound in the room, and it took him a second to realize it was her breathing. Shallow. With a rattle.

He had the insane urge to laugh. She had sacrificed *everything*—her humanity, her family—to be the most powerful witch she could be. To make others too scared of her to do anything but bend to her will.

And now she was little more than a skeleton, hanging on to life by a thread.

"What happened?" Nico asked, and Keegan finally looked away from his mother and noticed that Tashmica and Doc were in the room, standing off to one side. He stepped the rest of the way into the room, and Nico closed the door behind them.

"She was attacked," Doc said. "But I can't... There isn't anything I can do for her."

"Attacked," Keegan repeated, his voice sounding far away. "By who? Look at her."

Doc turned to Tash, and she stepped forward, coming over to Keegan and placing a gentle hand on his shoulder. "Our best guess? Another coven. They..."

"They ripped out her magic, didn't they?" he breathed, finally realizing what was missing from the room. For years, his mother's magic had been an oppressive presence in every room she was in, and it was just... gone. Reaching out with his own, all he felt was... nothing. A void.

"I'm so sorry, Keegan," Tashmica was saying. "There isn't

anything we can do. The trauma of it... It was too much for her. All we can do is make her comfortable."

"How did she even get here?" Nico asked.

"We think she got left just outside the border, and she walked into town, asking the first person she came across to call Rick Kincaid. By the time he and I got there, she'd collapsed. She's been unconscious ever since."

"So you didn't talk to her," Nico asked, eyeing the bed. "You don't know who did this?"

Tash shook her head and glanced at Doc before turning back to them. "No, but whoever did it is not only extremely powerful, they're sadistic. It would have been kinder to just kill her."

Keegan made a pained noise at that, an involuntary reflex. A call back to when he had been a child who actually loved his mother and not been terrified of her. Legs unsteady, he made his way across the room and collapsed on the edge of the bed. He stared at the hollowed-out form that used to be Beatrice Toussaint, the leader of the La Fleur Coven.

He was aware of the others still talking, but he couldn't hear it over the buzzing in his ears. He felt like he'd float away any moment, completely unmoored. After a while, he realized Tashmica and Doc had left, and then Nico's warm, comforting presence was right behind him. His big, strong hand landed on the back of his neck, and it was like he snapped back into his body, suddenly anchored once more.

He didn't know how long they stayed like that. Not talking. Not moving. Just... waiting.

He stared at his mother, thinking about the last time he'd seen her in that warehouse. She'd been larger than life. The most terrifying and beautiful person he'd ever seen. He remembered how he'd felt when he'd realized what she'd been doing to him, trying to break his mind like he was some enemy combatant and not her son.

He wondered when she'd stopped seeing him as her little boy and started seeing him as a threat. As much as she'd talked about him taking over for her in leading the La Fleurs, he knew she hadn't trusted him, and she'd proved it that day she'd found his dream walking ingredients.

As he looked over her sunken features, he tried to recall the last time they'd been happy as a family, but it was so long ago he could barely remember. Before his grann had died, he'd been happy, but even then, he remembered being a little scared of the things his mother was saying and doing in her bid to gain more power and control.

"I need to call my dad," he said with a jolt, trying to stand, but Nico easily kept him in place. "And Jocelyn."

"Later," Nico murmured, giving his neck a squeeze. He sat behind him and wrapped his arms around Keegan's chest and waist to hold him against his big body. Holding him together when Keegan felt like he would have shaken apart otherwise. "You can call them later. For now, I think you need to be here. In case she wakes up."

Squeezing his eyes shut, Keegan nodded jerkily. Of course, he was right. Taking a deep breath, he relaxed back against Nico and waited for her to open her eyes.

And waited.

And waited some more.

A couple of times, Nico urged him to drink or eat something, to go to the bathroom and stretch his legs, but he just kept coming back. Sitting on the bed, staring at her, he could barely look away, the sight of her so heinous and heartbreaking. It felt like she deserved his attention though. Even after everything she'd put him through, he felt like he *owed* her that. To stand vigil and pay witness to the horrors that had been done to her.

Sometime during the night, with a single lamp in the room turned down low, he noticed her eyes flutter and held his breath. It took several minutes, but her eyes finally opened. When her gaze met his though, he had to hold back a flinch and force himself not to look away.

They didn't look like his mother's eyes anymore. They were cloudy and unfocused. He'd been expecting them to be the same, to hold the same power and weight they had his entire life. To pin him in place as she demanded he avenge her.

"Keegan," she said, her voice barely more than a puff of air.

"I'm here." He saw her eyes drift over to Nico where he was standing just over his shoulder, but she didn't ask who he was, and he didn't offer. "What happened? Who did this to you?"

"The... O'Hares."

His eyes widened, every muscle in his body tensing. "Why? What possible reason did they have to do... this?"

The O'Hares were a coven even older than the La Fleurs, and one of the few that were more powerful. They lived in the same territory as a shifter pack, but they weren't a united force like the Kincaids and their coven. They were purists— they didn't have any seers, they didn't mix with shifters unless absolutely necessary, and they thought anyone who wasn't a witch wasn't worth anything. The only reason they hadn't driven away the pack they shared territory with was because they liked the added protection of what they considered "dumb beasts." And the alpha liked the prestige of having the most powerful coven in the western hemisphere "in" his pack. It was a strange, symbiotic relationship Keegan had never truly understood.

"I went to them... for help," she rasped out.

"Help with what?" But he had a bad feeling in his gut that he knew. He reached a hand back, grateful when Nico's warm palm met his, suffusing him with heat and comfort from that single touch.

"To... come here," she said. "To... take you back... and make an example... of this pack."

"I don't understand," he said, clenching his teeth. He'd known it would be something awful like that, but hearing the words was like a slap to the face. "You went to them for help, and they did this?"

"They said—" She was stopped by a horrible cough that racked her whole body.

Keegan reached over and grabbed the cup of water on the bedside table and extended it to her when she finally stopped, panting. She took several small sips from the straw before collapsing back on her pillow, eyes shut.

He waited a minute, worried she'd gone back to sleep, but she eventually reopened her eyes, and they seemed a little more clear and her voice more steady.

"They said they already had a plan for Kincaid. That he'd get... what was coming to him, and then they dismissed me... like I was nobody. Just some common witch off the street."

And that infuriated her. Keegan could easily imagine it. He had witnessed her fury at what she perceived as a lack of respect for her and her position many times over the years. Had felt her wrath on occasion too.

"I told them I would just do it... myself." She squeezed her eyes shut, face creasing with pain. "They..."

Unable to stop himself, he reached out and laid a hand over one of hers. Her fingers twitched, then lay still, her skin dry and cool. "It's okay. Why don't you get some rest?"

"No," she insisted, turning her hand over and gripping him with a strength he wasn't expecting. She speared him with a look that made his stomach cramp at its hard familiarity, and he heard Nico growl softly behind him. "You need to know... They're coming."

"The O'Hares?" Nico said, speaking for the first time in what felt like hours. There was an edge to his voice Keegan wasn't used to, and he knew it was costing his mate a lot to be civil to the woman who had hurt him so badly, and he loved him even more for it. "What grievance do they have against us?"

"They didn't say," she said, not even sparing Nico a glance. "The leader... she just said it was time."

"Time for what?" Keegan asked.

"To cleanse."

🐾

"To cleanse?" Tashmica asked as soon as she stormed into the Great Hall, Damien and Jessica behind her. Damien closed the door quietly before joining them at the circle of chairs. "What the hell does that even mean?"

"She wasn't sure," Keegan said, rubbing his palms on his thighs, grateful for Nico's steadying heat next to him. "Just that the O'Hare Coven had a plan to take out... Rick."

"Everything really is happening because of me," Jess whispered.

"This isn't your fault," Rick said immediately, his face creased with agitation.

"What isn't?" Keegan asked, looking around the circle. "What am I missing?"

"Jess used to belong to the O'Hare Coven," Nico said softly. "They were... upset we took her in."

"I was an abomination," she spat, wiping at her eyes. "My grandmother was an elder in the coven, and she hated me and what I was. A stain on her perfect family lineage."

"Because her father was a seer, not a witch," Tashmica clarified, putting a hand on Jess's shoulder in comfort.

She nodded. "As soon as I turned eighteen, my mom went

249

to the alpha of the pack, whose territory the coven resides on, and requested I be banished. Pack law complicated things and made it impossible for them to just get rid of me on their own."

"Your mom probably saved your life," Rick said, rubbing his forehead. "Your grandmother demanded your return as soon as word spread to them that you had found sanctuary here. She even had the leader of the coven reach out to try and convince me. I believe her exact words were something about stamping out the blight of the O'Hare line."

"But your last name is Macey," Kai interjected, then shook his head. "Sorry, not important."

"My father's name. Goddess forbid I carry the O'Hare name." Jess took a deep breath before letting it out shakily. "So they're the ones behind the Council. That's what we're all thinking, right? That my old coven wants me dead so bad they started a war between us and the Council."

Rick shook his head. "It doesn't make sense. No offense, but why do you mean so much to them?"

Keegan squeezed his hands into fists and stared at Jessica, trying to figure out what made her so special that her old coven would manipulate the Council, kill multiple people, and create beasts that went against nature just to get their hands back on her. To kill her. What were they missing?

"They know who she is... who she was." Every pair of eyes landed on Damien. He swallowed and bit into his bottom lip, gaze dancing over everyone but not landing on any one person. Then he dropped his head and twisted his hands in his lap. "They know how powerful Angeline Pierre-Louis was and have been preparing for her return since she died."

"Preparing?" Kai asked, glancing at Jessica, who was sheet white as she stared at Damien. "Like... to welcome her back?"

Damien shook his head. "The O'Hares... They don't like

anyone more powerful than them, especially not someone who's only half-witch. But they're... they're also scared of her."

He said the last part so softly, Keegan almost didn't catch it. Eyes narrowing, he tried to recall everything he'd learned about Angeline and her visions since arriving. He knew there were more journals somewhere, some containing the visions she'd had about her own reincarnation. But there hadn't been anything in them to rise to this level of fear. The only time he'd seen witches that scared had been some diehards who believed in some myth about—

No. It couldn't be.

It was just a story meant to keep witches in line. Make sure they never got too powerful. A cautionary tale...

"They think she'll be the one to do it," he said, voice incredulous. Damien looked up and met his gaze, his face calm, but his eyes... Fuck, he looked like he was dying inside. "That she'll become so greedy for power, she'll... she'll fucking corrupt magic and sever the connection to the source for us all. Erase it. They actually believe in the legend of the fall of magic? It's just a story!"

"*What?*" Jess choked out.

"How do you know that?" Rick demanded, pushing to his feet. Keegan realized Vanessa and Bennett had stood too, both of them moving around the outside of the circle of chairs toward Damien.

"I..." Damien stared up at Rick, his smooth face breaking and crumbling into despair. He buried his head in his hands, shoulders shaking. "I'm sorry."

Tashmica pushed to her feet. "Rick—"

"Did you know?" He turned on her with a snarl, baring his teeth.

"I knew he was hiding something," she said, stepping over to Damien and placing a hand on top of his head, offering him comfort the same way she had Jess. The way she had him upstairs. If anything, her touch made things worse though, a sob slicing through the tense air. "But I trust him."

"Tell me the truth," Rick ordered, crouching in front of Damien. He grabbed his wrists and forced his hands away from his face. "Did they send you here?"

Keegan sucked in a breath as Nico stiffened next to him, and someone growled nearby.

Face miserable, Damien nodded. "I'm sorry, Alpha."

Chair squealing on the floor, Jessica scrambled away from Damien, hands coming up defensively. Keegan could feel the fizzle of magic in the air, and he called on his own, just in case. Angeline Pierre-Louis reincarnated or not, if she lost control and became a threat to the people he cared about, Keegan wouldn't hesitate to stop her.

"Who are you?" she screamed, and he caught a spark of pink dancing between her fingers, the hairs on his arms standing on end. The only time he'd seen magic manifest like that was his own after he'd bonded with Nico. He'd seen her do spells and practice her active powers while he'd been working with Tashmica at the shop, and never once had she done *that*.

Dread pooled in his chest. Could the O'Hares be right?

Could Jessica really be a danger to them all?

Damien dropped his head once more, looking defeated. His voice, when he spoke, was a barely there croak Keegan had to strain to hear over his own thumping heart.

"I'm your brother."

CHAPTER TWENTY-ONE

"It feels weird to just... act like things are normal," Keegan said without looking up from the peanut butter he was spreading on a piece of bread for Rosie. He slapped it together with the piece already covered in jam and added it to the plate that held her cottage cheese and apple slices. "I can't believe Rick is still holding the pack run tonight."

Nico finished pouring Rosie's milk and handed it to her. He sat at the table next to her and leaned back in his chair, watching his mate and disliking how agitated he was. His wolf wanted to wrap himself around Keegan and cover him with his scent until he settled, but he'd already tried that.

Twice.

It only worked for a few hours, and then Keegan was right back to worrying. It wasn't that Nico wasn't too, but he trusted Rick to know what was best for the pack. Even if that trust had been stretched lately when Rick had finally agreed —after Tashmica had asked over and over—to move Damien from one of the cells in the manor's basement and into his own apartment on the condition Tash made it impossible for him to leave.

It had been nearly a week since Beatrice had shown up and Damien had dropped his bomb and then been thrown under house arrest. At first, Nico thought Keegan was upset over his mother dying. She hadn't woken up again, passing into the afterlife less than a day after arriving. But his mate had confessed that he was more upset that he *wasn't* more upset at her death and that it wasn't what was keeping him up at night.

He was worried about Damien, yes, but he was also freaked-out that Jess might destroy magic. Hell, so was she, it seemed. No one had seen her in the last week either, making it seem like she'd been magically confined to her small house too.

Even after reading up on the legend of how magic would be destroyed—which didn't actually name Jess *or* Angeline, yet no one else seemed to care about that—Nico couldn't help but scoff at the idea of sweet, funny Jessica Macey going all dark side and burning the parahuman world to the ground.

But Keegan wasn't so sure. After watching his mother be corrupted by power over the years, he was more inclined to believe such a thing was possible.

"Most people have no idea what's really going on," Nico reminded him. As soon as Keegan set the plate in front of Rosie and moved to walk away, Nico snagged him around the waist and pulled him down into his lap.

Rosie watched them, grinning, and shoved a huge bite of her sandwich in her mouth.

"What do you say, sweetie?" Nico reminded her.

"Thank you, Daddy! Thank you, Papa!" she said immediately, voice muffled with peanut butter.

"You're welcome," Keegan said, giving her a soft smile before turning to Nico.

Before he could say anything, Nico continued. "All that

shit about Damien and the O'Hares is need to know at this point. So it's important—"

"That things proceed as normal," Keegan finished, rolling his eyes, but there was a small tug on the corner of his mouth as he settled on Nico's legs, wrapping his arms around his shoulders. "I guess. It just…"

"Feels weird." Nico ran the back of his fingers down Keegan's face, tracing the path of his scar. "I know, mate. But people look to us for guidance. Even if they don't know everything, with the hunters and the Keshena Pack here, everyone is already on edge. A little normalcy is good."

"I know." Keegan sighed and leaned into him, tucking his head under Nico's chin. "I have a bad feeling though. Like something terrible is going to happen."

At the words, a shiver raced down Nico's spine, and his arms tightened on his mate, his instincts warning him that Keegan was right. They couldn't let their guard down because something bad *was* coming. The O'Hares were done hiding; they'd dumped Beatrice at their doorstep so they'd know who was targeting them.

So they'd be afraid.

And Nico would kill them all for making his mate feel even an ounce of fear.

Nico was exhausted and energized at the same time.

He always felt that way after a run with his packmates though. This time it had been even better thanks to Keegan being there. He turned his head a little where it rested on Keegan's stomach to see his face. They were sprawled out with some of the others, and it was late. The pack was too big for everyone to run together except on special occasions, so they split into a few smaller groups and spread out throughout the territory. Nico and the other Enforcers always ran—or flew in Fiona's case—with Rick though. It strengthened their bond in a way nothing else could.

The only thing missing had been Kai.

The pack's alpha-mate hadn't left the manor—or allowed Henry to leave it either—since learning about the Fourth King Prophesy. Rick didn't talk about it much, but they could all see the tension in him as Kai worried himself sick, digging into anything he could find to try and learn more. Both of them stared at the sweet little pup with a mixture of love, fear, and resolve.

Nico buried his snout farther into Keegan, not wanting to think about that while he was still enjoying the puppypile with his closest friends and mate. There would be time to find answers later.

"Oof. Easy, baby," Keegan murmured, sinking his fingers into the fur behind Nico's ears and scratching.

"I swear they don't know their own strength in this form," Gabriel muttered a few feet away underneath Drake's bulky cat, Jamie's hawk perched on the toe of his booted foot and surveying around them. When Drake hissed softly at him, Gabriel just chuckled. "I hear you, kitty cat. So ferocious."

"I love furry time," Robson chimed in from next to Keegan. Marcus's back was pressed against Nico's so they could touch each other and their mates at the same time. "Marcus turns into a cuddly puppy."

Keegan laughed, his body shaking underneath Nico, thankfully not enough to dislodge him. "Nico's always cuddly. Rosie loves it."

He lazily snapped his teeth at his mate.

"Yes, yes. I love it too."

Satisfied, he huffed out a sigh and resettled, just enjoying the way all of their scents mingled together and covered them. Most of all, he liked the way his and Keegan's bonded scent was strongest on his mate, filling his nose and easing the lingering tension in his body.

He ended up dozing for a while, Keegan's fingers gently moving through his fur. He roused when Marcus and Robson stood, murmuring soft goodbyes before heading into the darkness.

Nico lifted his head slightly to glance around and was surprised to find that Rick was gone too since he usually stayed until the last of them headed back. But he supposed with his mate back at the manor, he hadn't wanted to stay out so late.

"You awake?" Keegan murmured as he pushed up onto his elbows, one side of his mouth quirking up in a smile. "I have a surprise."

He cocked his head, staring at his mate. What kind of surprise could he have on him out here in the woods?

Biting his lip, Keegan looked around at the others, but no one was paying them much attention. Jamie had shifted back to his human form but had wedged himself as far as he could between Gabriel and Drake. Colt's and Vanessa's wolves were sprawled out on the other side, and Bennett's big tiger was curled around his mate's wolf next to him and Keegan. Fi was probably in the trees somewhere, keeping watch over them. Everyone else who'd run with them and puppypiled by the lake had left already.

"Come on," Keegan said, keeping his voice low. He climbed to his feet and waited for Nico to do the same, then led him away from the others and into the woods, but not in the direction of the manor where Nico's clothes were and they'd left Rosie.

Was Keegan turned around?

Before he could decide if he should shift into his human form to ask what Keegan was doing, his mate glanced back at him, grinned, then took off running.

Nico stood frozen for a second, shocked, and then a shot of anticipation spiraled through him, and he was off, sprinting after his mate, who'd gotten a decent head start. But he was no match for Nico's four legs. He was a pack Enforcer. There was no way Keegan could outrun him.

Keegan didn't play fair though, cursing and sending fallen logs and branches at Nico to try and slow him down, his purple magic dancing around his hands.

It was no use though.

As he closed in on Keegan, leaping over a fallen tree, he let out a bark of excitement. Keegan's laughter floated back to him in the air, ratcheting up his eagerness. His mate was *happy*, and that made Nico fucking ecstatic.

Keegan tried to feint to the right and then dodge left, but Nico was ready for him, launching himself up and taking Keegan to the ground.

"*Oof.*"

He didn't get a chance to worry he'd hurt Keegan, his mate flipping over beneath him and smiling up at him with a leaf in his hair. His smoky scent thickened in the air between them, and Nico stuck his nose into his neck, lapping at the skin to try and taste his mate's arousal.

Keegan laughed and pushed his head away. "That tickles."

Nico huffed at him, sending his wild curls dancing.

"Now that you've caught your prey, oh mighty wolf, what do you plan on doing with him?"

As Nico registered what Keegan's playful words meant— the full extent of his surprise for Nico—he jerked his head up and looked around, realizing that while he'd been completely focused on catching Keegan, his mate had just circled the clearing the others were still in. He could see them through the couple of trees separating them and hear snatches of the words Gabriel murmured to his mates.

Turning back to Keegan, he pulled at his other form,

needing only the tiniest tug now that he was full of Keegan's magic. As soon as his bare skin was available, Keegan reached up and ran his hands over him, humming in appreciation.

"This is a nice surprise," Nico said, diving down to kiss him and getting lost in Keegan's taste, staying for several long moments of hungry lips and wet tongues. While he'd imagined what it would be like to have a mate who'd enjoy celebrating pack runs the same way Nico had always dreamed of growing up, he hadn't let himself hope for it too much, not wanting to be disappointed if his mate wasn't open to it.

Based on the hard ridge digging into his hip, Keegan was *very* open to it.

"Can't stop thinking about it. I never would have guessed I'd be into exhibitionism before I met you," Keegan said, kissing his way down Nico's neck and nuzzling into the bite mark he'd left. "But it's exhilarating, knowing they can hear us. That they'll know you're staking your claim and knotting me after chasing me through the woods."

Nico groaned, gritting his teeth as his mate's words went right to his cock.

Keegan really was made for him.

When their frantic kissing had turned into a blowjob in the back of *Wicca We Can* the week before, he'd been surprised by how much Keegan had seemed to love it. Especially considering how he'd blushed when Damien had looked at them knowingly.

But apparently, the thrill of almost getting caught had led to Keegan wanting more, wanting Nico to take him just out of sight of their packmates.

"You're wearing too many clothes, mate," he snarled, pushing up to get some space between them and then tugging at Keegan's shirt. After he tossed it aside, he reached for his jeans, but Keegan stopped him.

"Hold on a second." He shoved his hand into his pocket and pulled out... lube. His mate really had planned this. "Gonna need that. Okay, off with the pants."

"So bossy," he muttered, leaning down to lick at one of Keegan's nipples, then bite it as he unzipped his jeans. When Keegan jolted and moaned at the hard press of his teeth, Nico snarled and did it again to his other one.

"Nico," Keegan gasped, clutching at his hair and bashing him in the head with the lube he was still holding. "Fuck."

He finally pulled Keegan's pants off his legs and threw them as far away as he could, then dropped down onto his mate's bare skin and rolled his hips against Keegan's. It was perfection. It was everything he'd ever dreamed of. It was—

"Ouch. Should have brought a damn blanket. A stick is poking me in the ass."

Nico dropped his head into Keegan's neck and shook with laughter.

"Quit laughing. Not all of us are used to running around in the woods naked." Keegan swatted at his shoulder, then squeaked in a totally manly and not at all adorable way when Nico jumped to his feet, taking Keegan with him. "Fuck! Warn a guy."

Grinning, he took two steps until Keegan's back was pressed against the trunk of a large maple tree, the others maybe ten yards past it. "Is that better? Or still too rough for your delicate skin?"

"You're such a fucking je—*mph*."

He used his lips to cut off his complaint, and his mate relaxed in his arms, wrapping his legs around Nico's waist. He kissed him deep and hard, savoring every hungry sound he coaxed from Keegan. His smoky scent was so thick Nico felt like he could drown in it.

Dragging his hands down Keegan's sides, he grinned against his mouth when his mate shivered and arched against him, rubbing his hot dick against Nico's abs. "So eager."

"I've been thinking about this for days," Keegan admitted, flicking open the lube and waiting for Nico to offer his hand. He squirted out more than enough, closed the top, then tossed the bottle away. "When I wasn't worried about every-thing else, I was imagining this. You going all he-wolf on me and marking me as your territory."

A low growl worked its way up from Nico's chest at the words. He reached down and slicked his cock quickly, then traced his fingertips up between Keegan's cheeks until he reached his hole and circled the tight pucker.

"You know how I feel about you calling yourself my terri-tory." Nico licked up the side of Keegan's neck as he pushed a finger inside his scorching heat.

"Yeah, I do. You love it, baby," Keegan said, tipping his head back against the trunk and tightening his legs around Nico with a ragged sigh. "You pretend you're above all that possessive shit, but you *love* getting your scent all over me." He leaned in and sucked Nico's earlobe into his mouth. "In me."

He wasn't wrong, and with his wolf so close to the surface, the urge to get his scent *inside* his mate was over-whelming. With a low snarl, he bit right over his bonding mark and worked a second finger into Keegan, loving the deep moan he got for his effort.

He loved having Keegan like this, writhing against him and gripping at Nico with need. The rest of the time, his mate was strong and independent and prickly. But in Nico's arms?

"Fuck. More, baby." Keegan gasped, riding Nico's fingers as he thrust in and out. The broken sound he made when Nico pegged his prostate had him biting down harder. "Fuck fuck *fuck*."

He was just thinking about pushing in a third finger, just to be safe, when Keegan gripped the sides of his head and pulled him off his neck. He released his teeth with a growl, then groaned when Keegan shoved his tongue into his mouth.

Keegan ripped his mouth away after stealing Nico's damn mind. "Turn me around."

The words didn't make sense to him at first, and he shook his head in confusion even as he pushed his fingers in deeper just to make him moan again.

"Won't get your knot deep enough this way," Keegan said, panting and loosening his legs. "Turn me toward the tree."

Groaning, Nico nearly dropped him in his haste to flip him around, and Keegan laughed as his arms shot out to brace himself against the trunk.

"Can lift a car with one hand and toss Rosie in the air with the other but nearly drops me in a sex haze." Keegan shot a fake annoyed look over his shoulder, and Nico pinched his ass in retaliation.

Keegan's brown skin was glowing in the moonlight, and Nico couldn't resist running one of his hands down his spine as he held him up by his hip with his other. His mate was so beautiful and all his.

As he gripped his cock, lining himself up and preparing to push inside Keegan's heat, his mate urging him on with filthy words, he glanced up and saw Colt watching them from where he still lay less than thirty feet away. The others were either ignoring them or oblivious, but Colt's glowing wolf eyes were locked on them, his head cocked to the side. Nico lifted his chin in acknowledgment, then thrust forward, baring his teeth as Keegan cursed loudly.

Holding him by his hips, Nico pulled almost all of the way out, then drove back in, Keegan's elbows bending with the force of it and his legs kicking helplessly.

"That's it," Keegan said, moaning when Nico's fingers dug into his hips. "Harder, Nico."

Always happy to oblige his mate, he sped up and thrust harder, their skin slapping together and building a symphony with their gasping moans and deep grunts. The pleasure was building inside Nico fast, rushing through his veins and landing in his aching balls.

When he changed his angle just enough that Keegan slapped at the tree and yelled, he threw his head back and howled. His packmates responded immediately, returning the call, and Keegan glanced back at him over his shoulder, a wicked smile on his face.

He needed to taste him again.

Driving deep into Keegan's body, he wrapped his arms around his waist and chest and tipped him upright so his back was pressed to Nico's front, his cock still throbbing inside him. Keegan reached behind him, grabbing at any part of Nico he could get his hands on, the faintest shimmer of purple beginning to dance around his fingers. Nico could feel his magic surging through their bonded connection, the sensation similar to how he felt after a long, intense workout where his muscles were swollen, and he felt stronger than ever.

Having free access to Keegan's thrumming magic was like having access to an untapped source of pure, raw power.

Terrifying and thrilling all at once.

He nosed at the side of Keegan's face until he turned enough that he could capture his lips, being extra careful of his fangs. Licking into Keegan's mouth as he ground deeper into his ass, he groaned, trying to stave off his impending orgasm, but he could already feel his knot beginning to swell at the base of his cock.

Panting against Nico's mouth, Keegan moaned and nodded. "That's it. I can feel it. Give it to me, baby."

He wasn't ready, not yet.

He slid one hand down to where Keegan's cock was rock hard and dripping with precome and gripped his shaft firmly. With a groan Nico could feel vibrate his body, Keegan let his head fall back onto Nico's shoulder. He stroked him, keeping his hold nice and tight the way Keegan liked and paying extra attention to his sensitive head.

Even one-handed, he easily lifted and lowered Keegan, driving his cock into him again and again. When he felt him getting close though, his ass gripping at him and dick swelling in Nico's hand, he slammed Keegan down once more, burying himself as deep as he could and letting himself finally come, his knot expanding and tying them together. He stumbled, his knees trying to give out as pure, exploding pleasure eclipsed everything else in his brain.

Keegan yelled, his whole body tensing and a purple shimmer beginning to swirl around them. "Yes! Fuck yes. Love that. Love you."

Panting, Nico laid his teeth right over his bonding mark again and bit down, his joints feeling loose as he started to come down, but still being extra careful of his fangs to not pierce the skin. But Keegan shook his head, grabbed his hair, and pushed him down.

"Do it. Do it. Do it."

"*Shit.*" He dropped to his knees on the rough ground, grabbed Keegan's throat, and forced his head farther to the side before sinking his teeth into his mate's skin. He moaned, long and low, as the smoky flavor of Keegan's blood coated his tongue.

"Fuck!" his mate yelled, his magic sparking in the air around them.

Nico felt Keegan's cock throb in his other hand as he gave him a few more quick strokes, then snarled with satisfaction as Keegan finally came, shooting against the base of the tree in front of them. He arched and gasped, holding Nico's head tightly against his neck as his hole rippled around Nico's knot, squeezing out another burst of come.

When his head started to clear, he released his teeth and tried to raise his head, wanting to check to make sure he was okay.

"Not yet, baby. Just… hold on to me." Keegan's words were a little slurred on the edges, his throat vibrating against Nico's palm where he still held him.

Unable to deny his mate anything, Nico wrapped his arm around him and held him as he knelt in the dirt, Keegan's come splattered against the bark of the tree like some new-age art piece.

Or maybe old-school.

That had felt… primal.

And perfect.

He pressed a kiss to the already healing bite on Keegan's neck, grateful for the added benefit of their bond. There would be another scar though, nearly overlapping the original, and Nico shivered at the idea of leaving more marks on his mate. "Okay?"

"More than," Keegan said, still panting. "Though you'll probably have to carry me home."

He'd be more than happy to do that. Humming, he nosed at the fragrant spot behind his mate's ear. "Thank you."

"For this? It was hardly a hardship. Pretty sure I lost a few brain cells I came so hard." Keegan squirmed a little, then sighed happily when Nico's knot held them together.

"No." He licked his lips, not sure how to explain the depth of his gratitude that Keegan was in his life, making it infinitely better in every conceivable way. "Thank you for choosing me."

Keegan's fingers tightened in his hair. He swallowed, but

his voice was still a little hoarse when he said, "Best decision I've ever made. Thank you for… saving me."

Nico knew he didn't just mean from his mother. His mate had needed saving from himself too. "I'll always be here to save you."

He wasn't going anywhere.

CHAPTER TWENTY-TWO

Rick never wanted to be alpha of a pack. He'd left his childhood one to get away from his abusive father, sure, but also because he hadn't wanted the responsibility once his old man died—or Rick put him in the ground. Whichever came first. He'd taken off and not looked back, and he'd felt *free* for the first time in his life.

For years, he and his friends did whatever they wanted, went wherever they pleased, and had been happy.

And then he'd decided to pass through Michigan and had come across the saddest-looking pack he'd ever seen. He might have even kept going, leaving them to their fate, but his best friend had looked at him in disappointment, and he'd caved.

Staring at his pups curled up together in Henry's crib, he felt his fucking eyes burning. He didn't know where he'd be without his mate and his family. He'd thought he'd known happiness when he'd been untethered from anyone and anything, but it was nothing compared to what he felt when he held his mate in his arms. When he played with his pups or made Samantha laugh.

He'd been *drowning* before Kai, lost in endless duties and struggling under the weight of a responsibility he'd never wanted. Finding his sweet mate had felt like taking a deep breath for the first time in years.

Henry made a snuffling noise, and Callie scooted closer without opening her eyes, and he felt like his whole world was falling apart. How could someone so small and sweet be the harbinger of the world ending or whatever the fuck that damn prophesy had been a warning of?

Henry was... he was everything good in the world, him and his siblings, and there wasn't anything Rick wouldn't do to protect him.

Even if his mate would never forgive him.

Silently, he walked over to the crib and reached in, gently running his fingers over their heads to leave his scent behind, hoping it would offer them comfort when they woke and he wasn't there.

If he didn't come back, would they forget him? Henry definitely would, he wasn't even two, but Callie might remember.

He hoped they'd understand one day why he was taking the risk of not coming back to them. Even if he survived, would Kai look at him the same way? Would he trust Rick anymore?

Grinding his teeth together, he stepped back.

He had to believe that Kai would understand.

He had to.

Since they'd had that fucking prophesy translated, he'd felt like there was a heavy weight on his chest, slowly crushing him. He could barely focus on anything else, especially since Kai was losing it, locking himself away in the archive room or the library to search for days on end for an answer that Rick wasn't sure was out there.

As he stepped into the hallway, he glanced toward his

bedroom, but it was empty, Kai still upstairs poring over books.

The manor was quieter than it usually was these days, most of the inhabitants either staying the night out in the woods or passed out in exhaustion in their bedrooms. He'd chosen the night of the full moon for that exact reason, knowing it'd be easier for him to slip away. It was only an hour before dawn, and no one would notice until he was long gone.

He took the back steps down to the main floor, then headed for the empty housekeeper's suite near the kitchen. There was someone moving around in the kitchen, probably getting a drink or a snack, but he slipped into the room without being noticed. He slowly closed the door behind him and only felt a little ridiculous for sneaking around his own house.

"Thought you might come this way."

Rick whipped his head around at the familiar Southern drawl. Gabriel was leaning against the far wall, arms crossed over his chest and one leg bent and propped up behind him. He was dressed in dark cargo pants and a black Henley, and Rick could actually see the weapons on him, which meant he was carrying even more than normal.

"What are you doing here?" he snarled, pissed that his plan to slip away was being thwarted by this fucking human who'd been a thorn in his side since day one.

"Tashmica called in a favor I owed her, so we're road trip buddies." Gabriel smiled, but it was little more than him baring his teeth.

Rick realized when he tried to scent the human that he wasn't putting one off again. He narrowed his eyes and took a step closer, inhaling deeper, but still got nothing.

"Oh, yeah, and she hooked me up with a few things to

help me go unnoticed by whoever the fuck shows up to this asinine meeting you set up."

Sighing, Rick rubbed at his forehead, his perpetual headache throbbing at the idea of spending hours in a vehicle with Gabriel. He shouldn't have told Tashmica when he was leaving, but he hadn't had much of a choice if he wanted her to deliver the letters he'd written if he didn't come back.

Besides, the whole thing had been her idea.

"Why did I just have a premonition of you driving away from the pack without telling anyone where you were going?" Tash had demanded as she'd stormed into the library three days ago, eyes blazing with fury. "I don't have enough to worry about without you jumping ship and abandoning us?"

Snarling, he'd pushed to his feet and stalked over, slamming the door shut. "How dare you even suggest—"

"I know what I saw," she'd spat, lifting her chin and meeting him head-on. "What are you planning?"

"Nothing." He'd held on to his outrage for a few seconds, and then the weight of everything had come crashing back down on him. Shaking his head, he'd collapsed back in his chair and covered his eyes. "I haven't decided anything for sure."

"Tell me what's going on, Rick." Tash had come over, settling on the couch next to him and placing a hand on his knee. "We need to stand together more than ever. Don't cut me out."

He'd exhaled, hard, then sat forward and leaned on his forearms. "I can't stop worrying about Henry."

She'd nodded. "Okay, but we don't even know that the vision was really about him."

He'd thrown her an incredulous look at that.

"Okay, fine. It probably is. But a seer's visions aren't the same as a witch's premonitions. You know that. We can change the outcome."

"How?" He'd burst to his feet again, pacing toward the window. "You yourself have said how powerful a seer Angeline was, how

accurate her visions were. How the fuck do I stop something I don't even understand?"

She'd been silent behind him for so long, he'd thought she'd somehow left while he'd been talking without him noticing. When he'd finally turned away from the window that overlooked the backyard where his pups had been playing with the rest of the youngsters, she'd given him an assessing look.

"There's only one way I can think of without knowing more about this seal or what birthright she was referencing."

He'd extended his arms, indicating not just the manor but the entire pack. "Isn't it obvious? Becoming the next alpha of the Kincaid Pack is his birthright."

She'd wrinkled her nose. "Except he wasn't actually born *for that, was he? He's not your blood—"*

Rick hadn't been able to hold back his snarl. "He's my *son!"*

Holding up her hands, she'd said soothingly, "I'm not arguing that. I'm questioning the assumption that taking on the mantle of alpha for the Kincaid Pack is what he was born *to do. His biological parents may hold the key to figuring that out."*

"They're dead," he'd reminded her.

"Well, as Keegan so aptly proved, dead doesn't mean much to the right witch with the right spell."

"Is that what you think will stop the vision from coming true? Summoning Kai's parents and interrogating them?"

She'd shaken her head. "No, that might help us figure out part of the vision, but it won't stop *it from coming true. For that, I think we need to stop other visions first."*

"What?"

"Hear me out. A seer, even one as powerful as Angeline, only sees one possible outcome. With her level of power, she saw the most likely outcome, but it still isn't set in stone. And, like other seers, I'd bet my life on the fact that her visions are built on top of each other."

271

Something like hope had started to bloom in his chest. "So if you take away one..."

"You could potentially prevent all of the ones that come after from happening."

"We could stop Henry from breaking the seal."

"Maybe. But the only other vision we know of right now—"

"Is the one about her reincarnation and the Council succumbing to its decay or whatever." He'd sighed and scrubbed at his face. "Are we sure Jess really is her reincarnated spirit?"

"I'm sure. I did a regression spell on a vial of her blood, and it... exploded. Someone or something in her past didn't want me poking around."

"Jesus."

"Yes, so I'm confident she's the one the O'Hares have been worried about for a century."

"And they let her slip through their fingers," Rick had grunted, sitting back down. "How do we stop it then? From where I'm sitting, the decay seems pretty rampant."

Looking him dead in the eye, Tashmica had said softly, "You have to save the Council from itself, Rick."

Because that would be easy.

"Look," Gabriel said, pushing off the wall, "I don't like this any better than you, but I pay my debts."

Rick thought about his poor mate, unable to eat or sleep he was so consumed with worry. He thought about his pups, too young to understand things like visions or prophesies, wanting nothing more than to snuggle with him and play on the swings. He thought about Samantha, just finding her footing and growing into a strong young woman.

He thought about Jess, terrified that she'd lose control of herself and become the thing the O'Hares were so afraid of.

He thought about his pack, full of men and women, elderly and pups, all of them depending on him to protect them. To always know what to do.

He hoped they never found out how terrified he was.

Swallowing, he met Gabriel's eyes and nodded. "Let's go."

He'd agreed to meet his father at a seemingly random spot in a federal nature preserve about an hour north of Springfield, Illinois. The coordinates were about a mile inside the preserve, far away from the empty farmland surrounding the woods. The sun had set a few hours ago, and Gabriel had left him to walk the last half mile himself, the hunter shouldering a backpack full of supplies and disappearing into the darkness without a sound.

He just hoped he wouldn't need his backup.

Double-checking he had the right spot, Rick slipped the GPS navigation tool Gabriel had given him into his pocket and glanced around, but he didn't see anyone. They'd left their phones in Michigan, not wanting their mates to be able to follow them, but he'd have given anything to talk to Kai in that moment. To hear his voice one more time.

"I wondered if you'd actually come."

It took a lot of effort to keep his lip from curling back in disgust at the sound of his father's voice, his wolf anxious to attack and neutralize the threat to his pack and family.

"I'm the one who asked you to meet." He folded his arms over his chest and waited for his father to materialize out of the trees to his left. Unsurprisingly, two figures followed Alistair Kincaid, taking up positions behind him. Scenting the air, he narrowed his eyes at the wolf and witch. "We agreed to come alone."

"Well," Alistair said, grinning and holding out his hands in a what-can-you-do gesture. "To be fair, the last time we were in the same place together, you promised to kill me if you ever saw me again."

He'd been an eighteen-year-old kid full of rage and power he didn't understand, and his father represented everything he hated.

Ignoring his father's words and his companions, he got down to business, pulling out Angeline's journal. "I assume you're familiar with this and the amendment to the original Council charter?"

Alistair narrowed his eyes and nodded, not saying anything. The witch behind him, though, took half a step forward, eyes locked on the journal with a look of shock on her face.

Interesting.

"Here." He tossed the book to his father, who caught it but didn't look down at it. "There's a piece of paper marking the prophesy about the Council, and the translation is written on it."

Alistair still didn't look at it, holding the journal out to the shifter behind him. "Thank you for returning Council property. Though I believe the scroll of the original charter also went missing just before poor Mikel's unfortunate death."

Rick squeezed his hands into fists at his sides but didn't rise to the bait. Gregson had been a friend, and they all knew Alistair and his cronies had been behind him dying. "Consider it an offer of truce. I want me and my pack to be left alone, and you want the Council to stay standing. We should help each other."

Taking a few steps forward, Alistair studied him, that same air of condescension he'd always had thick around them. "The Council is perfectly fine."

"No, it isn't," Rick snapped, taking a step forward himself. He stopped when the witch narrowed her eyes on him. "The prophesy is clear—the Council will fall to its own hubris if we don't do something to prevent it."

Both of his companions shifted uneasily at that, exchanging looks behind Alistair's back, but his father just scoffed. "Please. The Council has been in power for centuries, protecting and ruling the parahuman world. Some *seer*"—his sneer at the word drew the witch's attention again, but she still didn't say anything—"won't stop that."

Frustrated, Rick shook his head. "It's not her—it's you! It's the Council's lack of accountability, it's their willingness to use fucking *hunters* against their own people, and it's their failure to offer fair and impartial judgments." He took another step forward, pointing at his father. "You will be your own downfall if you don't let me help you."

Silence reigned for several long moments, and then Alistair rolled his eyes. "So dramatic. You're the one who picked a fight with the Council because you didn't like the verdict of the hearing regarding the McAllister Pack. Then again… you took care of them, didn't you?"

Gritting his teeth, Rick said, "I didn't pick a fight with anyone. I'm trying to help—"

"We don't need your help!" Alistair roared, his eyes flashing as he stormed forward. He stopped a couple of feet from Rick, chest heaving as he sneered at him. "You've always been a disappointment, but to come crawling to me to beg for help under these pretenses… For the first time, I'm glad you abandoned our pack."

Anger surged through him, but he held it back by sheer force of will. Seeing it explode out of his father was a grim reminder of where his own temper came from. He'd promised himself a long time ago he wouldn't be like him, and he intended on keeping that promise.

"What did they offer you?" he asked, really looking at his father for the first time. They looked similar, but whereas in Rick's mind, his father was always that towering figure above him, the picture of youth and vitality, the man in front of Rick looked... old. Worn-out.

Weak.

"Who?"

"The O'Hares."

The witch took a step forward, eyes on Alistair. "What's he talking about?"

"Shut up," Alistair snarled, not even bothering to look back at her. To Rick, he said, "Nothing I couldn't have gotten on my own. They'll just make it easier."

Rick stared at him, trying to figure out what he meant. When he'd found out a few years ago that his father had stepped down as alpha and joined the Council, he'd assumed it was what his father had wanted, the ultimate position of power and authority. He couldn't think of anything the O'Hares could have offered him that was better than a position on the Council.

But the way he was looking at Rick... the hunger on his face...

Fucking hell.

An alpha without a pack was nothing.

Powerless.

A figurehead.

"Killing me won't get you my pack," he said, voice steady, as he reached out with his senses to try and find Gabriel, but all he found were two more of his father's people hiding farther in the trees. "You'll never be alpha of a pack again. If you come after me and mine, I'll burn your precious Council to the ground."

"By the time the O'Hares are through with you and your pack, they'll be *begging* me to lead them."

Rick shook his head, fury shooting through him. At his father and at himself for playing right into his hands. "You're wrong."

"We'll see." His father stepped closer, his cloying scent of rage and desperation nearly choking Rick. "You should have stepped aside when you had the chance. Things would have been easier for everyone."

Muscles tensing, Rick bared his teeth. "You should have accepted my offer of help."

Alistair closed the remaining space between them, but Rick refused to step back. He unsheathed his claws though, and his fangs started descending from his gums as his father leaned in and whispered, "I'll tell your little half-breed mate you said goodbye."

He swung, his fist connecting with the underside of Alistair's chin even as he felt a white-hot burn in his gut and sending his father flying backward several feet until he landed on his back on the ground, a glint of silver clutched in his hand.

A knife.

Snarling, Rick started forward, uncaring about the cut in his side, but his legs wobbled and then gave out after two steps, and his vision began to darken. As he landed on his knees, he cupped the wound, warm blood soaking his shirt and making his hand sticky.

He heard a yell, but it sounded far away. Lifting his head was harder than it should have been, and he couldn't see very well, but utter chaos surrounded him. His father was gone, and the witch... Rick grimaced at her and the arrow sticking out of her forehead.

"*Where the fuck is he!*" someone screamed, and Rick tried to laugh, but it hurt. All of him hurt.

It felt like his blood was on fire, consuming him from the inside.

Fucking wolfsbane.

Grunting, he tipped over when someone pushed past him and hit the ground on his side, the landing so jarring he lost his breath. He tried to just focus on staying conscious, but it was getting difficult, numbness beginning to spread out from the wound in his side.

That couldn't be a good sign.

He wasn't sure how much time passed, but then he was being forced onto his back, and he groaned.

"Rick! You fucking asshole, don't you dare die on me!" Gabriel yelled at him, his voice ringing in Rick's ears and making him dizzy.

He wished he could smell him. That he could scent his pack one more time...

"Tell Kai—"

"Don't. I swear to god, I will stab you myself. Just... just stay awake. Please."

He couldn't see anymore, he realized. He was almost positive his eyes were open, but he couldn't see... anything. Not the trees or the moon or Gabriel's annoying face.

Fuck. He'd never see Kai again.

And he'd fucking failed Henry.

Searing pain hit his side again as Gabriel pushed on it, muttering something about Tashmica owing him.

Using the last of his strength, he found Gabriel's wrist and gripped it tightly. "Gabriel, please. Tell him... tell him..." He was starting to fade, but he fought it with everything he had. Kai needed to know. Gabriel *had* to tell him. "Love him... Sorry..."

"*Rick!*"

Don't miss the epic conclusion of the Kincaid Pack series! Preorder The Witch and His Doctor now and get it as soon as it goes live!

On your Kindle? Scan the QR code with the camera on your phone to jump to the Amazon page.

Want a little more of Keegan and Nico?
I've got a bonus scene available to my newsletter subscribers featuring a spicy moment between these two in Nico's office at the manor. *wink*
(You can always find all my extra scenes under the Bonus Content tab on my website, www.kikiclark.com.)

On your Kindle? Scan the QR code with the camera on your phone to jump to my website to sign up!

A NOTE FROM KIKI

THANK YOU. THANK YOU. THANK YOU.

Thank you for reading *The Enforcer and His Heart*. If you enjoyed Nico & Keegan's story, please consider leaving a review to help other readers find it.

Wanna never miss a release or sale?
Follow me on BookBub!

Come hang out in my group on Facebook, Kiki's Korner!

Free to download at www.kikiclark.com/newsletter!

Injured and terrified, Victor runs for his life and right into the arms of the last person he expected to find: his true mate.

Living in a pack who viewed imperfections as weaknesses that needed to be eliminated, Victor is lucky to escape alive. He's heard of the Kincaid Pack's strong but fair alpha, but he has trouble truly believing he won't be targeted once more if his shameful secret is discovered.

When Cole meets a young man with fear in his eyes and pain in his scent, he recognizes him as his mate on sight. His excitement is short-lived, however, when they find out Victor's life is still in danger from what his old pack did to him.

After a lifetime of being abandoned by others, Victor has an important decision to make: Will he choose to trust the mate fate gave him?

Or will he run again?

A New Pack for New Year *features an eighteen-year-old wolf in need of some TLC, a thirty-something lion dying to give it to him, sexy times in an inappropriate place, found family feels, and hurt/comfort that will warm all the corners of your heart.*

EXPAND YOUR TBR!

Once you're finished bingeing the Kincaid Pack series, you might like to try one of my contemporary romances!

Laying Pipe features an age gap, dad's best friend, bisexual awakening, and adorable rescue pets. All the books in my Blue Collar Hearts series can be read on their own and have characters who work blue collar jobs.

Available in eBook, Paperback, Audiobook, & Kindle Unlimited.

Reckless is the first in my Leather & Chrome series which focuses on the Devil's Hands Motorcycle Club and the exploration of kinks. Tank and CJ's story features a prison pen pal program, an age gap, exhibitionism, and a tough biker only soft for his kinky virgin.

Available in eBook, Paperback, Audiobook, & Kindle Unlimited.

ALSO BY KIKI CLARK

Kincaid Pack Series

FREE Prequel: A New Pack for New Year

The Alpha and His King (Rick & Kai)

The Second and His Bonded (Kieran & Bennett)

The Deputy and His Enforcer (Robson & Marcus)

The Hunter and His Mates (Drake, Jamie, & Gabriel)

The Enforcer and His Heart (Nico & Keegan)

The Witch and His Doctor (Doc & Damien)

Kincaid Pack Adult Coloring Book Vol 1

Blue Collar Hearts Series

Out In the Cold (Beau & Coop)

Laying Pipe (John & Lukas)

Banger (Hank & Kevin)

Leather & Chrome Series

Reckless (Tank & CJ)

Temptation (Six & Ollie)

Yearning (Houston & Kenneth)

L&C holiday novella

Joyful (Rooster & Emmett)

Many of my books are also available in audio! Check them out on Audible or on my website, www.kikiclark.com.

ABOUT THE AUTHOR

A small town Michigan girl, Kiki has enjoyed reading since she first picked up Harry Potter and the Sorcerer's Stone as a child. After that, she devoured everything she could get her hands on and dreamed of one time writing her own books that touched people's hearts.

In her early twenties, she discovered LGBTQ romances and had a realization: these were her people and this was where she belonged.

Nearly ten years later, she's proud to finally join the ranks of authors releasing character-driven, emotionally satisfying books showcasing that everyone deserves to find love.

To keep up-to-date with Kiki, sign up for her newsletter: http://www.kikiclark.com/newsletter or join her Facebook group: https://www.facebook.com/groups/kikiskorner.

Keep in touch by following her on any of these platforms:

- facebook.com/kikiclarkauthor
- twitter.com/kikiclark_
- instagram.com/kikiclark2017
- amazon.com/author/kikiclark
- bookbub.com/authors/kiki-clark
- goodreads.com/kikiclark

www.ingramcontent.com/pod-product-compliance
Lightning Source LLC
Chambersburg PA
CBHW050701290626
47170CB00016B/2561